drive me WILD

Special Edition

Melanie Harlow

USA TODAY BESTSELLING AUTHOR

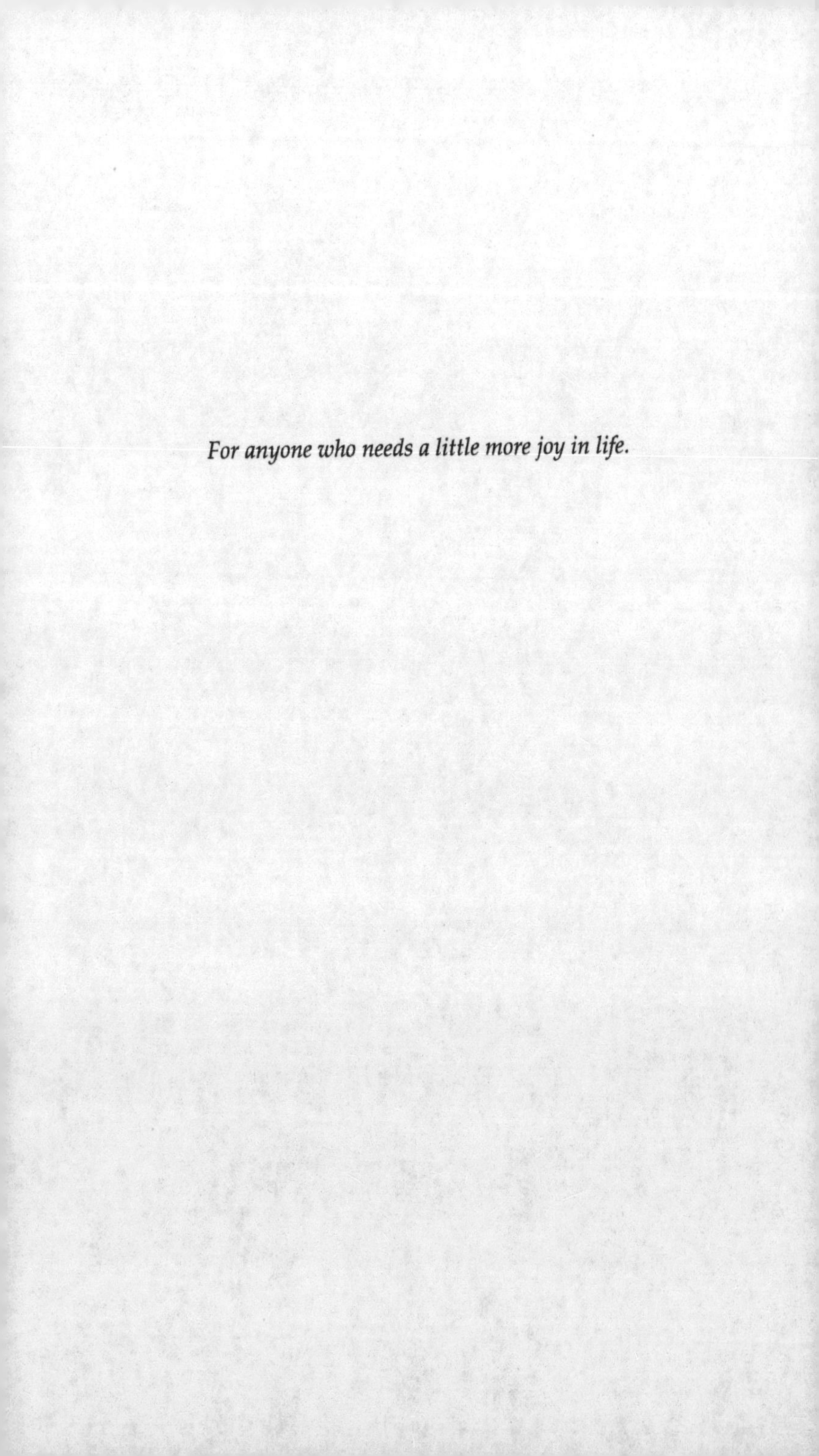

For anyone who needs a little more joy in life.

Let go of your umbrella
    'cause darlin' I'm just tryin' to tell ya
    that there's always been a rainbow
    hangin' over your head…

It'll all be alright.

"RAINBOW," KACEY MUSGRAVES

CHAPTER 1
GRIFFIN

A WATCHED POT NEVER BOILS, but a watched mechanic will.

I don't remember how old I was when I first heard my dad say it, but damn if he wasn't right. There was nothing worse than a hoverer, and old man Dodson was a serial offender.

"Are you sure you need to hit that so hard?"

Clench jaw. Count to three. "Yes."

"Is that really the right way to do it?"

Take a breath. Don't throw things. "Yes."

"Are you going to be done soon?"

Not if you keep standing there asking me stupid questions.

My temper was nearly at the boiling point, but since I really couldn't afford to lose customers, I turned around and attempted something resembling a smile.

"Shouldn't be too long now, Mr. Dodson. Why don't you take a walk? Maybe grab a cup of coffee and a donut at the diner? By the time you get back, I'll have your vehicle all ready for you."

The old-timer scratched his head and hitched up his kelly-green pants. "You know, Swifty Auto said they could have this done in half an hour. And their price was cheaper than yours."

I gripped the wrench I was holding even tighter.

Fucking Swifty Auto. The fast food chain of automotive repair. High volume, low value, shitty rush jobs done on the cheap—but customers didn't seem to care. Apparently, a chandelier in the lobby, glossy TV ads, and free cookies were more important than good service. "Well, they're a bigger shop. And they've got a different philosophy."

"But I've always brought my cars here, and your dad was a good honest guy. Knew what he was doing. I figure you're a good honest guy too."

"He taught me everything I know," I said. *In other words, I too know what I'm doing, asshole. Now go get a fucking cruller and let me finish this up. You didn't even have an appointment—I squeezed you in as a favor.*

Dodson exhaled and gave up. "Guess I'll take a walk then."

I watched him wander out to the sidewalk and begin his old-man shuffle down Main Street, then got back to work.

"Damn, that guy is annoying," called McIntyre, the other mechanic at Bellamy Creek Garage. I owned the place, but he'd been working there almost as long as I had. We also had a helper—a "stack the tires" guy—whose real name was Andy, but we referred to him as Handme, since we were always telling him to *hand me that wrench* or *hand me a towel* or *hand me the 10mm socket I just dropped in the engine bay and couldn't fucking find if my life depended on it.*

"Yeah, he is. But he pays his bill, at least." I checked the clock on the shop wall. "Hey, where the hell is Handme? I thought he was supposed to be here by seven. It's almost nine."

"I think he had to take Lola somewhere."

"Oh, right. He mentioned that yesterday." I shook my

head as I went back to work under the hood of Dodson's Buick. "Poor kid."

"What do you mean, 'poor kid'? He's getting laid all the time."

"I mean, he's a fucking mess over that girl."

"So?"

"So it's *Handme*. She's gonna eat him alive and spit out his bones."

McIntyre laughed from beneath a Ford Mustang. "He might enjoy that. I know I would."

"You and Emily fighting again?" McIntyre was engaged to be married in six months—if he and his high-maintenance fiancée could stay together that long.

"She broke up with me last night."

"What was it this time?"

"Hell if I know. I think her words were something like, 'Because you're an insensitive asshole who doesn't care about anything important.' But by *important*, she means shit like what color the flowers will be at the church or what flavor the wedding cake will be, or who sits where at the reception. What do I care about that stuff? It doesn't matter!"

I couldn't agree more, but I kept my mouth shut.

"It's all bullshit," he rambled on. "Why can't we just say 'I do' at city hall and go drink beers afterward like normal people? I'll even wear the suit."

I laughed. "Got me. You're the one who asked her to marry you."

"I know, but it's like she lost her mind with all this wedding stuff. She used to be so fun. We used to hang out and listen to music and talk about shit that matters, like cars and baseball. Now all we do is argue. I have to say I'm sorry like ten times a night."

"So stop apologizing. Let her crawl back to you for once."

"That could take weeks, Griff. I can't wait that long to

have sex. Not all of us have the discipline to be a celibate monk like you."

"I'm not celibate, asshole. I'm just not a slave to my dick like everyone else who works here."

"But don't you miss it?" McIntyre asked.

Was he kidding? Of course I did. But needing something or someone so badly made you weak, and I prided myself on being strong. Sure, I was human like anyone else, and occasionally a cute ass in tight jeans got the better of me, but I always followed my rules: I was a one-night-only attraction, I always used protection, and I never slept over.

"There are more important things in life than sex," I said.

"Like what?" McIntyre sounded genuinely curious.

"Like keeping this business alive despite the fact that we're bleeding customers and Swifty Auto is soaking them up. Like finding time and money for hands-on training so we can stay up to date with advanced diagnostics. Like getting that small business loan so I can afford advertising, another mechanic, and better tools and software." I straightened up and grabbed a blue shop towel. "Like winning the league championship."

He rolled out from under the Mustang and looked at me, his expression somber. "Amen, brother."

McIntyre and I played for the Bellamy Creek Bulldogs in a league my sister referred to as "old man baseball." It's true, we were all over thirty, not as agile or fast as we'd been in high school, and we consumed a *lot* more beer, but we took it very, very seriously. We lived for those Thursday night games, celebrating every victory—and drowning our sorrows after each defeat—at The Bulldog Pub, the bar that sponsored us. And it looked like this summer's championship game would be a match-up between us and our most bitter rivals, the Mason City Mavericks. We'd won the title the last two years, and they were anxious to get it back.

"You're coming to practice tonight, right?" I asked. McIntyre was our center fielder. He wasn't a big hitter, but he was quick and had a good throwing arm.

"Definitely." He paused. "If Emily says it's okay."

I shook my head—the guy was a hopeless case—and tossed the towel aside.

After closing the shop just after five, I locked the doors and re-entered the building from a door on the far left of the façade, which opened onto the staircase leading up to my apartment.

The garage was actually an old firehouse with two bays. It had been vacant for at least a decade before my grandfather bought it in 1955 and repurposed it into a service station. My father took it over in the early 1970s when my grandpa retired. Back then, they used the second story over the lobby as storage, but after I got out of the Marine Corps four years ago, my father offered to let me convert it into living space.

That hadn't been the plan, of course, but life as I'd imagined it was no longer an option. So I returned the ring, withdrew my offer on the house, drank myself into oblivion and generally behaved real fucking badly for several months before my dad and my three best friends told me to get my shit together, because life goes on.

Having a project helped, and my buddy Enzo Moretti was a builder, so he'd worked with me on the apartment after hours. There was something cathartic about spending my spare time putting up walls.

It was a cavernous space with high ceilings, exposed brick, and wide-plank wood floors. My bedroom and bathroom were at the back, and the front was basically one big rectangular room, with a kitchen in one corner and a seating area by the three front windows overlooking Main Street.

Thanks to Moretti's connections, I'd scored nice materials on a limited budget—leftover tile and granite from someone's new vacation home, reclaimed wood floors from a lumber dealer, doors and fixtures salvaged from old barns and farmhouses, even some of the original details from the firehouse itself. It might have been a little mismatched to an expert decorator's eye, but it didn't bother me.

The only thing I wished I had was some land. If I could ever afford it, I wanted a piece to call my own. All his life, my dad had talked about saving up enough to buy some decent acreage when he retired. He'd planned to move out to the country and spend his days tinkering with old cars in a barn, going fishing whenever he felt like it, and teaching his grandchildren how to play pinochle.

Unfortunately, a heart attack had claimed both him and his dreams too soon.

"He worked himself into an early grave," my mother said the day of his funeral. "Don't do it, Griff. He wouldn't want it for you. Find some other way to honor him."

But my dad had worked his fingers to the bone to keep *his* father's business alive, and I'd be damned if it was going to die on my watch. If it meant working longer hours to keep our customers loyal, so be it.

But tonight, there was baseball.

Hungry, I went to the fridge, hoping for a miracle, like maybe I'd forgotten there was a fresh-baked lasagna in there. Or a steak and potatoes. At the very least, a chicken pot pie.

No such luck. Clearly, I'd forgotten to grocery shop again.

But I had some lunch meat and half a loaf of bread, so I slapped a ham sandwich together and scarfed it down while changing out of my work clothes into some sweats.

I was hurrying around to the back of the building where my truck was parked when my cell phone buzzed.

"Hello?"

"How's my favorite big brother ever?"

"You mean your only big brother ever?" I jumped into the truck, tossing my glove onto the passenger seat.

"Seriously, Griffin, how *are* you? Have I told you how handsome you look today?"

"We're on the phone, Cheyenne." I started the engine. "You can't even see me."

"Then I think you should come over to the shelter so I can say it and mean it."

"And what else?" I asked, because I know my little sister.

"And nothing else," she said.

"There's always an *else* with you, Cheyenne." I shifted into reverse and backed out of my parking spot behind the building. "And you never say nice things to me. You must need something."

"So suspicious," she scolded. "Frankly, I'm offended."

"Uh huh."

"I was only hoping to see you."

"Right."

"And show you something."

"Something like an animal you want me to rescue?"

"No, Mr. Know It All, it's not an *animal* I want you to rescue." She paused. "It's just a kitten."

I groaned.

"A tiny little orphan kitten."

"Stop it. I'm not fostering any more animals. They poop on everything. They chew shit."

"Please, Griff? You're the one who brought in the stray pregnant cat."

"Because I didn't want a pet and she kept hanging around my door." Of course, that was because I'd been feeding her, but I'd felt sorry for the thing.

"Well, the babies are ready to be adopted, and it's breaking my heart to see them there every day. I'd take one but you know how allergic Mom is. And of course, I gave up my lease so I could move in with her after her surgeries."

"I am well aware of your sacrifice, Cheyenne." My sister loved to bring this up in order to guilt me into doing things. And it always worked—there was *no way* I could have survived moving back home. I loved my mother, but she drove me nuts. "How long would I have to keep it?"

"Not long, I promise. Just until I can find it a permanent home, which I'm sure I'll be able to do as soon as school starts up in a month." Cheyenne was a kindergarten teacher at our old elementary school.

"Fine," I said grudgingly, heading toward the ball field. "But I can't pick it up right now. I'm on my way to practice."

"I would not *dream* of interfering with old man baseball," she said, laughing. "Just come to the shelter tomorrow. I'll get the paperwork ready."

"You know, you shouldn't make fun of me after I just agreed to do you a favor. I could still change my mind."

She laughed again. "No, you couldn't. I know you, Griffin Dempsey. Granite on the outside, gooey on the inside. You're like a soft-serve ice cream cone covered with Magic Shell chocolate. You're like a Cadbury egg. You're like a—"

I hung up on her. Little shit.

After practice, most of the team met up at The Bulldog Pub for a few beers, some pizza, and a lot of trash talk about the Mavericks. I sat at an outdoor table on the sidewalk with Cole Mitchell, our star pitcher, and Moretti, our second baseman and fastest runner.

"We're gonna crush those assholes," said Cole. "They're

not gonna know what hit 'em." Then he winced as he adjusted the bag of ice on his shoulder.

Cole was a cop, widowed way too young, now a single dad with a little girl he adored. We'd grown up next door to each other and had been best friends from the day we met. His family had moved in when we were six, and he was the closest thing I had to a brother. He was also the best human being I'd ever known, straightforward and honest, even if he was slightly in denial about our team's ability to crush the Mavs.

Not that he was the only one.

"Fuck yeah," agreed Moretti, lifting his beer bottle. He worked for Moretti & Sons, his family's construction business, and we'd been buddies since his family had moved to Bellamy Creek when we were in middle school. "We're gonna decimate 'em. And I'm gonna steal home just like I did the last time." He shifted uncomfortably on his chair. "Hope my groin injury is better by then."

I laughed and took a long pull on my beer. "Don't fall apart on me now, assholes. We looked decent tonight. Solid hitting. Good pitching. The Mavs are tough, but I like our chances—if you don't turn into a bunch of old ladies in the next two weeks."

"Where's Beckett tonight, anyway?" said Cole, reaching for another slice of pizza. "He think he's too good for practice or what?"

Beckett Weaver was the only guy in our childhood foursome who'd left Bellamy Creek for college and hadn't come back—not right away, anyway. It didn't surprise any of us, since he'd always been the book-smartest in our group—straight A's, Valedictorian, scholarship to an Ivy League school. He'd gotten two degrees, moved to Manhattan to work in finance, and fucking hated every second of it. He'd grown up on a farm and decided he missed it too much, so three years ago, he'd left the Big Apple behind and moved back home to help run his family's cattle ranch.

It was awesome for the team, since Beckett had always been the biggest hitter of any of us. I was a close second, and a damn good first baseman, but against the Mavericks, we'd need all the muscle we could get.

"Nah, he just had something he had to get done tonight," I said.

"Move his cows, probably." Cole laughed and shook his head. "That guy spends more time moving his cows around his land than doing anything else. I don't know how he stands it."

"Beats being stuck behind a desk all day," I said. "I don't know how he did that as long as he did."

"I do—he was making millions of dollars," Moretti said, trying to catch the server's eye to order another beer. It wouldn't take long—his looks pretty much guaranteed him the eye of every female in the room between the ages of twelve and ninety. He'd always been the charmer of the group, able to flirt his way out of trouble with anyone—teachers, principals, coaches, girls. Even the mothers adored him. "It's those dark eyes," my mom said once, a little too dreamily. "They smolder."

Sure enough, the server, a pretty twenty-something with long blond hair and a shy smile, came rushing over to ask what she could do for him. Moretti gave her the smolder and asked for another beer, and she sighed before saying she'd be right back with it, hurrying inside the pub before anyone else could order anything. Cole and I exchanged an eye roll.

"Hey, has Beckett said anything to you about his dad?" Moretti asked.

"His dad?" I squinted across the table at him. "No, why?"

"My mom said she ran into him at the grocery store the other day, and he seemed confused. Like he couldn't remember how he'd gotten there."

"Huh. That's not good."

Cole moved the ice pack on his shoulder again. "Getting old sucks."

"We're not that old," Moretti said. "We're barely thirty."

"We're thirty-two," I pointed out.

"Okay, we're barely *over* thirty. But what's so bad about it? We still look good." He smiled at the server as she set down his beer.

"Could I get one more too, please?" I asked.

"Sure," she said, before glancing at Cole. "How about for you, Officer Mitchell?"

He thought about it and shook his head. "Nah, I better get home."

"Okay. I'll get your check." She gave him a smile and picked up his empty plate.

"I think she likes you, Officer Mitchell," I said, laughing as I tipped my chair back on two legs.

Cole rolled his eyes. "Fuck off."

"No, Griff is right," Moretti said with a grin. "She didn't call *me* by name. Maybe you should ask her out."

"No." Cole was adamant.

"Why not?"

"Well, besides the fact that she barely looks older than Mariah, I don't even remember how to ask a girl out. I haven't had to do it since high school."

"It hasn't changed," Moretti assured him.

"How many times do I have to say it—I'm good," Cole insisted, holding up his palms. "I don't want to date anybody. I live with my mother. I'm raising a daughter. I've got enough women to deal with."

Moretti looked at me. "What about you? What's your excuse?"

I shrugged. "I'm smarter than the rest of you assholes."

Moretti shook his head. "Jesus. You guys really are a couple of old men. You're gonna end up like those two crotchety dudes on the Muppets, Statler and Waldorf, sitting alone up in the bleachers, watching Bulldogs games and complaining about everything."

Cole laughed. "And where are you gonna be?"

"Oh, my wife and kids will have driven me into an early grave by then."

I cocked a brow. "I didn't realize you had a wife and kids."

"I don't. Not yet, anyway. But it's inevitable. In my family, you have a wife—preferably Italian, definitely Catholic—and a bunch of kids. They're expensive, loud, and they drive you crazy, but then you get to spend the rest of your life making them feel guilty about shit." He shrugged and picked up his beer. "That's how it goes. It's the Moretti circle of life."

I laughed. "And where are you going to find this wife? You know every single Italian girl in this town, and half of them are related to you."

"I'm not worried," Moretti said, lifting his bottle toward the sky. "I figure as long as I have faith, she'll show up when I least expect it."

Right then, we heard a huge boom next to us on the street. Since sudden loud noises trigger a hyper-alert response in me —a remnant of my three deployments in Afghanistan—I jumped to my feet and assessed the situation, my adrenaline pumping. But it was immediately apparent that the source of the explosion was a blown tire.

Cole and Moretti stood too, and we watched as a red vintage MG wobbled precariously before jumping a concrete chock block and coming to rest on the sidewalk in front of the Bellamy Creek Credit Union, which told me that the driver did exactly the thing you're not supposed to do after blowing a tire—panic and slam on the brakes. Luckily, no one was parked in front of the credit union at this hour, and the sidewalk was empty as well. Still, the driver had to be pretty shaken up, if not injured.

Without exchanging a word, the three of us took off toward the car. As soon as we got close, we could see it had been the MG's rear passenger-side tire that had blown. The driver opened the door and got out of the little car, which took some effort since she appeared to be wearing . . . a big, white wedding gown.

"Holy shit." Moretti put both hands on his head. "I was kidding."

We stared as the woman approached us, taking in all the details. The long strapless dress. The tiara perched on top of her dark blond hair. The white gloves covering her arms to the elbow. The shocked expression. She looked like a very confused Disney princess, as if she'd been well on her way to the Magic Kingdom and had no idea how she'd wound up here instead.

But she was undeniably beautiful, with wide-set green eyes and a full lower lip, and even though something about her spelled T-R-O-U-B-L-E, my gut instinct was protective.

"Are you okay?" I asked.

She blinked at me. "Is this heaven?"

"It's Bellamy Creek," said Cole. "Ma'am, do you need help?"

"I . . ." she started. Then her eyes fluttered shut, her knees buckled, and her body began to collapse into the massive cloud of white.

I moved fast, catching her as she fell.

CHAPTER 2
BLAIR

ADMITTEDLY, I am not a very good driver.

I have a terrible sense of direction, I know nothing about cars, and I have an unfortunate tendency to hit things like curbs, other people's bumpers, and random stationary objects like telephone poles or fire hydrants. Once I accidentally collided with a lovely old magnolia tree, but I sincerely believe that was not my fault, since I'd pulled into the wrong driveway and the tree appeared without warning where no tree had ever appeared before.

But I could have *sworn* there was nothing on the road in front of me, when BOOM! It was like something *exploded* beneath my car.

I freaked out and slammed on the brakes, which suddenly ceased to function as brakes should, which prompted further panic, which resulted in my car jumping one of those parking curb thingies and landing on the sidewalk.

Now, here's where my memory gets a little hazy. I vaguely remember turning off the engine and sitting there for a moment, breathing hard, gripping the steering wheel, and listening to the rapid gunfire of my heart. Then I got out of the car, gathering the full tulle skirt of my dress in both hands, and making my way onto the sidewalk.

That's when I saw them.

Three *ridiculously hot* guys standing there staring at me. For a moment I wondered if I'd hit my head and this was sort of a Wizard of Oz moment, where nothing was real.

"Are you okay?" asked the one in the middle. No joke, he looked like James Dean, only taller and more muscular, with tattoos covering one arm. I didn't even know guys that hot existed in real life.

That's when it hit me—I was dead and didn't know it.

I blinked at him. "Is this heaven?"

"It's Bellamy Creek," said the one to the right of James Dean. He had the brightest blue eyes I'd ever seen. "Ma'am, do you need help?"

"I . . ." Help? Yes, I needed help, but for the life of me, I couldn't remember why. My head began to spin, my vision went foggy, and my knees gave out.

I sank into a puddle of tulle.

When I came to, I was cradled in someone's arms. I opened my eyes and realized that James Dean must have caught me before I hit the ground.

"Set her down on the bench," said a voice from behind. "Elevate her feet."

I felt myself being gently lowered onto a hard surface. Someone grabbed my feet and held them up by the heels of my sandals, and someone else snatched my wrist and took my pulse. "Ma'am! Can you hear me?"

I nodded. "Yes."

"Cole, should we call 911?" James Dean knelt down next to me.

"No—please," I said. I wasn't sure if calling 911 cost money or not, but on the off chance it did, I couldn't let it happen. "I'm okay. I just got dizzy."

He studied my face, his expression skeptical. "You sure?"

I nodded, noticing his eyes for the first time. They were blue too, but not a piercing blue like his friend's. They were a softer, smokier blue. Hazy and beautiful.

I may have moaned.

"I don't smell alcohol, pulse is normal," said the guy holding my wrist.

"I haven't been drinking," I said, my voice hoarse. "I'm probably just dehydrated."

James Dean looked toward my feet. "Moretti, will you run into the Bulldog and get her some water?"

"On it. Cole, you want to take over here?"

The guy who'd checked my pulse gently set my arm on my stomach and moved to take my feet. "Ma'am, do you have any medical conditions?" he asked. "Are you diabetic?"

I shook my head.

"Do you feel any pain?"

"No. Are you a doctor or something?"

"I'm a police officer. My name is Cole Mitchell, and this is Griffin Dempsey. Can you tell us your name?"

"Blair Beaufort."

"Where do you live, Ms. Beaufort?"

"I'm currently between addresses."

"And what brings you to Bellamy Creek?"

I tried to remember. "I think it was the pie."

"The pie?" James Dean—I mean, Griffin Dempsey— sounded confused. "What pie?"

"Can you help me sit up, please?"

He took my hands and slowly pulled me into a seated

position, while Officer Mitchell gently brought my feet down to the cement.

"Thank you." I closed my eyes and took a couple deep breaths as the last hour pieced itself back together in my mind. "I was on the highway and I saw this sign for the Bellamy Creek Diner advertising the best apple pie in the Midwest since 1957. I happen to adore apple pie, so how could I resist?"

"Oh, *that* pie." Officer Mitchell sighed and shook his head. "Yeah, that's an old sign."

"You mean, there's no pie?" I asked incredulously. Was that even legal? Surely you couldn't keep advertising a pie that no longer existed.

"Well, there's pie," he said. "But not *thee* pie. Not the pie from the sign. We haven't had that pie since Betty Frankel died and took the recipe to her grave."

"Seriously?"

"Yep." He shook his head and sighed tragically. "Damn, I miss that pie."

"Me too," said Griffin.

Their dark-haired friend who'd gone for the water appeared and handed me a tall Styrofoam cup with a cardboard straw. "Here you go."

I stared at him for a few seconds, a little in awe of his dark, smoldering eyes and exquisite bone structure. Jeez, what the heck was in the water around here? "Thank you. I appreciate it."

Grateful, I took a few sips. Then, just in case it was from some mythical Fountain of Beauty, I took a few more.

Griffin pulled his wallet from his pocket. "Hey Moretti, do me one more favor. Can you go settle up my bill? I'll run over and get the tow truck."

"Sure." Moretti took the cash he was offered but stood there a moment longer, looking at me like I might be a ghost.

"What?" I asked, unnerved by the intensity of his stare.

"You're not Italian, are you?"

"No."

"Are you even Catholic?"

I shook my head. "Sorry."

Moretti looked relieved. "I'll be right back."

"I'll go settle up too," said Officer Mitchell. "Griff, you good here? Soon as I'm done, I'll stay with her while you go get the tow truck."

"Okay."

A tow truck.

Crap.

I was positive *that* would cost money, although I had no idea how much. The truth was that I'd been raised with every advantage wealth could buy but remained pretty much clueless about what basic things cost.

I had a lot to learn now that I was on my own.

The reality of my situation sank in hard. I sucked down some more water, wishing it was something stronger.

"So, Blair Beaufort. Is someone waiting for you somewhere?" Griffin Dempsey glanced at my dress. "Like . . . at the *altar*?"

I gave him a funny look. "This isn't a wedding dress."

"It's not?"

"No, it's my debutante gown."

He barely hid a smile. "Of course it is."

"I'm only wearing it now because it didn't fit in my suitcase."

"And the crown?"

"It's a *tiara*, and it's my best one. I didn't want to crush it."

He adjusted the ball cap on his head and squinted at me, clearly wondering if I was one brick short of a load.

I sighed heavily. "My car is tiny, so my suitcase is small. Not everything fit in it."

"Why not get a moving van?"

I shrugged. "I don't have any furniture."

"You own a ball gown, but not a couch?"

I sat up taller. "This isn't just a *ball gown* to me, mister. I wore it on the most special night of my life, okay? I danced in it and felt beautiful. Inspired. Hopeful. Like my life was just beginning. That's a feeling I need to hold on to, especially now."

"Why especially now?"

I sniffed and looked away from him. "It's personal."

"Okay."

I fully expected him to press for details and was slightly annoyed when he didn't. "If you must know, my life circumstances have changed of late, and I no longer possess the resources I once had."

"Sorry to hear it."

"My family has fallen upon hard times," I went on, as if he'd asked for more.

"It happens."

"My father made some . . . creative accounting decisions, which turned out to be called tax evasion, and now he's awaiting trial. But he's not a bad person—he just made some bad choices."

The poor guy clearly didn't know what to say, but I couldn't seem to stop talking (this is a recurring problem I have).

"We had to sell pretty much everything we owned, right down to the furniture, just to cover the back taxes and legal fees. My mother moved back in with my grandmother, who said 'I *told* you not to marry a Beaufort' and offered to set me up with some crusty old tycoon at her country club, but I said no thanks. I'd rather be poor than be someone's trophy wife."

"I don't blame you."

"Then we had a huge fight, because my family isn't used to me standing up for myself. They thought I would just do what they told me to do, because I always have. But not this time." I lifted my chin. "*This* time, I'm doing what *I* want."

"And what's that?"

"To start over somewhere fresh. I'm going to run my *own* business."

"What kind of business?"

"A bakery."

"A bakery?" Griffin sounded surprised.

"Yes." I sipped up the last of the ice water. "I've always loved to bake, and I'm actually really good at it, but my parents said I wasn't allowed to go to culinary school."

"Why not?"

"They said I had to go to a university and pick an appropriate major like history or French. So I did."

"Which one?"

"French." I smiled mischievously. "And during my junior year abroad, I secretly studied with a Parisian pastry chef. Of course, after graduate school, I took the cushy job my parents wanted me to, lived in the fancy apartment they provided, and attended all the boring social events they insisted upon, where I sipped expensive champagne, danced with men in tuxedoes, and pretended to have a good time."

"Sounds like torture."

"It was," I said, although he might have been kidding. "Because inside, I was slowly dying. I kept asking myself, 'Is this it? Am I just going to be bored and unfulfilled the rest of my life? Is being rich worth the price of my *soul*?'"

"I don't know. Your soul is probably more expensive than mine."

"So I decided to do something about it, and for the last couple years I worked in the kitchen at a coffee shop every morning on the sly, from five to eight a.m. Then I'd run home, clean up, and make it into the office by nine. My family never knew."

"Good for you." He chuckled, and I noticed the dimple in his chin.

"What's funny about that?"

"I don't know." He adjusted his cap again. "It's just that a job is an odd thing to have to hide from your parents."

"Not if they're *my* parents. Anyway, when this huge reversal of fortune happened, I decided to take it as a sign I needed to escape my old life and start a new one somewhere else. So that's what I'm doing."

"Good luck."

"Thank you." I studied him then, waiting for him to tell me *his* story. It was only polite to reciprocate, right? "Sooo," I prompted.

"So what?"

"So what about you?"

"I'm a mechanic. My parents approved."

I waited for more. "That's it?"

"That's it."

"Did you always want to be a mechanic?"

He gave me a funny look. "You talk a lot."

"Conversation is a lost art."

"I think you found it."

I sighed, giving up on art and moving on to more practical matters. "So how bad is the damage to my car? Will it be expensive to fix? How long will it take?"

"Hard to say." He studied my MG for a moment, then got down on his hands and knees and looked at the ground beneath it. "Thanks to the pothole you hit, you definitely need a new tire and some work on your front end, but I think you might need brakes too. How old is this car?"

"Old."

"Do you know what year?"

"I think 1971."

He looked over at me. "You *think*?"

I shrugged. "That's what the guy said."

"What guy?"

"The guy who sold it to me last week. I got a really good deal on it because it had been in his barn for a while."

"Oh, Jesus." Griffin got to his feet and brushed off his hands. "I'll look everything over tomorrow. Make sure it's safe."

"But how much is that going to *cost*? As I've mentioned, I'm not particularly liquid at the moment."

"We'll figure something out." He glanced down the street toward the pub and rubbed the back of his neck. His clothes were kind of dirty and he looked like he might have gotten sweaty earlier, but I found myself admiring his broad shoulders and trim waist. I bet he had those six-pack ab muscles too. I'd never actually seen any in person, but he seemed like the kind of guy that would have them.

"Would you like to sit down?" I scooted over to one side of the bench to make more room.

He ambled over and sat, crossing his arms over his chest. "Thanks."

I couldn't stop staring at his thick forearms, his wide hands. "Thanks for not letting me hit the ground, by the way. You must have fast reflexes."

He shrugged. "More like good instincts."

We sat in silence for a moment, and I looked up and down the street. "This looks like a cute little town. Did you grow up here?"

"Yep."

I waited for him to ask me where I'd grown up.

He didn't.

"Belle Meade, Tennessee," I announced anyway. "That's where I'm from. And I'm headed in the direction of a place called Cloverleigh Farms."

"Never heard of it."

"Really?" I frowned. "Shoot, I hope I was going the right way."

"Where is it?"

"The Leelenau Peninsula."

He nodded. "You're good. That's about three hours north of here."

"Whew," I said, peeling off my gloves and fanning my face.

After a minute he asked, "You're moving to a *farm*?"

I laughed. "Does that surprise you?"

"Actually, yes."

"Well, it's not *just* a farm. It's also an inn with a winery and a restaurant. It's run by the Sawyer family, and I stayed there once several years ago for a wedding and fell in love with it. It's *beautiful*. And it gave me the most incredible feeling. If a place could love you back, or like, grow arms and hug you, that's what this place would do. So that's why I'm going there."

"To feel the hug."

I couldn't tell if he was teasing me or not. "Yes. If I feel it again, I'll know where I belong."

"Sounds like you've got things all figured out."

I didn't, not even close, but I crossed my fingers and hoped he was right.

"Hey. Sorry that took so long." Officer Mitchell and the dark-haired friend came jogging back over. "Moretti was sweet-talking the server."

"What else is new?" Griffin muttered, rising to his feet.

"Listen, I shaved like five minutes off the usual time I spend getting someone's number," Moretti said. "You're welcome."

Griffin rolled his eyes. "I'm gonna go over to the garage and get the truck. Back in ten minutes."

"Sounds good." The cop sat down on the bench, and we watched Griffin jog across the street and get into a white pickup truck.

"Don't worry about a thing," Moretti said. "Griffin is the best mechanic there is. He'll have you fixed up in no time."

"I hope so," I said. "Do you think he'll be able to fix it tonight?"

"If anyone can do it, Griffin can." Officer Mitchell sounded confident, and it made me feel a little better.

Those big hands *had* looked awfully capable.

"Ready to go?" Griffin asked me once they were finished getting my poor little MG hooked up to the tow. It took some serious effort, thanks to the awkward angle at which I'd, um, "parked."

"Yes," I said. "Should I ride in the truck with you?"

He looked amused. "Unless you want to walk. But I won't be around to catch you if you fall."

"Very funny. I'll take the ride, thank you."

He opened the passenger door, and I noticed the blanket over the front seat. Had he done that for me?

Touched, I hitched up the bottom of my dress and climbed in, although it took me a few hops on one foot, and I almost asked him for a boost. But once I was seated on the blanket, I gathered up all the tulle around me and nodded at him to shut the door. I could tell he was trying not to laugh.

The cab of the truck was dark and smelled like gasoline and leather, which was a strangely pleasant and masculine combination. On the drive to the garage, I snuck a peek at Griffin's profile and thought again how handsome he was. Chiseled jaw, strong, straight nose, full lips. I wondered what color his hair was beneath his cap. I remembered the blue of his eyes, and my belly performed a little flip.

But he was probably a big jerk. Had I ever been attracted to a nice guy? That was another thing I planned to change in my new life—no more dating commitment-phobic playboys or lazy, entitled assholes. I wouldn't be distracted by pretty lies or empty promises anymore, and I certainly wouldn't care about a big bank account. I knew better than anyone how quickly money could disappear.

I wanted someone *good*. Someone *real*. Someone *honest*. Someone with a big heart and big dreams, and if he happened to have a big dick too, well, I wouldn't complain.

But there would be time for all that later. My first order of business was to work on myself.

Just beyond the downtown area, Griffin slowed down and we passed in front of a tall brick building that looked at least a hundred years old. It was two-and-a-half stories high and had two huge, arched bay doors. The façade was illuminated by streetlamps, and a sign across the front read BELLAMY CREEK GARAGE. Above that, etched in the cement, I could barely make out lettering that said Ladder Co. 3.

"Was this a firehouse?" I asked.

"Yeah." Griffin turned into the lot next to the building and expertly maneuvered the truck into position, while I admired the old firehouse's Beaux-Arts architectural details.

"It's a beautiful building."

"Thanks. My grandfather bought it in the fifties. By then it had been vacant and crumbling for years. Nobody knew what to do with it, and it was about to be torn down."

I gasped. "Thank goodness he saved it."

"Everyone told him the idea was crazy, but he mortgaged himself into the ground and bought it anyway."

"He took a leap of faith," I said, gooseflesh rippling down my bare arms.

"Or he was just stubborn." Griffin put the truck in park. "My dad was the same way when he got his heart set on something."

I looked over at him. "What about you?"

"Me?"

"Yes. Are you willing to take a leap of faith when you get your heart set on something?"

"I've learned not to get my heart set on anything."

Our eyes met in the dark. "Why not?"

For a moment, I thought he wasn't going to answer, or might even tell me to mind my own beeswax, but he surprised me. "Because it never ends well."

I wanted to ask him what he'd gotten his heart set on in the past that hadn't ended well, but even *I* realized it was too personal a question, so I buttoned my lip.

It was a very difficult moment for me.

Griffin cleared his throat. "I'll open up the lobby and you can wait there while I get your car unloaded."

"Thanks."

"Is there anything you need out of it?"

I bit my lip. "It won't be fixed tonight?"

He looked at me like I'd sprouted a second head. "Um. No."

"Then I should get my suitcase. Is there a Hilton in town?" I asked, hoping I had at least one credit card that wasn't maxed out.

He laughed like I'd told a great joke. "No, but there are a couple of bed and breakfasts and a motel not too far up the highway."

"Okay."

"I'll bring your suitcase into the office when I'm done out here. It's in the trunk?"

"Yes."

He opened his door. "Do you need help getting out of the truck?"

"I think I'm okay." But when I opened the door and looked down at the pavement, it seemed like an even bigger drop than it had when I'd gotten in. I peeked at him over my shoulder. "You don't happen to have a step stool handy, do you?"

He shook his head, chuckling a little. "Stay there, Cinderella. I can't have you losing a shoe or twisting your ankle."

"Thanks." I swiveled in the seat to face outward, and when Griffin got around to my side, he reached for me—then stopped.

"Is this okay?" he asked, his fingers hovering an inch from my waist.

I nodded. "Yes."

He wrapped his hands around my sides and easily lifted me out of the truck and set me on my feet. I'd never been much of a dancer, but I imagined this was how Ginger Rogers must have felt every time Fred Astaire swung her through the air.

Like just for a moment, the two of you could defy gravity.

He left me sitting inside the small waiting room for about ten minutes. It was small and sparse, not unclean or untidy, but not terribly warm or welcoming either. It smelled like stale coffee and something chemical and metallic—sort of like hairspray from a can. The magazines, though neatly stacked, were all dog-eared and outdated. The chairs were the metal folding variety with padded vinyl seats. One had a rip. The rug appeared clean enough, though frayed at the edges, and one sad, thirsty plant hung on a ceiling hook in the corner.

I took out my phone, prepared to hop on Google Maps and search "places to stay," but because this was obviously not my day, the thing was dead. I shoved it back in my bag and fought off tears. I did not want Griffin to see me crying, and even more than that, I was determined to be the kind of woman who solved her own problems.

Pausing for a few deep breaths, I made a plan. I would get something inexpensive to eat, ask someone at the restaurant if I could possibly charge my phone while I ate, and then secure a place to stay the night. Of course, I still wasn't sure how I'd manage to pay for it—and car repairs too—but one crisis at a time, right?

When Griffin returned, he asked for my license, wrote up some paperwork for me, and said he'd look the car over first thing in the morning.

"Thank you," I said, tucking my license back into my wallet.

"Can I give you a lift somewhere?"

"No, thank you. But could you recommend a restaurant nearby?"

He checked the old clock on the wall. "I'm pretty sure the diner stays open until ten on weeknights during the summer. But it's nine-thirty now, so you'll want to hurry."

"Is it within walking distance?"

"Yes. Just a few blocks west. Turn left when you leave here. But I'd be glad to drive you."

"No, no. That's okay." Determined to appear plucky and independent, I picked up my suitcase, and he crossed the lobby to open the door for me.

But I couldn't move. It was like my feet were stuck in cement.

That's when I realized I didn't want to leave him.

Crazy as it sounds, I felt safe in the care of this small-town mechanic with the movie star face and the dimple in his chin and the tattoos and the deep voice and the big, strong hands and the heart he'd learned not to set on anything. I had no real reason to trust him, yet I did. And I kind of wanted to know more about him.

For a second, I thought about asking him if he wanted to come with me.

But just as quickly, I shut that idea down. He'd only been

doing his job tonight. He didn't really care about me. He was holding the door open for me to leave, wasn't he?

He was holding the door open for me to leave because he probably thought I was a silly, spoiled debutante who couldn't do anything for myself—a girl who owned a ball gown but not a couch, who fainted on sidewalks, talked too much, and wasn't even sure what year her car was, let alone what it would cost to fix it. I couldn't tell him I was scared and had nowhere to go. I wanted him to think I was brave. Resourceful. Adventuresome. All the things I planned to become in my new life.

Besides, I wasn't his problem, and he'd done enough.

He was holding the door open for me to leave, and there was nothing left for me to do but walk through it.

CHAPTER 3
GRIFFIN

I WATCHED her walk down the sidewalk in the dark, carrying her suitcase and wearing that ridiculous white dress. She almost looked like a ghost.

When she was completely out of sight, I locked the door, turned off the lights, and headed up the stairs to my apartment.

It was strange how bad I felt letting her wander off alone —I had to remind myself she was a grown woman, she'd refused my offer of a ride, and "crime" in this town was generally confined to kids with toilet paper and too much time on their hands.

Still, I hoped she would be okay. She didn't strike me as helpless, exactly—she was obviously intelligent and probably always landed on her feet, but I definitely got the sense that she lacked some basic street smarts. The fact that she spoke perfect French wasn't really going to help her in her post-debutante life. But I didn't blame her for wanting to escape her family, especially if they really expected her to marry someone for his money. It sounded like a soap opera to me.

Then again, I thought as I tossed my dirty clothes in a laundry basket, I didn't know that many super rich people.

Maybe that was normal in their world. I mean, her middle name was Peacock, for Christ's sake. I'd seen it on her license and nearly laughed out loud, but I hadn't wanted to make her feel any worse. Hopefully, I could get her car fixed up and send her on her way without too much hassle.

Problem was, it wasn't just a blown tire. The fluid I'd seen leaking onto the sidewalk earlier told me the MG's hard brake line had probably rusted through. And getting parts for a 1971 MG wasn't going to be quick or cheap. But I'd do the best I could for her.

I jumped into the shower and rinsed off the day's grime and grit, wondering if she'd made it to the diner and whose ear she was talking off there. It made me smile.

The girl had gumption, as my mother would say.

I admired what she was doing. It took guts to leave behind what you knew and start over somewhere else. I liked that she wanted to start her own business and was willing to work for it. And damn, she was beautiful. Maybe the most beautiful woman I'd ever met. I mean, she was a little bit crazy, and she talked *way* too much, but those big green eyes? Those full lips? That curvy little body? I kept thinking about what she felt like in my arms . . . and wishing it could have happened some other time, some other way.

A way that involved being naked in the dark, where I'd shock her sweet little rich girl sensibilities with my filthy mouth, my rough hands, and my big, hard—

I stopped myself before my thoughts went any further, turning off the shower before my hand wandered to my dick.

There was no point in fantasizing about it. Blair Peacock Beaufort did not look like the type of woman who'd be interested in one night of hot, dirty sex with her mechanic. Or with anyone, for that matter. She was undoubtedly pure vanilla between the sheets. She'd probably insist on wearing the white gloves to bed. Maybe even the tiara.

Then again, that might be kind of fun.

I woke up with a start—I'd heard something.

I lifted my head off the pillow in the dark and stayed completely still, my ears pricked up. At first, I heard nothing but crickets. I glanced at the digital clock on my nightstand—it was just after midnight.

Then, through my bedroom window screen, I heard the sound again—it sounded like someone was opening and closing car doors in the lot. A drunk looking for spare change? Teenagers causing trouble in the dark? A thief attempting to make off with a client's vehicle?

Not on my fucking watch.

Jumping out of bed, I threw on a pair of jeans and some boots, moving quickly and quietly down the stairs and out the door. Pausing only to lock the door behind me, I jogged around to the back of the building to approach the lot from the alley.

I scanned the shadowy lot from the back, seeing no one. Hearing nothing. But my skin was blanketed with gooseflesh in the heat—something wasn't right. I could sense it.

Slowly, I walked toward the front of the lot, which was dimly lit by streetlamps. Movement caught my eye, and I turned my head sharply to the right.

A flash of white inside the MG.

My shoulders and neck lost their tension. What the fuck was she doing, trying to sleep in her car?

Running a hand through my hair, still damp from the shower, I wondered what to do. I didn't want to scare her, but I couldn't let her stay out here in the parking lot. As I approached the driver's side window, I saw her trying to unzip her dress in the back. But she wasn't having much luck, either because she couldn't reach the zipper or the front seat of the MG was too small, and suddenly she dropped her forehead to the steering wheel and began banging it in frustration.

That's when I tapped on the window.

She screamed, of course. I held up my hands and backed away from the glass. "Shhh. It's okay. It's okay. It's just me."

She put a hand on her heart and closed her eyes, breathing hard. Then she opened the car door and got out, looking embarrassed and guilty and maybe a little bit scandalized at the sight of me without a shirt on. I noticed she'd removed the tiara and let her hair down. It hung in long, messy waves past her shoulders.

"Sorry," I said. "Didn't mean to scare you."

"It's okay. I know I shouldn't be here." She eyeballed my bare chest, then quickly looked away.

"Why *are* you here? I thought you were going to find somewhere to stay."

"Well, after I got something to eat at the diner, I tried calling both inns in town, but they were booked." She looked me in the eye. "Truth be told, I can't really afford their prices anyway. So I just came back."

I folded my arms over my chest. "Well, I can't let you sleep in your car."

"But I have nowhere else to go. Can't you just pretend you don't know I'm here?" she pleaded.

That was out of the question. But what was I supposed to do with her? It was too late to call my sister. Should I drive her out to the motel on Highway 31? And then what? Pay for the room myself? Then I'd have to go out there and get her tomorrow. I could let her stay on the couch at my place, but was that too weird? I was debating calling Cole and asking for his advice—he always did the right thing—when I saw a tear slip down her cheek.

"Hey, it's—it's okay," I said. "Don't cry."

"It's not okay," she said, weeping into her hands. "My

new life is already just as big a mess as my old one. I'm trying so hard to be brave and handle things on my own, but maybe this is a sign I can't. Maybe I should just go back to Belle Meade and marry the tycoon."

"Don't say that."

"But it's true. And it's my own damn fault. I mean, I'm thirty years old! I should have my life figured out by now. But I was a coward. And I was complacent. I could have walked away when I wasn't so desperate, but I never did. I deserve to sleep on the street like a vagabond."

"For fuck's sake, Blair." I rolled my eyes. "You're not going to sleep on the street."

"I have no choice," she sobbed. Then all of a sudden, she moved so close the backs of her hands were resting on my chest.

I could smell her perfume—sure enough, there was something vanilla about it—and her bare, trembling shoulders were begging me to put my arms around them. I had to shove my hands in my pockets to keep from embracing her.

"Look, you can—you can stay with me," I choked out.

"What?" She sniffed and looked up. "Stay with you where?"

"My apartment. I live above the garage."

"Oh, I couldn't do that." She backed up and touched her collarbone. "It wouldn't be right."

I rolled my eyes. "You don't really have a choice, Blair. I'm not leaving you on the street, you don't have money for a motel, and it's the middle of the night."

She blinked. "I guess you're right. But I hate to impose. It's so tacky."

Impose, as if she'd shown up uninvited to a garden party. "Just . . . get your stuff and come on," I said gruffly.

"Okay. My suitcase is in the trunk."

I got it out for her, brushing away her hand when she reached for it. "I'll carry it," I said.

"Thank you." She followed me down the sidewalk to my apartment door and stood at my side while I unlocked it. A car drove past us as I was pulling it open, and I cringed when it slowed down. Hopefully, it was no one I knew—I didn't need to be the subject of any gossip tomorrow.

"Go on," I said impatiently. "Get inside."

She held up the bottom of her dress and started up the stairs, while I took a moment to lock the door behind us before going up two steps at a time, her bag still in my hand.

I hadn't left any lights on, so when I reached the top, I bumped into her from behind. She stumbled forward, and I instinctively reached out, catching her around the waist.

"Sorry," she said. "It's just so dark."

It *was* dark. And I had her clutched against my bare chest so tightly I could smell her perfume again. Or was it her hair? Blood rushed to parts of me that didn't need encouragement right now, and I let her go.

"Give me a second." Sidestepping her, I moved to the wall and flipped a switch.

"Oh—oh, wow," she said, moving deeper into the room and turning in a slow circle. "This is beautiful."

"Thanks." I turned on a couple more lights, suddenly wary of being alone with her.

"No fireman pole?" she asked, shooting me a smile over one shoulder that I found alarmingly seductive.

"Not anymore." Trying to remain businesslike—not easy when you're shirtless at midnight—I set her suitcase down and stood a good ten feet from her, crossing my arms over my chest. "You can stay on the couch. I'll get you a pillow and some blankets."

"Thank you."

"If you want to use the bathroom, it's through there." I gestured toward the hallway leading to my bedroom and quickly folded my arms again.

"Thank you. I would like to get out of this dress. Could I borrow a hanger please?"

"Sure. In the closet." I was hoping she'd head straight for the bedroom but instead, she came toward me and reached out, placing a palm on my shoulder.

"I really appreciate this."

Heat rushed my entire body. "No big deal."

"It is to me," she said, and I was terrified she was going to hug me, but she didn't. She picked up her suitcase and headed down the hall into my room.

When I heard the door shut, I exhaled in relief and went over to the chest beneath the front windows where I stored spare blankets. Since it was so warm, a sheet would've been better than a blanket, but my extra sheets were in my bedroom. I'd have to wait until she came out to get one. I stood there wondering if she was topless in my bedroom right this second, and my cock was hard in seconds.

The bedroom door creaked open again.

"Griffin?"

"Yeah?"

"Um, I need some help."

"Help?"

"Getting this dress off."

I looked up at the ceiling. *Really, God? Really?*

Cursing under my breath, I adjusted the crotch of my jeans and walked back to my bedroom, my heart beating an uncomfortably hard, fast rhythm. When I reached the doorway, I kept my eyes on the floor. "Is it okay to come in?"

"Yes. I'm sorry—this whole situation is awkward enough —but the zipper is stuck."

Tentatively, I entered the room and saw her standing with her back to me, holding up her hair. A few more steps and I was close enough to reach for the zipper, which was concealed behind a column of what looked like fabric-covered buttons. Holding my breath, I concentrated on pretending the job was just another mechanical task, like tightening a bolt.

The zipper's slider was tiny and definitely stuck, but I managed to grasp it in my fingers and get it moving—the dress parted and her naked back appeared. I stopped when my hand reached the curve of her waist. "Is that okay? Can you reach it from there?"

She let her hair fall and reached around her back, but I was standing so close she accidentally brushed against my crotch, which had a pretty good bulge going.

Gasping, she pulled her hand away and whirled around. "Oh God! I'm so sorry."

"It's okay." I cleared my throat and backed away. "I think you'll be able to reach it now."

She tried again and was able to grasp the slider without a problem. "I'm good. Thank you."

"No problem." I turned around and left the room, pulling the door shut behind me.

Out in the living room, I dropped onto the couch and tried not to think about her bare limbs, the scent of her skin, the brush of her fingers over my cock.

Stifling a groan, I laced my fingers behind my head and tipped it back, staring at the rotating ceiling fan above. Its whir was hypnotic, and I was so tired . . . my breathing slowed, my eyes closed, and before I knew it, I was out.

When I woke up, rays of early morning light were just starting to slip through my front windows. For a few seconds, I was confused about why I was sitting out here wearing boots and jeans but no shirt.

Then I looked over to my left, where Blair was sound asleep in a chair, and it all came back to me.

She was curled into a ball, her head resting on a small throw pillow wedged between her knees and her cheek. Her arms were wrapped around her legs, and one bare foot was crossed over the other. She wore a T-shirt and shorts, but they were so short I saw a lot more of her bare thighs than I needed to. I tried to tear my eyes from them before they telegraphed a message to my cock about the way they might feel beneath my palms or under my lips or wrapped around my waist, but I was too late. At the telltale twitch of morning wood, I jumped off the couch so suddenly it startled her.

Her eyes opened, and she picked up her head. "Oh. Hi."

"Hi." I moved behind the couch, not that it was tall enough to conceal an erection if I couldn't prevent it. Jesus Christ, it was like being sixteen again and having no control over my body whatsoever. How bad would it be to grab a pillow and cover my crotch?

I forced myself to focus on her face, but that wasn't helpful either—she looked even prettier this morning than she had last night, her face bare of makeup, her hair a tousled mess. I suddenly wanted nothing more than to scoop her off that chair and carry her back to my bedroom. Toss her onto the mattress. Make her scream my name. So what if she'd never slept with someone who didn't wear a suit to work? I'd show her a good fucking time.

Her lips curved into a smile. "You were asleep by the time I got changed last night. I didn't know whether I should wake you or not."

I ran a hand through my hair. "Sorry I crashed—I meant to make up the couch for you. Your legs are probably all cramped up from sleeping like that."

"It's okay." She unfolded them and wiggled her toes. "Beggars can't be choosers, right? I'm just grateful I had a roof over my head. If you weren't so nice, I'd still be stuck in my car in that uncomfortable dress. Thank you."

"Glad to help." I glanced toward my bedroom. "I'm gonna get dressed and head down to the garage so I can take a look at your car. But it's still early. You don't have to get up."

"I like getting up early. I used to go into work at the bakery at five, remember?" She rose to her feet and stretched with her arms over her head, her nipples visibly poking at the thin white cotton. "I'll get dressed and clear out of here."

"No rush." Trying not to drool, I started for my bedroom. "Stay as long as you like."

Just stay away from me. You're making me want things I can't have.

I had planned to check out Blair's car first thing, but it turned into one of those mornings where nothing went right.

My cousin Lanette had taken over as receptionist while my mother was recovering from surgery—and by "taken over," I mean she sat in the chair three days a week and answered the phone. Sometimes she filed her nails, but never the paperwork. But Lanette didn't work on Wednesdays, so of course the phone wouldn't stop ringing and we were inundated with walk-ins as soon as I unlocked the door.

Which all would have been fine—great, even—except somehow they were all the worst kind of customer.

Like the lonely old lady who wants to tell you her life story instead of what's wrong with her car. Or the shifty-eyed guy who's hiding the fact that he already tried to fix the problem himself and made it worse. Or the guy in the suit who's currently suing the three previous mechanics who have worked on his vehicle.

And it seemed like all of them had already gotten an estimate from Swifty Auto that was cheaper than mine, and a guarantee it would be done by the end of the day. Then there were the customers picking up their cars who were upset at being charged for labor in addition to parts—as if the parts had magically installed themselves and didn't take hours of skilled diagnostic and technical work on our end.

To make things worse, the desk was a mess, I couldn't find anyone's invoices because nothing had been filed for weeks, and no one had told me we were out of coffee.

By the time Blair walked through the lobby door carrying a bakery box and a drinks tray with two tall cardboard cups in it, I was ready to torch the whole operation.

"Hi there," she said, setting the box and tray on the counter. She wore a short yellow flowery dress, and her hair was pulled back in a ponytail. "How's it going?"

I rubbed my face with both hands. "Shitty. I'm sorry, I haven't had a chance to look at your car yet. It's been fucking chaos in here for the last two hours. This is the first time the lobby has been quiet."

"That's okay. I can wait. I went down to the diner for some coffee and realized you hadn't eaten anything before you left this morning. Thought you might like some breakfast." She opened the box to reveal a dozen donuts. "I know it's not the best apple pie since 1957 or anything, but these looked okay."

"Thanks. Coffee up for grabs too?"

"Of course. I wasn't sure how you took it, but when I mentioned to Louise at the diner where I was bringing everything, she said you just took it black. That one's yours." She pointed to the cup with a G on it before pulling one labeled with a B from the carrier.

"Perfect." I grabbed the cup she'd indicated was mine and took a gulp. "I needed this."

"Can I help?"

"Nah, that's okay." I reached into the box, pulled out a glazed donut, and took a bite. It was oddly tasteless.

"I really don't mind. Is your receptionist late or something?"

"We don't have one full-time right now. My mother has worked the desk here for years, but she's out because she had a hip replacement recently. My cousin Lanette has been working part-time, but . . ." I frowned at the disaster area in front of me. "She doesn't get much actual work done."

Blair peeked over the counter. "Yikes. How do you find anything?"

I took another gulp of coffee. "Sometimes we don't."

"Well, listen. I don't have anything to do while I wait for you to fix my car, and I owe you a big favor for offering me a place to stay last night. Let me take over here and get all this stuff filed, so you can get to work in there." She gestured toward the service bays.

My first instinct was to say no, but I gave myself a minute to think as I polished off the rest of the boring donut. I did not want to spend my entire day out here listening to people gripe. I did not want to stay after hours filing paperwork. And I sure as hell didn't want to hear the words *Swifty Auto* again today—my temper was already threatening to blow. "Are you sure?" I asked.

"Of course I'm sure."

"And you're okay answering the phone too?"

She rolled her eyes. "Seriously?"

"Sorry, but you don't strike me as the type to have had a lot of experience being a receptionist."

"I'm pretty sure I can handle it."

"Okay. I'm going to get a few quick things out of the way and then I'll look at your car. I'll discount the labor in exchange for your work at the desk."

"Perfect." She smiled brightly at me, and my stomach

muscles tightened up. I turned away and headed for the garage, coffee cup in hand.

"Oh, Griffin?"

I looked back at her and felt the tightness expand into my chest. "Yeah?"

"Should I answer the phone in French or in English?"

I stared at her for a full five seconds, wondering if she was serious, before she lost it and burst out laughing.

"Oh my God, you should see your face," she said, shooing me out. "Go on, get out of here. I have work to do."

Shaking my head, I turned around and walked out. It was the first time I'd smiled all morning.

Inside the first service bay, Handme was fixing a coolant leak on a Honda and McIntyre was hunting around the floor near the tool cabinets for something he'd dropped (probably the 10mm socket).

"You really need to think about hiring a full-time desk person," McIntyre said. "We're getting behind back here without you."

I frowned. "I can't afford one. I'm still paying my mother."

"Is she ever coming back?"

"Why? Do you miss her nagging?"

McIntyre laughed. "She nagged you more than me."

"Hey, Griffin?" called Blair from the doorway.

"Yeah?"

"Someone from the bank is on the phone. Do you want to talk to him or should I take a message?"

"I'll talk to him. I'll pick it up back here."

"Okay. I'll ask him to hold."

"Who is *that*?" McIntyre's eyes were wide.

The female voice had drawn Handme's attention too, and he moved closer to hear the answer.

"For the moment, that's our receptionist."

"But who is she?" McIntyre was still staring after her.

"Her name is Blair Beaufort," I said. "That's her MG outside. She blew a tire last night, but I need to look over the entire vehicle as soon as I can. I'm just trying to make space in here."

"Is she new in town?" he asked. "I know I've never seen her before. I'd remember."

"She's just passing through," I told them. "I'll explain it after I talk to the bank."

"Is this about the loan?" McIntyre wondered.

"I hope so."

"Think they approved it?"

"Guess we'll find out." But I didn't allow my hopes to rise as I headed for the phone at the back of the garage. I knew better.

This was the third time I'd tried to get a loan in the last year. Swifty Auto was hurting us badly. Plus, my dad had struggled to pay back loans he'd gotten years ago, and I'd inherited a lot of debt along with the business. I was sure he'd planned to get it all straightened out before he retired, but he'd died before he had the chance, and now I was supporting my mother too.

Banks all said the same thing—I was too big a risk.

I knew we could improve with some investment in training and tools, and my sister was always on me about renovating the lobby. "People want to see a nice, welcoming room when they come in," she'd say. "You don't need a fancy chandelier, but would it kill you to get some nicer chairs? Some better coffee? A new rug?"

I always argued back that it shouldn't matter what the damn lobby looked like. The important thing was the *work*, and I knew we did good work—excellent work, in fact. And we could be even better. But without the loan, it wouldn't happen.

This was exactly why I didn't get my heart set on anything that mattered.

You wound up feeling like a failure every fucking time.

CHAPTER 4
BLAIR

THE FIRST THING I did was water that poor plant in the lobby.

Grabbing my empty coffee cup, I found the tiny bathroom down the hall and turned on the faucet. As the cup began to fill, I glanced at my reflection in the mirror above the sink. I'd done the best I could with my hair, which definitely could've benefited from some shampoo and conditioner, but I hadn't felt right using Griffin's shower without permission. I wasn't a homeless person. I was just . . . temporarily *sans maison*.

That wasn't the same thing at all, was it?

I'd wanted to do something nice for Griffin this morning, since he'd seemed a bit moody and distracted when he left for work. He'd barely looked at me and only mumbled something undecipherable when I'd thanked him again. I thought maybe he was annoyed with my being there, but then again, he might simply have been tired. He couldn't have been too comfortable all night, trying to sleep sitting up like that. I hoped the coffee and donuts would perk him up. He really was a nice guy.

With a hot body.

And a huge package.

My core muscles clenched up, as they had been doing every time I recalled accidentally grabbing at his crotch. My God, it was so embarrassing! He knew I hadn't meant to do it, right? Every time I thought about it, I sort of wanted to die—but also sort of wanted to do it again. It was so cute the way he'd practically run out of the room afterward. It had made me feel even safer with him.

Turning off the tap, I carefully carried the full cup of water back out to the lobby and dumped it into the dry dirt. I did the same thing two more times before tackling the desk.

Griffin was right—it was a mess.

Stacks of invoices littered the surface, piles of folders threatened to topple over, paper clips and pencils and several staplers were scattered everywhere. It was the complete opposite of Griffin's apartment, which was completely clean and uncluttered.

I got to work filing and organizing immediately, stopping only to answer the phone the few times it rang. Once a customer came in to pick up her vehicle, and I'd poked my head into the garage to let Griffin know, but it was a younger, skinnier mechanic who came to the desk with her keys.

Once the customer was gone, he turned to me and smiled. "Hi, I'm Andy."

"Nice to meet you, Andy. I'm Blair."

"I know. I mean, that's what Griffin said." He glanced over his shoulder. "He's looking at your car now."

"Great." I smiled. "Fingers crossed it isn't too bad."

"Yeah, I'm—I'm not sure." Andy looked a little uncomfortable.

"What's wrong with it?"

"Like I said, I'm not sure, I just . . . hear a lot of cussing back there today."

I bit my lip. "More than usual?"

"A lot more. He's in a real mood. But that might be because of the bank."

"Oh?"

"Yeah. Business isn't so great these days because of Swifty Auto. And he's been trying to get this loan forever, see, and—"

"Hand me!" bellowed a deep voice.

I looked over Andy's shoulder and saw Griffin's huge frame filling the doorway. *Hand me what?* I wondered.

"What the hell are you doing up here?" he demanded, his eyes shooting daggers at Andy, his forehead creased with anger. It was the most intimidating I'd ever seen him.

"I was just giving Mrs. Stephens her keys."

Griffin crossed his arms over his bulging chest. "I don't see Mrs. Stephens here anywhere."

"She only left a minute ago. I was introducing myself to—"

"Yeah, well I don't pay you to stand around running your mouth," Griffin barked, moving into the lobby and jerking his head toward the garage. "Get back to work."

"I'm going, sorry." Andy hurried back into the service bay.

I felt bad for him, and I was about to apologize and take the blame for keeping him out here, but I didn't have a chance.

"Your car won't be ready today," Griffin announced abruptly.

My heart plummeted. "It won't?"

"No. I don't have the parts. And I won't be able to get them quickly."

"How . . . how long?" I swallowed hard. "A day or so?"

"Probably more like a week."

"A week!"

He cocked his head. "You think parts for fifty-year-old British cars grow on trees around here?"

"No, I just—"

"You're just used to getting everything you want exactly

when you want it because no one has ever said no to you. I get it, princess. Welcome to the real world." And with that, he stormed back into the garage, pulling the door shut behind him.

I stood there for a moment in complete shock, one hand over my mouth, one flattened against my stomach. No one had ever spoken so rudely to me before. I sank onto the chair behind the desk, my face burning.

What had I done to make him so angry? Wasn't I the customer? And wasn't the customer always right? No wonder business hadn't been so great lately, if he spoke to people like that. And how dare he make fun of me!

This Griffin was nothing like the guy from last night—obviously, he had a mean streak. Or maybe last night had been an act. Figured! No one was ever who they pretended to be, millionaire or mechanic.

My first instinct was to get the hell out of there, leaving him high and dry without a receptionist, but as I was grabbing my purse, I realized I couldn't leave.

Not only did I have nowhere to go and no way to get there, but I'd offered to do a job, and I wasn't the kind of person to go back on my word. Not to mention the fact that I needed him to repair my car and give me a fair price on it—if I abandoned the desk, he'd have no reason to offer me a discount. But I didn't have to let him speak to me like that. He had no right! And since I'd never been one to stay quiet when I had something to say, I marched into the garage all fired up to speak my mind.

I spotted him at a tool cabinet in the back. "Excuse me!" I yelled.

He turned around and frowned at me. "What now?"

I stuck my hands on my hips as I approached him. "For your information, I've been told no *plenty* of times in my life."

"Oh yeah?"

"Yes," I snapped. "Just because I grew up with money

doesn't mean I always got everything I wanted. I told you yesterday how my parents ran my life according to their rules —what I wanted never even mattered!"

He sneered. "Tell me you never had a pony."

"I never had a pony!" I paused and sniffed. "I had a *horse*."

Griffin rolled his eyes.

"But that's not the point!" I yelled, throwing my arms up. "Okay, yes, it took losing everything I had to realize I had to stop letting my family call all the shots. And *yes*, I am somewhat clueless about mechanical things like cars and how they work. *Yes*, I had a horse."

"You realize all those yeses are making *my* point, not yours."

I stopped moving and held up my palms. "I know there's a lot I need to learn about the real world. But I'm trying, okay? I want to start a new life, one where I don't depend on other people's money or connections to fix my problems, so it really stinks to be so broke and stranded and helpless right now." I crossed my arms over my chest and lifted my chin. "I don't need your rudeness on top of it."

Griffin stared at me, his scowl deepening. "Fine."

"Fine!" Angry that I hadn't heard an apology, I whirled around and stomped toward the lobby door.

"Are you leaving?" he shouted.

"No!" I called over my shoulder. "I said I'd do the job, and I'll do it!" Then I yanked the door shut behind me with quite a bit more force than necessary.

I'd never slammed a door before. It actually felt pretty good.

But the satisfaction dissipated pretty quickly. In fact, I started to feel bad about mouthing off to him. He'd been so nice to me last night.

Maybe he was just having a bad day. Maybe the call from

the bank had been bad news. Maybe Andy was always slacking off and needed to be kept on task.

Bottom line, he was the closest thing I had to a friend in my new life so far. And friendship took patience and understanding.

By one o'clock my stomach was growling, and I decided I'd offer an olive branch in the form of lunch. Maybe I could bring him a sandwich or something—I'd seen a little place called Main Street Delicatessen while walking back from the diner this morning. I was just about to get up from the desk and go ask what he'd like when the phone rang again.

I picked it up. "Good afternoon, Bellamy Creek Garage."

"Hello, Lanette?" said the woman loudly. "It's Doris Applebee." Right away I had the feeling she was older and hard of hearing, so I spoke up.

"Lanette isn't here today, Mrs. Applebee. This is Blair."

"Oh, hello there! You must be the lucky lady. I heard the big news this morning—congratulations!"

"Thank you," I said, although I had no idea what she was talking about. "Can I help you?"

"Well, I don't know," she went on. "My car is making that noise again."

As I was picking up a pen to take notes, I saw Griffin open the lobby door and lean against the frame. We made eye contact, and my stomach flip-flopped, but his expression revealed nothing. "What kind of noise, Mrs. Applebee? Can you describe it?"

"You know. The *noise*. The same one it always makes. The clunk-clunk noise."

"The clunk-clunk noise?" I frowned and wrote down *Doris Applebee, clunk noise*. As I did so, Griffin started mouthing something at me.

"Yes. I remember Griffin fixed it for me last time," Mrs. Applebee said, "but I can't recall exactly what the problem was. He was so sweet, he didn't even charge me."

"I'm sure he can fix it again."

Griffin was still trying to tell me something, but I frowned at him and held up one finger.

"Mrs. Applebee, could you hold on for just one second, please?"

"Certainly, dear."

I covered the mouthpiece of the phone and whispered, "What?"

"It's her bowling ball," said Griffin wryly, something close to a smile on his face. "She goes bowling with a bunch of old ladies on Tuesday nights and sometimes forgets to take the ball out of the trunk."

"Seriously?"

He nodded. "I guarantee it."

I uncovered the mouthpiece. "Mrs. Applebee? Griffin is here, and he wonders if it's possible you forgot to take your bowling ball out of the trunk?"

In the silence, Griffin's eyes held mine, and for a second I couldn't catch my breath.

And then in my ear, "Oh, my stars, that's right! *That's* what the noise was last time! Heavens to Betsy, if my head wasn't attached to my neck, I'd probably forget that too. That's what happens when you're eighty."

I laughed. "We all forget things sometimes."

"Well, you tell Griffin I'm going to bring him some nice cookies this week."

"I will."

"And make sure he shares them with you. How lovely he's finally found a bride!"

I glanced up sharply at him. "Um . . ."

"He was my student, you know. Tenth grade English. He sat in the back row and he was always late, but he was always so apologetic about it, I could never be mad at him. Plus, he used to fix my broken pencil sharpener for me all the time. He was so handy!" She laughed. "You'll appreciate that around the house, I'm sure."

I thought about correcting her on the whole bride thing, but she was eighty years old and obviously confused, so I didn't think it would be worth it. "Yes," I said. "Well, have a nice day."

"You too, dear. Thank you again."

I hung up the phone, tossed the note I'd written about the clunk-clunk noise in the trash, and looked over at Griffin. He was back to leaning on the door frame again, arms crossed. "I take it she's a frequent customer."

"She is."

"She says she's going to bring you some nice cookies this week."

"She'll forget."

I smiled. "She also mentioned tenth grade English class."

"She was my teacher. Funny how she could probably name every kid in that class from sixteen years ago, but she can't remember to take her bowling ball out of the trunk."

I smiled. "For some reason, she thinks we're married."

He groaned, his expression pained. "Jesus. I really hope that rumor is not going around."

"She was probably just confused. She's eighty, after all." Taking a deep breath, I put the pen down and tightened my ponytail. "So I was just about to ask you—"

But at the same time, he spoke up too. "Look, I wanted to apologize for—"

We both stopped. Our eyes met, and my heart skipped a beat.

"Sorry," he said. "What did you want to ask me?"

"Just, um, about lunch. I was going to ask you if you wanted me to go get sandwiches or something?"

"Oh. Sure." He came off the door frame and moved toward the desk, putting both hands on the counter. "Listen,

I'm sorry about earlier. I was pissed about something and I took it out on you."

"What happened?"

He exhaled. "It's complicated, but the short version is that first my dad died, and then Swifty Auto happened. We've lost a good amount of business to them."

"Why?"

"They're cheaper and faster. And they have a fancier lobby. Gourmet coffee and fucking cookies." He frowned. "But their work is shit. People don't realize they're going to have to go back there twice as often, because they're thinking short-term—they want it done *now*, for as little money as possible. It's hard to compete with that." Pausing, he took a breath. "But that's not your problem. And I'm sorry my temper got away from me. It sometimes does."

"Well, I shouldn't have come back there yelling and pointing my finger. I'm sorry too." I shrugged. "The truth is, for all I know, car parts *do* grow on trees."

He shook his head. "Not for your car, they don't."

"What's wrong with it?"

"I'm still checking things out, but in addition to the tire and brakes, you've got damaged cylinders, some corrosion, plenty of rust. There's a lot of wear and tear on a car this old, and this one obviously hasn't had a lot of maintenance."

"No wonder I got it so cheap." Closing my eyes, I put my fingertips at my temples. "God, I'm so stupid."

"You're not stupid. You just didn't know what to look for. What to ask. I'll give you the best deal I can on the labor and make sure it's safe to drive, but I can't get the parts here any faster."

"I understand. Thank you."

Griffin looked slightly uncomfortable. "Blair, do you have somewhere to go in the meantime?" He rubbed the back of his neck. "Somewhere to stay, I mean?"

"Not yet. But I will," I said firmly. "Don't worry about me."

"I'd be glad to help you find—"

I shook my head. "No. I don't need rescuing. I am not a helpless fairy tale princess trapped in a tower."

That made him smile.

"What's funny?" I asked.

"Don't take this the wrong way, but that's exactly what you looked like last night when you got out of your car in that dress—a lost fairy tale princess."

"Oh." I tried not to be offended. "Well, maybe that was the *old* me, but it's definitely not the *new* me. I can take care of myself. I just might . . . need help." I sighed, feeling my pride deflate. "Do you think that's the same as being rescued?"

"Not at all. If you *were* trapped in a tower and someone offered to lend you a ladder, it would be stupid not to use it, right?"

"Right. It's just not how I wanted things to go." I caught myself. "But it's okay—not everything in life is going to go exactly like I want it to. I'm tough. I can deal with setbacks."

"We all have them."

"And this is temporary, right?" I perked up a little. "I'll get through it."

"I have no doubt."

I opened my mouth to ask the next question, then hesitated.

"What?" he asked.

"It's just . . ." I took a breath and told myself to be brave. "I hate asking you this. But do you think I might continue to work for you at the desk until my car is ready? I'm worried about being able to afford a place to stay *and* the repairs."

"Actually, that's perfect. Lanette was sort of an emergency hire. Every qualified person we interviewed wanted a permanent job, and my mother is planning to come back as soon as she can. In fact, I'm still paying her."

I smiled. "I'll take the temporary position, if it's available."

"It's all yours. But after lunch, I should probably show you how to schedule appointments in the computer."

I smiled with relief. "Great! I'm starving, and I saw a little deli this morning that looked nice."

"Main Street Deli. They make great sandwiches."

"Got a favorite?" I picked up my pen again.

"I like the roast beef. With spicy mustard."

"Got it. How about Andy?"

"He brings his lunch." A grin appeared. "Pretty sure his mom makes it for him every morning. Probably cuts the crust off his sandwiches."

I laughed. "What about your other employee? I haven't been introduced yet, but would he like a sandwich?"

Griffin shook his head. "Nah, McIntyre goes home for lunch to let his dog out. He lives close."

"Okay, then it's just you and me." I smiled and slung my purse over my shoulder. "I'll be right back, boss."

"Just a second." He pulled his wallet from his jeans and set a twenty-dollar bill on the counter. "You don't have to buy lunch. You're covering for me today."

I rolled my eyes. "Because you gave me a place to stay last night. I'm trying to pay you back. I might be low on funds, but I can afford a couple sandwiches."

"I don't want your money, okay? Take this." He shoved the twenty closer to me. "I'm buying lunch."

"*No*, Griffin."

His eyes held mine for a moment. "Don't make me come behind that desk."

The flirty threat, delivered with a straight face and gruff tone of voice, ignited something inside me. "You're a tough boss, you know that?" But I picked up the twenty and tucked it into my purse.

He leaned a little closer over the counter. "And don't you forget it."

CHAPTER 5
GRIFFIN

BLAIR HAD BEEN GONE ABOUT twenty minutes when my cell phone rang.

"Hello?"

"Hello, dear."

I grimaced. "Hi, Mom. How are you feeling?"

"Fine, fine. Just got back from physical therapy. The therapist says my hips will feel good as new soon."

"That's good."

"But listen, dear. I didn't call to talk about me."

"No?" I had a sinking feeling I knew exactly what she was calling about.

"Who is she?" she asked, confirming my suspicion.

Leaning back against a workbench, I decided to play dumb. "Who is who?"

"Don't play games with me, Griffin Dempsey. I ran into Yvonne Davies at the physical therapist's office. Her daughter Natasha works at the Bulldog Pub, and she told Yvonne there was some sort of accident last night involving a mysterious woman in a wedding gown. And then late last night—after midnight, in fact—Natasha was driving home from her shift and saw you and the mysterious bride going into your apartment. Then this *morning,* Louise from the diner told Fern Walton—she's the nurse at my physical therapist's office—that the mysterious woman had supper alone there last night but that she was back again this morning ordering coffee for two and a dozen donuts to take back to the garage. And she specifically mentioned you by name!"

I exhaled, pinching the bridge of my nose. Fucking small towns. "Are you done?"

"No, because I just got a call from Neona Pappas, who said she was at the Main Street Deli just now and she saw a mysterious light-haired woman ordering sandwiches for two, and one of them was roast beef with spicy mustard, which I happen to know is your favorite."

"Jesus, Mom. She's not even back from the deli yet."

"*So,* who is she?"

"She's a—"

"Why haven't I met her?"

"Because I—"

"Griffin Dempsey, if you got married without telling me, I will march over to that garage and blister your hide!"

"For Christ's sake, Mom, I didn't get married!"

"Are you sure? Because Natasha *saw* you—"

"Yes, I'm sure." I held the phone away from my ear and stared at it for a second in disbelief. "Have you lost your mind?"

"Well, it's not like you ever tell me anything. For all I knew, you've had a secret fiancée all this time."

"No secret fiancée, no sudden wife. She's just . . ." I tried to think of what to call her. "A friend."

"Oh." Her tone went sulky. "Well, I won't say I'm not a *little* bit disappointed."

"Mom, you just said you were going to blister my hide if I got married without telling you."

"Well, I'm not getting any younger, you know. I'd like one of my kids to give me some grandchildren before I go."

"I thought you felt fine."

"I do. But life is short, Griffin. You can't keep letting it pass you by."

"I'm not. I'm perfectly happy with my life just the way it is."

A dramatic, heavy sigh, which would be followed—as always—with her addressing my late father. "Where did we go wrong, Hank? Why don't our kids want to have families? What happened to our dream of growing old with a dozen little Dempseys running around?"

"A dozen, Ma? Really?"

"We liked to aim high."

"So talk to Cheyenne. I'm pretty sure she's good for at least two or three."

My mother clucked her tongue. "That girl is hopeless. She's way too picky."

"It's good to be picky. There's a lot of jerks out there."

"You know why? Because the good guys like you have decided you're not interested in family values. You're just interested in—in—"

"In what, Ma?" I couldn't help smiling.

"In shacking up!"

I burst out laughing as Blair poked her head into the garage and held up a brown paper bag from the deli. Nodding, I held up one finger. She smiled and disappeared into the lobby. "I'm not shacking up with anyone, I promise."

"Well, what about the mystery bride? The *friend*? Is she new in town?"

"She's just passing through."

"So I won't even get to meet her?"

"I don't think so."

"Oh." Another sigh. "That's too bad. Guess I got my hopes up for nothing. Again."

My left eyelid twitched. "I have to go, Mom. I'm supposed to be fixing her car so she can get back on the road."

"What's the rush?" she asked. "Why can't she stay awhile longer?"

"Because she doesn't belong here."

"Are you sure? Because I think she might."

"Goodbye, Mom." I ended the call and shoved my phone into my back pocket as I headed for the lobby.

Blair Peacock Beaufort did not belong in Bellamy Creek—that much I knew for sure.

But when I opened the door and saw her sitting at the desk, charming a new customer with her welcoming smile and polite laughter, my stomach muscles balled up.

And just for a moment, I almost wished I was wrong.

Handme and McIntyre were both back from lunch and said they'd handle any walk-ins, so I asked Blair if she wanted to eat with me in the break room.

She sat across the table from me, pulling a sandwich and small bag of salt and vinegar chips from the bag and handing them over. "Here. The lady at the deli counter said these are your favorite. And here's your iced tea. She said that's what you drink with your lunch."

"Thanks."

"You're welcome." She unwrapped her sandwich, which looked like a BLT, and pulled a second bag of chips—barbecue—and a bottle of peach tea from the bag. "So everyone in Bellamy Creek knows everything about everyone else, huh? Right down to your favorite kind of chips?"

I nodded. "Yep. In fact, my mother just called me asking about you."

She paused in the middle of chewing. "Are you serious?"

Nodding, I took a bite of my sandwich. "She'd already

heard about the mysterious woman in a wedding gown who got into a car accident, had a late supper at the diner, entered my apartment after midnight, purchased coffee and donuts this morning to take back to the garage, and was seen at the deli ordering two sandwiches, including roast beef with spicy mustard, which everyone knows is my favorite."

Blair looked outraged. "It's *not* a wedding gown!"

Laughing, I took another bite. "*That's* what gets to you about that story? What you were wearing?"

"Well, the rest of it is kind of true, right?" She unscrewed the bottle cap and took a drink of her tea. "Guess that explains what Mrs. Applebee said on the phone."

I shook my head. "It drives me insane the way gossip spreads in this town. People should mind their own business."

"Does that mean I shouldn't ask you about the phone call with the bank?"

I didn't answer right away. I took a drink, opened my bag of chips, took another bite of my sandwich. Then I figured, what the hell—I was pissed, but I wasn't ashamed. "Not much to tell. They just keep denying my loan application."

"Why?"

"Too big a risk. Not enough income. Too much competition."

She thought for a minute, munching on her chips. "Swifty Auto?"

"That's a big part of it. Like I said, we've lost some customers to them. But we've also gotten some back—the ones who realize that investing in your car pays off in the long run."

"What makes them go to Swifty in the first place?" She picked up her sandwich again. "Is it *just* a lower price and quicker turnaround?"

I thought about it for a minute. "I don't know. My sister claims if I had a nicer lobby, it might help."

"Well, that's an easy fix. Appearances *are* important."

"I don't have the time or money to redecorate the damn lobby," I said, annoyed because I didn't want her and Cheyenne to be right. "It shouldn't matter whether I have fucking cookies and coffee as long as we can fix their car—and we can."

"Okay, okay," she said gently. "Don't get upset. I believe you. So let's say you got the loan. What would you do with it?"

"Invest in training and tools."

"Is that going to attract customers?"

"It should," I huffed, but in all honesty, I wasn't sure. Training and tools probably didn't sound that exciting to people.

Blair appeared deep in thought as she finished her sandwich and picked up her chips again. "I think one thing might have to happen before the other."

"Huh?"

"Do you think if you could show income increasing and business coming back the bank might reconsider?"

"Maybe," I said, distracted by the way she was licking barbecue flavoring off her fingers. "But at this point, I'm getting worried about having to lay off Handme, which will make us even slower. Or fuck, maybe just sell the building and walk away from the whole thing." Angry, I balled up the empty chip bag and tossed it onto the table. "Sixty-five years of my family's blood, sweat, and tears, gone."

"That's not going to happen."

"No?"

"No. Because we're not going to let it. I have an idea."

I picked up my iced tea and took a drink, surprised she'd used the word *we*. "What's your idea?"

"What if you took a little money and renovated the lobby—nothing extravagant, just a makeover."

"A makeover? That doesn't really sound like my thing."

"I'll help you."

"You're leaving," I pointed out.

"Not right away. And it won't take long, I promise." She smiled with satisfaction. "Then once the renovation is complete, you throw an event."

"An event?"

"Yes." She ate another chip, her eyes narrowing in thought. "Some kind of celebration. Like a reopening. Do you have an anniversary coming up, perhaps?"

I tried to focus on the discussion at hand instead of the way she kept licking her lips and fingers. I liked her appetite. "Sixty-five years in business? Something like that?"

Her face lit up. "That's perfect! It'll be a great reminder of how long you've served this town, how small businesses like yours are really the fabric of the community. We'll create a feeling—a sense of happy nostalgia, remind them why they still live in a place like Bellamy Creek. Swifty Auto does not represent their values—you do. You've always been here for them. You're part of their history. You're home. You're family. *That's* the message we send."

I studied her across the table. "You're good at this idea stuff."

Another smile, this one shyer, sweeter. "Thanks."

"And then what? How does it help?"

"It helps because you're going to get people back. Or maybe get new business. Income will go up. And then you can apply again for the loan."

I wasn't positive she was right, but if the cost wasn't too much, I supposed it was worth a try. "So you'll help me with the lobby? And the event?"

"Of course." She sat up taller in her chair. "I happen to have excellent taste, and I'm newly familiar with . . . a *budget*, I think you call it?"

I grinned. "Yeah. That's what we call it."

"And the food—let me take care of catering this event. I'll

give them a taste of something that'll put those Swifty Auto cookies to shame."

"Oh yeah?" I asked, thinking I'd like a taste of the baker herself.

"Any ideas when this could happen?" She picked up her tea. "Ideally, it would be great to have it coincide with a time when the town is busy—say a street festival or something?"

I thought about it as I polished off the rest of my sandwich. "Maybe Labor Day weekend? There's always a lot going on—it's sort of the last really busy weekend of tourist season. There's a parade, the baseball championships, sidewalk sales, a street fair."

"That's perfect!" She began shoving our trash back into the paper bag. "Although it doesn't give us much time—not even a month. We need to get to work right away."

"Just tell me what to do."

She stood up and pushed her chair in. "Okay, let me think some more this afternoon. I'll write up a list. And as long as I can find somewhere to stay until then and keep the job at the desk, I'll stick around until then."

"Really?"

"Sure. It's not like anyone is expecting me someplace else. And I think it'll be good for me, seeing how you run your business. I already know how to bake—what I need to learn is all the other stuff."

"There's a whole lot of *other stuff* to running a business," I said. "Way more than I can show you in three weeks."

She sighed. "I'm beginning to realize how impulsive this whole leap-of-faith move was. I'm not sorry I did it, but I really should have planned better. I just . . . got impatient. I didn't want to wait any longer for my real life to start."

"That's understandable," I said. I'd felt the same way once.

"But it's not as easy as it looks in the movies."

I shook my head. "It never is."

"Well . . . I guess I'll get back up to the desk. Thanks for lunch."

I watched her drop the paper bag in the trash and head for the door. "Hey, Blair?"

She looked back at me. "Yes?"

"You did the right thing. Leaving your old life behind."

Her smile made my heart beat quicker.

A month, I thought with sudden alarm. An entire month during which she'd be right here, and it would not be okay to put my hands on her.

I wasn't sure I'd make it.

I worked a little later than usual, long after Handme left to pick up his girlfriend and McIntyre had gone home to his dog and whatever tonight's fight with Emily would be. Earlier I'd heard him grumbling about a couples shower, which he'd apparently agreed to one night but did not turn out to be the sexy private occasion he'd imagined.

"Guys do not belong at wedding showers," he griped into his cell. "Even my mother agrees with me."

My guess was that Emily had gone off on him for that comment, because he'd had to hold the phone away from his ear for a solid thirty seconds. After they hung up, he looked over at me. "Just shut up," he said, frowning.

"I didn't even say anything."

"But you were thinking it."

I'd shaken my head and gone back to work putting a new tire on Blair's MG. Luckily, the tires were not original stock so that was an easier fix than the other issues would be. But she seemed okay with the idea of sticking around while waiting for parts. And God knew I could use her help around here.

Earlier I'd shown her how to use the online scheduling tool on the desktop computer in the lobby, and she'd picked it up with no problem at all—which was a good thing, because standing over her shoulder so closely made it difficult to breathe. Every time I caught her scent, I broke out in a sweat.

Around six o'clock, I was thinking about calling it a day when I decided to stop ignoring my phone. I'd turned it off after lunch to avoid my mother, but when I checked the missed calls and texts, I discovered that my sister had been desperately trying to get ahold of me. At first, her two phone calls and four frantic texts didn't make sense, but then I remembered—the kitten.

Grimacing, I called her back.

"Nice to hear from you," she said coolly.

"Sorry. It's been a weird day."

"I bet. I heard you got married last night."

"Oh, Jesus."

She laughed. "I have a wedding present for you. Her name is Bisou."

"For Christ's sake, I did *not* get married, Cheyenne."

"I know, and Mom's heartbroken about it. But you can still have your kitten. Isn't that nice of me?"

"Do I have a choice in the matter?"

"No. But you better hurry and come pick her up, because I already stayed late at the shelter for you. Technically we closed at six, but Bisou has been waiting for you all day, and I know you wouldn't want to disappoint her."

"Okay, okay. I just have to close up the shop and grab a shower. Give me half an hour."

"Works for me. Thanks, big brother."

We hung up, and I quickly tidied up the benches and tool cabinets before scrubbing my hands and heading into the lobby.

Blair, still seated at the desk, looked up and smiled. "Hi."

"Hey." I glanced around the lobby. It looked different

somehow, but I couldn't put my finger on it. I sniffed—it smelled like lemons. "Is . . . is there something new in here?"

She laughed as she stood up and came around the desk into the waiting area. "Not new. I just rearranged the furniture a little. I also tossed the raggedy magazines, watered your plant, dusted everything, and gave the windows a good cleaning."

"You did all that today?"

"Yes." Looking proud of herself, she clasped her arms behind her back.

"And worked the desk too?"

"Well, I wasn't really that busy at the desk," she admitted, her eyes dropping to the floor.

I frowned. "Oh."

"But the customers I *did* interact with, I learned something from! I started asking people how long they'd been coming here, what brings them back, what they're looking for in a repair shop. It was fascinating, really. And it gave me some more ideas for your rebranding."

"My what?"

"Your rebranding." She cocked her head. "Although I'm not sure you have a brand now, so maybe we should just call this your first branding."

"This sounds . . . a bit more *painful* than what I agreed to," I said, scratching my head as I pictured Beckett branding his cattle. "I don't really want to be branded."

Blair shook her head. "You have no choice. Swifty Auto is branded and believe me—they've got an entire team of people working on it."

My frown deepened into a scowl.

"You shouldn't make that face so often. It's going to give you wrinkles." She winked at me. "And you're kinda cute when you smile."

"*Cute?*"

"Something wrong with cute?"

"Cute is for babies and kittens, not mechanics," I said cantankerously, feeling hot beneath my clothes. "And speaking of kittens, I have to go pick mine up."

Her jaw dropped. "You have a kitten?"

"Temporarily. My bleeding-heart sister volunteers at the animal shelter, and she conned me into fostering a kitten until she can find it a permanent home."

Blair put her hands on her cheeks. "I'm going to melt. It's so sweet."

"No melting, please. I'm not sweet, I'm just doing it because my sister made me feel guilty. She moved in with our mom after she had eye surgery and both hips replaced. I wouldn't have survived."

"I still think it's sweet."

"Yeah, well . . ." I grumbled. "Like I said, it's temporary."

"It counts." Her eyes held mine, and my body temperature ratcheted up even higher.

I cleared my throat. "So listen. You're welcome to stay here, or wait at my apartment, while I run over to the shelter. I wasn't sure if you'd made arrangements for tonight yet."

"I made a couple calls but haven't had much luck. The bed and breakfasts in town are booked solid through Labor Day, the motel just out of town is full until next Tuesday, and Airbnb has no listings in Bellamy Creek. The closest is Holland, but seeing as my job is here and I have no transportation . . ." Her face fell, and she studied her shoes again. "I'm really sorry. I didn't want to come to you for help again, but maybe you know someone with a room for rent?"

"I don't, not off the top of my head, but that doesn't mean we can't find someone. Look, why don't you just hang out at my place while I go get the cat, and then we can grab dinner and I'll make a few calls."

Her face lit up. "Really?"

"Really. This is a small town, but there must be something." I grimaced. "If it comes down to it, I can ask my mother. She knows everything and everyone."

She clapped her hands and rose up on her toes. "Perfect!"

Just then the bell over the entrance rang, and we both turned to see a delivery guy walk in carrying a giant basket full of fruit, snacks, and what looked like a bottle of champagne. "Oh, good you're still open," he said with obvious relief. "This order came in last minute and I thought I'd be too late."

"What is it?" I asked.

"It's a wedding gift." He glanced at the name on the card. "For Mr. and Mrs. Dempsey."

I swore under my breath.

Blair winked at me. "Oh, honey, how nice! Our first wedding present! Who's it from?"

The delivery guy, whose polo shirt had a Bellamy Creek Gifts Galore logo stitched on it, set the basket on the counter and handed me the card.

I opened it and rolled my eyes. "Mrs. Applebee, of course."

Blair giggled. "Isn't she sweet?"

"Mrs. Applebee, the English teacher?" the delivery guy asked.

"Yeah." I looked at him. "You have her too?"

He shrugged. "Didn't everybody?"

I had to laugh. "Probably. Well, thanks for the delivery."

"You're welcome." He headed for the door and pushed it open. "And congratulations. I've been married twenty-two years. Best thing I ever did."

Blair and I looked at each other, and I shook my head. "I need a fucking beer," I told her, "but first I have to go get a kitten."

"Let me come with you," she pleaded, grabbing her bag from the desk. "You can introduce me to my new sister-in-law."

"Don't even joke about that."

"Why? Are you getting cold feet already?" she teased as she walked by me, giving me a sassy little look that made me want to throw her up against the wall and show her exactly how hot I was—all over.

I watched her push open the glass door and hold it for me, but I stayed where I was for the moment, studying her on the sidewalk. I liked the way the sunset turned her hair a coppery color.

"So what exactly did you do in your former life?" I asked. "After the French, but before the change in your circumstances?"

"I was in charge of brand management for my father's media company."

"Were you good at it?"

"I was, not that anyone ever listened to me. The board was full of pompous men who looked at me like I was a cake decoration. They never took me seriously."

"Even your parents?"

"Especially not them. It was a placeholder job, as they saw it. They were just waiting for me to get tired of working for a living and find a rich husband, fill my days with charity work and lunching with the ladies." She shook her head. "I can't believe I ever thought that would be my life."

"You don't miss the money?" I asked.

She laughed. "Oh no, I definitely miss the money. But I don't miss what came with it—all the bullshit rules. I want to make my own rules."

Switching off the lights, I followed her out onto the sidewalk, locking the door behind us. "I need a quick shower and change of clothes. Want to come up with me?"

"Sure."

I was following her up the stairs to my apartment, looking at her ass and wondering if she had *sexual* rules and how long it would take me to break them, when I realized she was still talking.

Shit, had she just asked me a question?

At the top of the stairs, she turned around and faced me. "So? Are you going to?"

I stood close. Ridiculously close. So close I could smell her —vanilla and lemon—and she could probably smell me— sweat and motor oil.

"Am I going to what?" I asked, looking at her lips.

She licked them. "Listen to me."

"Oh. Yeah. I am." But at that moment, I was pretty sure I was going to do something else to her too.

Suddenly she stepped back. "Good," she said, her cheeks flushed pink. "On second thought, I think I'll wait outside. I'm a little warm, and there's a nice breeze."

"Okay. I'll be out in a few minutes."

Nodding, she turned and descended the stairs so slowly, I wondered if she was dizzy. I watched her hand sliding along the wooden rail, thinking dirty thoughts.

On the landing, she pushed the door open and disappeared from view, but I still couldn't breathe right.

What would she have done if I'd put my mouth on hers like I'd wanted to just now? Would she have kissed me back? Would she have welcomed my hands on her skin? Or would she have kneed me in the balls and told me to keep my filthy fingers to myself?

She wasn't like any other girl I'd ever met, which was both the problem and the allure. I didn't know how to read her.

But damn, I wanted her something fierce.

I took an ice cold shower, hoping it would help.

It didn't.

CHAPTER 6
BLAIR

I PUSHED the door open at the bottom of the stairs, thankful for the soft breeze that cooled my skin. Griffin had a way of making me feel hot and bothered just by standing next to me.

Was I imagining the flicker of interest in his eyes? The chemistry between us? The way it sometimes felt like he was fighting the urge to put his hands or his mouth on me? I sighed, dropping onto a wrought-iron bench on the sidewalk and slipping my sunglasses on. It had to be in my head.

If he wanted to kiss me, he would have done it a minute ago. Our lips had only been inches apart. But he hadn't, and I'd felt stupid standing there waiting for something that wasn't going to happen.

To distract myself, I looked at my phone and saw I had new messages from my mother demanding to know where on earth I'd run off to and when I was coming home, peppered with words like *childish*, *tantrum*, *absurd*, and *unsafe*. Too angry to write her back yet, I stuck my phone in my purse again and took some deep breaths.

Griffin came out a minute later. "Hey. Ready to go?"

"Yes." I got up and followed him around the back of the

garage to the alley, where a white pickup truck was parked. He opened the passenger door for me, closing it once I'd hopped in.

While he walked around to the driver's side, I looked around the front and back seats. The truck was as nice as his apartment inside—the beige leather interior was perfectly clean, the dash was free of dust, and no trash littered the floor mats. It even smelled good.

So did the driver himself. I caught a whiff of cologne as Griffin slid behind the wheel, and I kind of wanted to bury my face in his neck. He looked so cute all cleaned up, with his damp hair, dark jeans, and fitted black T-shirt.

But he was frowning again as he checked his phone. "Fuck."

"What?"

"My sister," he said. "She said she couldn't wait any longer at the shelter and she had to bring the kitten home. Which was against the rules, so she's making me feel even shittier about it."

"So can't you pick it up from her house?"

"I can, but we'll have to deal with my mother."

"Is she that bad?"

"She's just . . . intense."

"I can handle it."

He gave me a disbelieving side-eye.

"Listen, my major was French, but I should have a PhD in grace under pressure. I can handle anybody."

He laughed a little. "You probably can. And I guess we can use the opportunity to ask her if she knows anyone renting a room in town."

"That would be great." I reached over and laid my hand on his forearm. It was warm beneath my palm. "Thank you."

His eyes dropped to my fingers against his skin and stayed there so long I grew self-conscious and took my hand back. Maybe he didn't like to be touched?

He started the truck without another word.

On the ten-minute drive to his mom's house, he remained silent except when I asked him a question, but even then, his answers were short.

"Is that the lake over there?"

"Yes."

"Is this where you went to elementary school?"

"Yes."

"Why does it smell so good here?" I stuck my head out the open passenger window and inhaled.

"Lavender farm."

"I didn't know lavender grew in Michigan."

"It does."

"Why are you so tense?"

"I'm not."

I stared at his handsome profile and sighed heavily.

The set of his jaw grew stubborn. "My mother thinks she knows better than I do how to run my life. It gets to me."

"I understand. Believe me."

He glanced at me. "Yeah, maybe you do."

A few minutes later, he pulled up in front of a charming two-story Arts and Crafts-style home with a deep front porch and well-tended lawn. The house was painted a cornflower blue and all the trim was white. "Did you grow up here?" I asked as Griffin parked along the curb.

"Yes."

"It's so pretty!" I got out of the truck and looked around at the neighborhood. The houses were close together, and they had small front yards but big front porches, and groups of kids were out playing all along the block. Girls with sidewalk chalk and jump ropes, boys riding bikes, a game of basketball happening in someone's driveway. It looked homey and safe, like everyone in the neighborhood was sort of like family. So different from the gated community full of McMansions where I'd grown up, with all the houses set far apart on a golf course.

"It wasn't pretty where you grew up?" he asked.

"It was, but in a different way. I didn't have friends right in my neighborhood. I never played hopscotch on the driveway or rode bikes to the ice cream store or had a lemonade stand with friends. I had no siblings either. I had to be the voices of *all* my Barbies—maybe that's why I talk so much."

Griffin laughed as I followed him up the brick walk. He waved to a group of young girls running through the sprinkler on the front lawn next door, and one of them waved back. "Hi, Uncle Griffin!"

"Hi, Mariah," he called back. "Your dad home?"

She shook her head, her hair throwing water droplets. "He's at work. Grandma is here."

Griffin nodded. "That's Cole's daughter," he said to me. "My goddaughter."

"Adorable." I smiled at her. "How old is she?"

"Eight. They moved in with his mom after Cole's wife died."

I gasped. "How did she die?"

"Giving birth to Mariah, actually."

My heart ached for the handsome police officer I'd met last night, and for his cute young daughter. "God, that's awful. He never remarried?"

Griffin shook his head. "Nope."

We climbed the steps onto the front porch, and I noticed the pretty hanging baskets of flowers and white rocking chairs and the welcome mat that read *Fáilte*. Before we could even knock on the wooden screen door, someone pulled it open.

"Well, hi there, big brother." A pretty woman with a long, caramel-colored braid over one shoulder and wide brown eyes grinned at us. She had the same dimple in her chin that

Griffin did. "Glad you could make it." She winked at me. "And this must be your bride."

"Don't start," he warned her. "Blair, this is my sister, Cheyenne."

"Nice to meet you," I said.

"You too." She stood back, holding the door. "I was hoping to set eyes on the girl who made Griffin break his number one rule. Come on in. Mom's in the den if you want to say hello."

"Is it optional?" Griffin muttered.

Cheyenne laughed. "Probably not."

Griffin looked at me. "One last warning. My mother can be overbearing. And dramatic. And she plays dumb even though she's not."

"It's her favorite game," confirmed Cheyenne.

I laughed, still wondering what the number one rule was that Griffin had broken for me. "I'll remember that."

Cheyenne led the way through the living room and dining room toward a small den that looked like it had been added on to the back of the house at some point. A woman with a messy cap of silvery hair was resting on the sofa watching television, but she immediately got up when she saw us. Her face, gently lined with age, lit up with excitement. Right away, I saw where Griffin's blue eyes had come from.

"Well, hello," she said with enthusiasm, ignoring Griffin to take both my hands in hers. "What a lovely, lovely surprise!"

"Mom, this is Blair," he said.

"It's so nice to meet you, Blair. I'm Darlene Dempsey."

I smiled. "Nice to meet you as well, Mrs. Dempsey."

"Please, call me Darlene." She squeezed my hands. "Aren't you adorable! Look how adorable she is, Griffin. Isn't she adorable?"

"Where's the cat, Cheyenne?" Griffin asked.

Darlene glared at her son. "I asked you a question."

Griffin rolled his eyes. "She's adorable," he grumped.

"Can I get you something, Blair? Tea? A snack? Some cookies? I made chicken salad for dinner. Do you like chicken salad?"

"We're not staying, Mom." Griffin's tone was firm.

His mother shot him a dirty look. "You have somewhere so much better to be?"

"We're just picking up the kitten."

"You have to eat dinner, don't you?"

"We're going out."

Darlene sniffed. "Well, I think you can spare a few minutes for your mother. You haven't been to see me in days."

"I was here Monday to mow the lawn, Mom. It's only Wednesday."

"That's what I said. *Days.*" She looked at me again and smiled sweetly. "Come sit for just a moment. I don't have company too often, and it does get lonely. I thought I'd have grandchildren to spoil by now, but . . ." Her expression turned mournful. "Alas. I remain bereft."

Behind me, Cheyenne sighed heavily. "Griff, why don't you come sign the paperwork? Then we can get your new best friend all loaded up."

"That's fine," Darlene said, taking a seat on the sofa again and patting the cushion beside her. "Blair and I will just take a moment to get better acquainted."

I glanced at Griffin, who looked reluctant to leave me alone with his mother. *Sorry,* he mouthed, but he followed Cheyenne out of the den, and I lowered myself onto the sofa, knees pressed together, hands clasped around them.

"So," Darlene said brightly, patting my leg. "Tell me how you and Griffin met. Have you known each other long?"

"We met just last night, actually. I was driving down Main Street and blew a tire."

"My goodness! Were you hurt?"

"I was fine, just a bit shaken up. When I got out of the car, Griffin and a couple friends were standing there. And then . . ." I wrinkled my nose. "I fainted."

Darlene gasped, steepling her fingers over her heart. "You fainted!"

"Yes, but Griffin caught me before I hit the ground."

"The Lord at work!" she exclaimed, looking toward the ceiling.

I laughed. "He towed my car back to his garage, and then he was nice enough to let me stay over, since I had nowhere to go."

"You stayed the whole night at his apartment?" Darlene was clearly shocked at the news.

"Yes. But only because he felt sorry for me. You see, I'm sort of between living situations right now, and I need to save every penny I have—which isn't very many, to be honest—in order to get on my feet somewhere new. Griffin caught me trying to sleep in my car and offered his couch. But he was a complete gentleman, I assure you."

"Of course he was." She nodded with satisfaction. "He was raised right. Of course, there was a lot of nonsense when he was growing up. My stars, that boy could find trouble with his eyes closed! His father and I were beside ourselves for years wondering if he was ever going to straighten himself out."

The screen door creaked open and slammed shut again, startling us both.

"Anyway," Darlene said, waving a hand in front of her face. "I'm just so pleased to see him out and about with a nice young lady such as yourself."

"Oh, well, I wouldn't say we're out and about *together*, exactly. He's just helping me out while I'm here. I'll be gone soon."

"And where is it you're headed, dear?"

"That's a bit up in the air at the moment, but when I left

Tennessee yesterday morning, I was heading for a place called Cloverleigh Farms. I was there once for a wedding years ago and fell in love with it."

"Oh yes, I know it. That's a beautiful place." She hesitated. "Of course, the nearby town is much less charming than Bellamy Creek."

"Is it?"

She nodded. "Yes. And quite small. They only have one harbor, and we have two."

I laughed. "Seeing as I don't have a boat at the moment, it's probably okay. What I'd like to do is open up a bakery once I'm on my feet."

"Ready to go, Blair?" Griffin appeared at the doorway.

"So soon?" Darlene sounded dismayed. "We're just getting to know each other. Did you know Blair wants to open a bakery?"

"Yes."

"I was just thinking she could open one up here in town. Or a pastry shop! We haven't had good pie in this town since Betty Frankel passed, God rest her soul." She crossed herself.

"She's not staying here."

"You don't know that for sure," Darlene said irritably.

"Actually, Griffin's right," I said. "I'm only here for a few weeks."

"A few weeks?" His mother looked hopeful again.

"Yes. It's going to take Griffin some time to get the parts he needs to fix my car, and in the meantime I'm going to work at the desk and help out with a new marketing strategy at the garage."

"Was there an old marketing strategy?" joked Cheyenne, coming into the room and dropping onto a leather recliner.

I smiled. "It's centered around an event we're going to plan for Labor Day weekend. Sort of an open house to reintroduce the business to the town. But first, we're going to renovate the lobby a bit."

Cheyenne's jaw fell open. "You convinced him to renovate the lobby? Wow, he really did fall under your spell."

"It was Blair that fell," Darlene said. "Did you know that? Fainted *dead away* at the mere sight of him, and he *caught* her."

"Really?" Cheyenne looked back and forth from me to Griffin, whose mouth was set in a grim line.

"No," he said, annoyed. "She was dehydrated."

"I heard she was wearing a wedding dress." Darlene looked smug as she pointed a finger at her son. "Now you tell me *that* isn't divine intervention."

"Jesus Christ, Ma. It wasn't divine intervention, it was a flat tire."

Darlene quirked a brow. "You say tomato, I say tomahto."

"Anyway," I went on, rising from the couch, "I'm really grateful for the short-term work at the garage. I feel very lucky."

"Well, I'm tickled pink that Griffin has someone to help out while I'm laid up." Darlene fell back on the couch and made a big show of lifting both legs onto the cushions, even though she'd seemed fine a moment before. "You never know how long I'll be out."

"Mom, you just said earlier the doctor said you could go back to work sometime next week," Cheyenne said.

"You hush, Cheyenne Dempsey. That's not at all what the doctor said."

"I was in the room, Mom."

"You must have misheard, darling." Darlene shot her daughter an evil look. "So thank the Lord for sending sweet, lovely Blair to fill in for me as long as we need her."

Griffin cleared his throat. "So, Mom. Blair needs somewhere to stay while she's in town. Know anyone who's renting a room?"

"I thought she was staying at your place."

"That was an emergency situation."

"Well, you can't just kick her out, Griffin. What's the matter with you?"

Griffin breathed heavily through his nose. "No one's kicking anyone anywhere, Mom. Now do you know someone renting a room or not?"

"Well, I'm not sure. I need to think about it." She smiled indulgently at him. "You're always such a bear when you're hungry. How about some nice chicken salad?"

"No, thank you." Griffin came over and grabbed me by the forearm. "Let's go, Blair."

"Nice meeting you, Darlene. Cheyenne," I called over my shoulder as Griffin dragged me toward the front door. His legs were much longer than mine, and I stumbled once or twice.

"You too!" Cheyenne shouted. "And congrats again on tying the knot!"

Griffin shook his head as he pulled me onto the porch, the screen door slamming shut behind us. He held my arm as we went down the steps, then he stopped short. "Oh my God."

I looked in the direction of his gaze and saw that someone—probably Cheyenne—had tied several aluminum cans to the bumper of Griffin's truck, and a sign that said JUST MARRIED was stuck in the rear window. Mariah and her damp little friends stood giggling next to the car, and when they saw us, they came running.

"Congratulations!" they shouted, showering us with handfuls of rice. "Yay! You got married!"

"We didn't get married," Griffin barked at them.

Mariah looked crestfallen. "But Miss Cheyenne said—"

"Miss Cheyenne lies."

Laughing, I stumbled forward through the shower of rice as he started marching across the lawn. His grip on me was tight but not painful, and I sort of liked how worked up he was. He was cute when he smiled, but he was smoking hot when he was mad, and the stubborn clenched jaw was doing things to me.

"Sorry, girls," I said with a smile. "It's just a joke. We aren't really married."

The three girls looked disappointed. "Nothing fun ever happens around here," one of them complained. But a minute later, they were tossing the rice at each other, shrieking and racing back toward the sprinkler.

"I'm going to throttle my sister," Griffin grumbled, pulling his keys from his pocket.

"Come on, she's funny."

"She's a pain in the ass." He let go of me when we reached the truck. "Grab the sign please. I'll untie the cans."

I opened the slightly smaller back door on the passenger side and peeked at the black and white kitten in a travel carrier. "Hi there, cutie. Are you excited about your new home?" Climbing onto the seat, I pulled the sheet of paper from the window where it had been taped. "Don't mind your new daddy. He's grumpy right now, but I promise, he's a nice guy."

"Can I have that, please?" Griffin asked from behind me.

I backed out of the truck, embarrassed that I'd probably just flashed him my underwear, which was not particularly sexy. "Here you go."

He took off with the cans and sign, marching onto the porch and dumping them right inside the screen door. I got into the truck's front seat and waited for him, listening to the kitten meow in the back. "It's okay, kitty," I said, wondering if it was a boy or girl and if it had a name.

Griffin got behind the wheel and slammed his door shut. "Told you my family is obnoxious."

"They do like giving you a hard time, don't they?"

"Yeah." He turned on the engine but left the truck in park. "Somehow it was easier to take when my dad was alive. Now it always feels like two against one."

"How long has he been gone?"

"A little over two years."

"I'm sorry."

He shrugged. "That's life, I guess. I just wish he could have lived long enough to retire. Enjoy his life more. He worked so hard every day of his life. For what?"

I stared at him. Did he really not know? "For *this*, Griffin." I gestured to his house, the neighborhood, toward him. "For his family. For security. For a business he was proud of and could pass on to his son."

"I guess."

I thought of my own father and how *he* did business. "I bet your dad was honest."

"Always."

"And paid his employees fairly."

"He did."

"And never completed a job he didn't stand behind. Never scammed anyone. Never did things the easy or cheap way when his reputation was on the line. And I bet he paid his taxes, even if he didn't like it."

"He definitely did not like it. But you're right, he never cheated."

"And do you think if he were here right now, he'd tell you he had regrets?"

"No," he said grudgingly.

"Because he was a good man. A good father. I bet your mother would say he was a good husband too. That's worth a lot."

Griffin continued to stare out the windshield.

"I mean, I think about my dad, and I feel . . . ashamed. It doesn't mean I don't love him—he's still my dad. But I'm not proud of the things he did. He cared more about money than what was right," I said, getting all worked up. "I never want to be that person."

He looked at me. "You're not, Blair."

"And as for my mother, she told me I was being a complete *imbecile* when I left. She said I was delusional and naive and wouldn't last a month on my own."

"She's wrong."

"What if she isn't?" I fretted, knitting my fingers together, feeling my heart begin to race. "What if she knows more because she's older and wiser and raised me to be this one specific way in a specific type of environment where everything is handed to me, and all these setbacks I'm facing are just the tip of the massive iceberg lurking beneath the surface and I'm doomed to fail?"

"Hey." He reached over and took one of my hands. "She's wrong, okay? Stop talking and take a breath."

Closing my eyes, I inhaled and exhaled slowly a couple times. When I looked at him again, I felt silly. "Thanks. Sorry for the panic attack—that conversation was supposed to be about you."

"It's okay. I don't really want to talk about myself anyway." He squeezed my hand. "Now listen. I only just met you last night, but I can already tell you are not the kind of person to turn around and run scared when you face a problem. Maybe you're a little bit, uh . . ."

"Careful," I warned.

". . . *inexperienced* in the real world," he finished, in what I considered a triumph, "but you'll learn fast. You're smart, you're determined, and you can talk to anyone—in two languages, no less."

"Three, actually."

"Three?"

"I speak Latin too."

"*Latin?*"

"It's the universal language of western civilization," I said defensively. "Although not terribly useful in modern life, I admit."

Griffin shook his head and gave me a disarming smile.

"You're going to be okay, Blair."

"You really think so?"

"Yes." He looked down at the inside of my forearm, which bore a couple faint brown scars. "Jesus Christ. What happened?"

"Oven rack burns. Professional hazard."

"Oh." He brushed his fingertips across them, which I thought was sweet, then let go of my hand. "You good now? You're not going to faint or anything?"

I laughed. "No. I'm good."

"Okay, then let's take this cat home and go get some food."

"But what about finding a place for me to stay? I feel like an orphan right now. And I'm not as cute as a rescue cat."

"Food first, or I won't even be able to think." He shook his head, and pulled away from the curb. "My mom's right about one thing—I get hangry as fuck."

After we'd been on the road for a few minutes, I looked over at him. "So what did your sister mean about breaking your number one rule for me?"

"Nothing."

"Oh, come on." I reached over and poked his shoulder. "What's your number one rule?"

He exhaled. "No sleepovers. I don't bring women back to my apartment."

"Ah."

"Not that last night was a sleepover in *that* way," he said quickly. "So I didn't really break the rule."

"Definitely not," I said.

But I turned my face toward the window and smiled.

CHAPTER 7
GRIFFIN

I CARRIED the kitten's crate up the stairs, and Blair followed behind, toting the bags Cheyenne had given me with food and supplies.

"My sister said to keep her confined in one room to start, so I guess I'll put her in the bedroom," I said.

Blair set the bags on the kitchen counter. "How cute. You can cuddle with her at night."

I glared at her over my shoulder.

"Let me guess—mechanics don't cuddle," she said, trailing me into my room.

"This one doesn't." I set the crate down in one corner and opened it up, but the kitten didn't come out.

"So is it a boy or a girl?" Blair asked.

"Girl. Her name is Bisou."

"Bisou?" She laughed and wandered over to where I stood. "That's adorable."

"It is?"

She turned to face me. "Yes, it's French. It means kiss."

Again, I found myself staring at her lips. Dying to taste them. Should I just fucking do it?

In the end, she saved me by dropping down and patting

the floor, trying to coax the cat out of hiding. *"Viens ici, ma petite Bisou,"* she crooned. *"Ma choupinette. N'aie pas peur."*

Suddenly I thought of those old scenes in the Addams Family when Gomez would lose his mind when Morticia spoke French. If I never got it watching reruns as a kid, I got it now. It didn't even matter I had no clue what she was saying. Just the words on her lips were sexy.

Blair sighed and sat back on her heels, looking up at me, her lips in a pout. "She won't come out."

Christ, she was adorable. And why was it so hot in here? "Maybe she just needs to get acclimated. Ready to go? I could use a cold beer."

"Sure." She took the hand I offered and rose to her feet. "Thanks. Have I told you yet how nice your manners are?"

"I don't think so." I dropped her hand before I started kissing my way up her arm, Gomez-style.

"Well, they are. I feel like all the guys I've met in the last few years are Neanderthals with expensive shoes." She shrugged. "Or maybe I just attract the jerks who think having money is the same thing as having class."

"I don't have much of either."

Blair laughed. "Doesn't matter. I'd rather be with you than any one of them tonight. Hey, listen. Do you mind if I use your bathroom real quick to freshen up before we leave?"

"No, go ahead. I'll wait outside." As I left the room, I glanced at the ball gown hanging on the back of my closet door.

"Want me to put my wedding dress back on?" she teased. "Seems like it was a big hit around here."

I looked back at her menacingly. "Don't you dare."

"I love it when you go all mean boss on me." Her grin was full of mischief, daring me to come at her and throw her down on that bed like I wanted to.

I left the room before I said—or did—something I'd regret.

Outside, I called my mother.

"Hello?"

"It's me. Did you think of anyone who might have a spare room to rent?"

"Not yet. But I'm thinking *very* hard. In the meantime, though, I think she should probably just stay with you a little longer."

"Stop trying to play matchmaker, Mom. It never works."

"Because you're so stubborn," she chided. "You don't even *try* with the women I introduce you to, and I've set you up with some perfectly lovely girls!"

"Name one."

"What about that nurse from Urgent Care? She was darling."

"She spent the entire dinner crying over her ex-husband. No, thanks."

"What about the new bank teller at the credit union? She was definitely single."

"She didn't like baseball. That was DOA."

"Well, how about the lawyer I met at the gardening center? She seemed outdoorsy."

"She likes women, Mom. Which she said she told you right away when you mentioned setting her up with your son."

"Well, sometimes people are just confused, or in denial."

"In this case, that person is definitely you."

"Don't change the subject! We were talking about Blair. If you'd just try to get to know her, I think you two could be good for each other."

"I am getting to know her. Because I *hired* her. I don't generally invite my employees to live with me."

"Well, this isn't a general kind of situation, is it? This is special." She sighed dramatically. "But if she doesn't feel welcome at your place, I suppose she can stay here in your old room."

I cringed at the thought of my mother filling Blair's head with nonsense about me, but figured it might be best for the time being. "Thank you. I appreciate it. I'll bring her over after dinner."

"Oh, not *tonight*," she said. "That room is full of junk. I need at least a day or so to clean it out. You can be a gentleman for one more night, can't you?"

"Stop playing games, Mom." I didn't trust myself to be a gentleman for one more night. One more hour was going to be hard enough.

"Griffin Dempsey, you heard what I said. Now mind your manners around that young lady, and at least *try* to be charming. You might not think her showing up here was a sign, but I do! And if you're not careful, someone else is going to come along and sweep her off her feet—someone like Enzo Moretti! Now *there's* a gentleman!"

I was so annoyed and hungry, I lost it. "Oh yeah? Well, Moretti was just telling us last night about a threesome he had recently. Is that the kind of gentleman you think I should be?"

My mother was silent for a moment, and I squeezed my eyes shut, picturing her having a heart attack. And then.

"That is *exactly* what I'm talking about! He charmed *two* women into being with him. All I'm asking you to do is work on one." Then she hung up.

I was still standing there staring at my phone when Blair came hurrying outside. "Thanks for waiting," she said breathlessly. "I'm ready now." She stopped, noticing my aggravated expression. "What's wrong?"

"My mother."

"What about her?"

I shook my head. "You know what? Never mind. Let's go eat."

Side by side, we walked a few blocks down to The Bulldog Pub. It was a warm night, and on the breeze I caught the scent of vanilla again.

"So listen," I said, putting a little more distance between us. "My mom is still going to make some calls in the hunt for a room for rent until Labor Day, but in the meantime, she offered the spare bedroom at her house."

"She did? Oh my goodness, that's so sweet of her!"

I frowned. "She can absolutely be sweet when she wants to, but I need to warn you, she has ulterior motives where you're concerned."

"Ulterior motives like finding you a wife so she can finally get those grandchildren she wants?"

"Exactly."

Blair laughed, elbowing me in the ribs. "Don't worry. I'm not looking for a husband. Establishing my independence and getting a business up and running are my priorities for the near future."

"I know that, and you know that, but she can be ruthless when she gets an idea in her head."

"I'll be fine. I'm just so grateful to have somewhere to stay. And of course, I'll pay rent. Did she mention how much the room would cost?"

"No, but that's something you can work out with her. That reminds me—I don't normally pay my employees cash under the table, but since you're here such a short time, I'll do it that way if it works for you."

"That's perfect."

"There's just one more thing," I said as we neared the pub. "What's that?"

I turned to face her. "My mother says the spare room won't be ready until tomorrow. It's probably just one of her little games, but she asked if you'd mind staying one more night with me."

Blair looked surprised, maybe even happy. "Of course I don't mind. But is it okay with you?"

"It's fine." In my head was my mother's voice telling me to be a gentleman, contrasting sharply with the fantasy of banging Blair on my dining table. "I'll make sure to give you the couch this time."

Without warning, she put a hand on my chest, rose up on her toes and kissed my cheek. "Thank you so much for everything, Griffin. I don't know what I'd do without you."

God, she was beautiful. And sweet. Smart. Sexy. And endearingly in need of protection without acting needy. The combination was driving me crazy. "Let's sit down. I really need a beer."

We grabbed a table for two on the pub's outdoor patio. "Is this where you were sitting when I drove by last night?" she asked, setting her purse by her feet.

"Not this exact table, but yes."

She cringed. "So you saw the whole thing?"

I grinned. "We all did."

"God." Closing her eyes, she shook her head. "So embarrassing. I mean, I've never been a very good driver, but last night was particularly humiliating."

"You're not a good driver?"

"No. I mean, I don't habitually speed or anything. Things just tend to hit me."

"Things tend to hit *you*? What kind of things?"

"Oh, you know, stop signs, bike racks, the occasional parking garage wall."

I laughed. "Blair, those things don't move."

She sighed and rolled her eyes. "Okay, fine, maybe it's me hitting them. But no one ever gets hurt. Except possibly that one bus driver who claimed to have a stiff neck, but I swear I was *legally parked* when I backed into her bus."

I laughed again. "I didn't think there was a worse driver than Mrs. Applebee, but you might have her beat. How do you even have a license at this point?"

She gave me a coy smile. "I used to have a *very* good attorney."

The server came by and took our drink orders, leaving us with a couple menus to look over. I ignored mine—I had the thing just about memorized—but Blair opened hers up.

"So what's good here?"

I answered her questions about the menu without even looking at it, and she teased me for knowing it so well. "I don't really cook," I said with a shrug. "And this place is close, quick, and reliable. Plus, they sponsor our baseball team, so I like giving them the business."

"You're on a baseball team?"

"Not just any baseball team." I leaned back, crossing my arms over my chest. "I will have you know you're sitting across from the first baseman of the one and only Bellamy Creek Bulldogs, the two-time champions of the Allegan County Senior Men's Baseball League."

"Well, my goodness." Blair fanned her face like a swooning Southern belle. "I do declare, Mr. Dempsey, that *is* impressive."

I smiled, realizing it had been a long time since I'd taken a woman to dinner—and even longer since I'd enjoyed someone's company so much. The waitress returned with our drinks—a beer for me, vodka and soda with a lime for Blair—and took our orders.

"So are you a baseball fan?" I asked when we were alone again, imagining her in the stands cheering us on.

"Hmm. I think so." Blair pretended to think about it, tapping that puffy bottom lip with one finger. "Baseball is the one played on a diamond, right?"

I laughed, picking up my beer. "That's the one."

"Then yes, definitely. I'm a fan of anything that involves

diamonds." She lifted her glass and clinked it against my bottle. "Cheers to a third championship, slugger. Now let's talk business."

While we waited for our food, Blair and I discussed ideas for revitalizing business at the garage, including the lobby makeover, the Labor Day event, and a social media campaign.

"I don't have social media, though," I told her.

"That's part of your problem—you need it." She took a sip of her drink. "You've got a website, and it's fine, but ideally it needs a makeover as well. Do you know any website designers?"

I thought about it and tipped up my beer. "You know, Handme's girlfriend Lola might do something like that. I can ask him."

She blinked. "Who?"

"Handme. Oh, sorry—Andy. We call him Handme at work."

"Why?"

I explained the nickname to her and she laughed, shaking her head. "That's mean. Poor Andy."

"Listen, we've all been that guy at the garage who hands the wrenches and stacks the tires. You have to start somewhere."

"Did you start there?"

"Hell yes, I did. My dad was not about to spare me just because I was his son. If anything, he worked me harder than he worked the other guys."

The server arrived and set down our plates of burgers and fries. "Another round?" she asked, picking up my empty beer bottle and Blair's glass.

"Sure," I said.

Blair bit that lip. "I shouldn't."

"It's on me," I told her, assuming she was worried about the cost. "Have another one."

"Thanks." She smiled, but she still looked uncomfortable.

And she stopped talking—the server came back with our second round, and she still hadn't spoken.

"Hey. What's up?" I nudged her foot with mine under the table.

"Nothing." She sprinkled a little salt on her fries. Pushed them around on her plate.

"I don't buy it. You've been silent for like four entire minutes. That's got to be a record." I was hoping it would make her laugh, but she gave me only a half-hearted smile.

"I'm feeling bad about myself."

"Why?" I picked up my burger and took a bite.

"I guess I was just thinking about how hard you've worked your entire life. Everything you have, you earned. And I had everything handed to me. It doesn't seem fair."

"Who said life was fair?"

"You know what I mean." She picked up one fry and ate it slowly, like a rabbit nibbling to the end of a carrot. "Tell me more about how you grew up."

"Like what?"

"I don't know. Were you good in school?"

I shrugged. "Good at what? Behaving? No."

"Did you get good grades?"

"When I tried."

She sighed in exasperation. "Did you try?"

"Sometimes." I took a few more bites and thought about it. "There were some subjects I liked, some teachers I liked. I worked hard for the ones whose approval mattered to me."

"What was your favorite subject?"

"I spent a lot of time in detention. Does that count?"

She laughed. "What did you get detentions for?"

"Mostly for being late for school. I'm an early riser now, but back then, I constantly overslept. I also got in fights sometimes. I'd mouth off when my temper got the better of me. My friends and I pulled pranks and got caught." I shrugged.

"Nothing serious. Just too much testosterone bottled up in a small town."

"You got in fights?" Her eyes were wide. "With who?"

"I don't know. It was just stupid guy stuff. Someone would say something that pissed me off, I'd say something back, and it would get physical. I was trying to be a rebel all the time."

"So you had a bad temper?"

I tipped up my beer. "You could say that. Yeah."

"Do you still?"

"Sometimes. But I've learned to control it."

"How?"

"Eight years in the Marines."

"Oh. You're a Marine." She glanced at my arms. "Is that where you got all the tattoos?"

"I had a few before. Most of them I got when I came home."

"I've never seen so many on one person," she confessed, looking a little scandalized by it. "Did they hurt?"

"I've been through worse."

"You were deployed?"

I nodded. "Three times."

"That must have been . . ." She stopped and sighed. "I don't even know how to finish that sentence. I was going to say *hard*, but that seems like a stupid remark. Of course it was hard. It's war."

"It was a lot of things. Hard is one of them."

"Do you hate talking about it?" she asked quietly.

I didn't respond right away. I took a few more bites of my burger and drank some beer, and thought about how to answer the question. Usually I kept my barriers in place with silence, but there was something about Blair that made me want to lower them a little.

But just a little.

"I'm sorry," she said when I didn't answer the question immediately. "I didn't mean to bring up bad memories."

"It's okay. I was just trying to put my thoughts into words. Some of us don't have three languages at our disposal," I said, nudging her foot again. "Most days, I feel like I don't even have *one*."

She smiled. "Well, anytime you want your thoughts translated into Latin, I'm your girl."

Leaning back in my chair, I turned the conversation onto her. "What about you? You were good at school, I take it?"

"Yes, I was."

"And I suppose you never once had a detention?"

"Not once."

"And probably stayed out of fights, the principal's office, and tattoo studios?"

She swirled the ice cubes around in her drink and stared into the glass. "Guess I've led a pretty boring life."

Immediately, I felt bad. "I didn't mean it like that. I just meant . . . I don't know. We're different. We've had different life experiences."

"I guess that's true. The most rebellious thing I've ever done is take a secret job at a bakery." She looked so down about it, I had to smile.

"I don't know. Look at the way you up and left your old life without knowing what the future would bring."

"Some people would call that stupid."

"Well, I don't." Impulsively, I leaned forward and took her hand. "I think it was brave. I think somewhere inside you is a rebel Blair that's dying to get out and show the world what she can do."

She brightened up so much she nearly glowed. "Do you think I should get a tattoo?"

I had to laugh. "Let's not go overboard. Why don't we start by teaching you how to change a tire or something? Or how to jumpstart your car in case the battery ever goes dead.

Those are two of the most common reasons people call for a tow."

"That would be great," she said. "Then I could help other people too, not just myself."

I nodded. "There you go."

She looked down at our clasped hands. "What am I going to teach you? How to speak French?"

"Hmm. Not sure that would come in too handy."

"You're right." Then she giggled. "Remember that episode of Friends where Phoebe tries to teach Joey how to speak French?"

I shook my head. Right then I couldn't think of anything except the way she was playing with my fingers, threading them through her own. My dick was reacting as if her hands were in my pants, not on the table.

"Anyway, it did not go well. I'll think of something else. Oh!" She took her hand from mine and held up one finger. "I'll teach you to cook something! Then you won't have to order so much takeout."

"That works," I said, grabbing my beer and finishing it. "Although I'm not sure I'll be a very good student."

"You'll be at least as good in the kitchen as I am in the garage," she said. "And I bet you're great with your hands."

Our eyes met. Slowly, I set my empty bottle back on the table. The crotch of my jeans was hot and tight.

Her cheeks flamed. "I'm sorry, I didn't mean it like—not that you wouldn't be—I mean, I wouldn't know if you're—" Flustered, she flapped her hands at the wrist in front of her chest. "Help me, I'm talking, and I can't shut up."

I laughed. "It's okay. I knew what you meant." Lowering my voice, I said, "And just so you know, that's a safe bet—I'm excellent with my hands."

She remained flushed in the face as we finished eating, sneaking peeks at my fingers.

I fucking liked it. A lot.

When the bill was paid, we started walking back to my place.

After a couple minutes of silence, she looked over at me. "Can I ask you something?"

"Sure."

"It's kind of out there."

"Now I'm nervous. But go ahead."

"If you knew that in one year you would die suddenly, would you change anything about the way you're living now?"

I glanced at her with concern. "You okay?"

She laughed. "I'm fine. But it's a question someone once asked me, and I said no. It was a lie, of course. And it haunted me for a long time."

"Ah."

"So what about you? Would you change anything?"

"Nope. My life is exactly the way I want it."

"That's amazing. I really admire the way you've always known what you wanted, and you just went for it."

I thought for a moment. "I don't know about that. I mean, I was an idiot for a lot of years." We were approaching the door to my apartment, and I pulled the keys from my pocket.

"An idiot how?"

I shrugged. "When I was younger, I thought I knew everything. I didn't."

"Everything about what?"

"Life. And when I got an idea in my head, I just ran hard at it, top speed, balls out. I had no self-control whatsoever."

She was quiet again for a moment. "I get what you mean. Not that I had balls, of course. But I thought I knew everything too."

I laughed. "Probably everyone does when they're eighteen

or twenty-one, or even twenty-five. It takes maturity to see things more clearly. Learn the right lessons." I unlocked the door and opened it for her, then followed her up the stairs, inhaling her vanilla-scented wake.

At the top of the stairs, she turned to face me. "What lessons have you learned?"

"Huh?" Moving past her, I switched on a light in the kitchen. I could *not* be alone with her in the dark.

"About life. What are the most important lessons you've learned?"

I walked over to the lamp next to the couch and switched it on. "I've learned that inner strength is just as important as outer strength, maybe more. I've learned that getting attached to people or things or ideas gives them too much power over you. And I've learned that the only person you can truly rely on is yourself."

She stared at me across the room. "Wow, Griffin. That's really bleak."

"No, it isn't," I said defensively. "It's practical. And it's freeing. When you realize that you don't need anyone else to be happy, you stop feeling like you're missing something. You stop looking for it. You realize you're fine with what you have."

"But how do you keep yourself so unattached?"

"That's what the rules are for."

"I take it you're not a relationship person."

"Nope."

"But don't you get lonely, relying only on yourself for everything?"

"Being alone is not the same as being lonely," I told her. "I promise you, I'm fine. But if you keep talking like this, I'm going to start calling you Darlene."

She laughed and put up her hands. "Okay, okay. I'll stop."

"Good." I moved toward the back hallway, anxious for the

conversation to be over. I was talking way too much. "I'll get a sheet and make up the couch for you."

"Thanks. Hey, do you think I might be able to take a quick shower?"

"Sure." I kept moving, ignoring the blood rushing to my crotch. She was going to get naked in my bathroom. She was going to take off every stitch of clothing, get in my shower, and put her hands all over her body. Right where I stood naked earlier and would stand naked tomorrow, jerking off at the thought of it. "I'll leave a couple towels on the bed for you," I said, my voice cracking, my dick getting hard.

"Thank you."

With my breath coming hard, I pulled my two nicest bath towels, the white ones Cheyenne had gotten me for Christmas that had no frayed edges, down from a shelf. I'd never even used them because pure white towels scared me—I'd ruin them in *one* shower after a day on the job. Running my hand slowly over the top, I couldn't help thinking that this material was going to be all over her bare skin. Up and down her legs, all over her back and thighs, back and forth across her stomach and ass and breasts. Then she was going to come out of the bedroom all showered and clean and smelling delicious, probably wearing those tiny little shorts and that T-shirt that showed her nipples poking through.

It was going to take the strength of twenty men to keep my hands off her.

I didn't have it in me.

CHAPTER 8
BLAIR

NOT GONNA LIE, I got a kick out of taking off all my clothes in Griffin's bedroom. I even stood there naked for a minute—the door closed tight, of course—daring him to walk in on me.

He didn't.

Grabbing the towels off the bed, I hurried into the bathroom. "*Que diable, Bisou*," I whispered to the kitten, who was still hiding in her crate. "Why am I acting so crazy?"

The shower felt incredible—I washed my hair, shaved my legs, soaped up and rinsed off two days' worth of road trip grime and sticky summer sweat. I used my own vanilla bean body wash, but I admit I picked up Griffin's bar of Lava soap and sniffed it. The scent was subtle, but it was enough to send a tingle directly between my legs.

I thought about those big strong arms . . . was it wrong to want them to manhandle me a little between the sheets? I recalled the way he'd grabbed my elbow and yanked me through his mother's house today, and my insides caught fire.

He had manners, but he didn't always use them.

Gah, that was so hot!

I made up my mind—I had to seduce him. But how?

I kept thinking about it while I dried off, rubbed body lotion into my skin, put on my pajamas, and brushed my teeth. In the end, it was my reflection in the mirror that brought me to my senses.

For God's sake, I was wearing an old Snoopy T-shirt and a faded pair of boy shorts. My hair was soggy, my underwear was plain old granny panty pink cotton—which you could see through a hole in my shorts—and I could no longer afford real pedicures, so my toes felt naked and unsexy.

Everything about me felt unsexy.

Giving up on the idea of seduction, I switched off the light, packed up my things, and went out to the living room.

Griffin was sitting in the chair I'd slept in. The kitchen lights were out but moonlight streamed in through the tall front windows, illuminating the room in a silver sheen. Just the sight of the back of his head and his neck did things to me. As I got closer, I could see a sheet spread neatly over the cushions and a pillow at one end.

"Thank you," I said.

He rose to his feet and faced me. "No problem. All done in the bathroom?"

"Yes." Self-conscious, I touched my wet, bedraggled hair. "I really appreciate the shower. I feel much better."

"Good." He glanced down at my bare legs for a moment and then back toward his bedroom. "Guess I'll feed the cat and go to bed."

"Okay." But I didn't want him to go. "I wish . . . never mind."

"What?"

I shook my head. "It's stupid."

"Tell me."

I stared at his chest as I spoke—at the biceps bulging against his sleeves, at the ink on his muscular arms, at the broadness of his shoulders. Desire was pooling at the center of me, bubbling like thick, hot, chocolate sauce. "I wish I'd met you under different circumstances, that's all."

He took a step closer to me. "Why?"

"Because I hate being dependent on you this way. It's not that I don't *want* to stay another night with you—it's just that I wish it wasn't because I *needed* to." Our eyes locked. "I wish it was because you wanted me to."

"What if it was both?"

"Huh?"

"What if it was that you need to *and* I want you to?" His hands moved to my hips.

"I hadn't thought about it like that." I slid my palms up his chest, rising on tiptoe. My stomach quivered. "*Do* you want me to?"

He pulled my body flush against him, and I felt the answer before he said it. "Yes."

Our mouths came together, hot and searing. He kissed me the way I'd always dreamed about being kissed—wild and savage, like a starving animal devours its prey. Twenty-four hours of pent-up longing overwhelmed us, and our hands tore at clothing—whipping off T-shirts, yanking at shorts, unbuttoning, unzipping, shoving down jeans. When we were naked, the full lengths of our bodies pressed against each other, our hands sliding over hot, sweaty skin, he groaned and moved his mouth down the side of my throat. I tipped my head to the side and sighed at the decadent swirl of his tongue on my neck.

Reaching between us, I sheathed his thick, towering cock with one hand, rubbing my thumb over its tip, moving my fist up and down its length, murmuring in appreciation and excitement.

He growled and slipped a hand between my thighs, caressing me with surprisingly soft, gentle strokes until I thought I'd die if he didn't penetrate me. I rocked my hips over his hand and he gave me what I wanted, sliding one long finger inside me, using the heel of his hand against my clit. Then he withdrew his finger and rubbed the warm, silky wetness in quick little circles and I felt like an oven buzzer was about to go off inside me.

"Oh God," I whispered, embarrassed that I might come this fast. I had to grip both his shoulders to even stay on my feet. "That feels so good. I haven't—so long—don't stop—yes, yes, *yes*—" I exploded in hot, pulsing beats, my core muscles clenching again and again. But I was greedy and desperate for more. I wanted him inside me. I wanted him to lose control the way I had. I wanted to make him come.

But first, my legs gave out.

He caught me—of course he did—grabbing me around my lower back and hoisting me up his body. I wrapped my legs around his waist as our mouths collided again, tongues searching, teeth bumping, lips opened wide. With my elbows on his shoulders, I threaded my hands through his hair as his hands kneaded my ass. Trapped between us, his cock was long and slick, and my entire body radiated with the need to take him in deep.

"Would it be too forward of me to tell you I want you?" I panted against his mouth. "Like right now?"

Instead of answering, he moved toward the couch and knelt on it with one knee, setting me on my back on top of the sheet. "Don't move," he ordered.

Propped on my elbows, I stayed where I was, watching him stride quickly back to his room. His naked back was perfection—the wide shoulders, the narrow waist, the perfect ass. My hands clenched into fists, eager to dig into that muscular flesh.

He returned a moment later, and the sight of him in the moonlight stole my breath. Good God, did any man deserve such physical perfection? I thought I might hyperventilate as he tore open the condom and rolled it onto his dick. My toes were curling already.

He knelt above me. "You're so beautiful."

"I was thinking the same of you."

"No. I'm a dirty mechanic who can't keep his hands to himself. Or his dick."

I opened my knees a little wider. "Don't tease me."

He lowered his mouth to one breast, teasing my nipple with his tongue. He brought his hand to the other, filling his palm, flicking its stiff peak with his thumb. I groaned as he sucked and pinched and tormented me, my hands cradling his head, my body aching for him.

"Griffin, please," I begged.

He finally gave in, inching into me slowly, his eyes closed, his mouth open. He growled and cursed, fighting for control.

I was struggling to breathe as he stretched and filled me, my body tightening up reflexively before it began to relax.

"Are you okay?" he asked.

"Yes. Are you?"

"I'm not sure. Give me a second."

Inside me, I felt a single telltale throb, heard him mutter a string of curse words, and I laughed. "Close?"

"Shhh."

Just to be wicked, I rocked my hips beneath his. "You're so big it hurts," I whispered in his ear. "But your body is making me crazy. I've never wanted anyone so badly in my life."

"I knew you were trouble," he said as I kissed his jaw, stroked his neck with my tongue, moved my hands to his lower back and down over his ass. "From the moment I saw you get out of that car, I swear to God I knew."

"Are you going to punish me for it?" I teased, pulling him in deeper, making both of us gasp.

"You don't know what you're asking for, princess," his voice gravelly with the struggle for control.

"Then I guess you better show me."

It was like a switch in him flipped—his body roared to life above mine, and suddenly I found my wrists crossed and pinned above my head, my arms immobilized by his strength. He drove into me with deep, powerful thrusts—slowly at first, making me inhale sharply with every one. But somehow he was rough and commanding without being mean, and the pain began to blur with the pleasure of knowing everything I felt was at his whim. Knowing every ragged breath he took was for me. Knowing every agonizing groan meant he was torturing himself, holding back to make it last.

Sometimes he'd pause, buried to the hilt, and perform some magical spiraling motion with his hips that made my body hum with hunger and desire. The base of his cock rubbed against my clit and I couldn't speak, couldn't beg, couldn't breathe. I struggled to get my arms free, to no avail. My head thrashed from side to side—he was so unbearably deep—everything within me tightening and tightening—my insides a vise around his cock—the tension in me rising to impossible heights—and then suddenly I was riding out the most intense and glorious orgasm I'd ever experienced.

Or maybe it was his climax I felt—deep and rhythmic and thunderous—the throbbing force behind it jarring my bones, shaking my core, tearing my body to pieces that scattered like stars all over the sky.

Was this even real?

I wasn't sure—not even when he collapsed above me, not even when the scent of vanilla and Lava soap and sex mingled in my head, not even when he finally released my wrists and I could move my arms again.

It was only when he lifted himself off my chest and asked if I was okay that I felt myself returning to earth.

"I don't know," I said, still out of breath. "I might have just had an out-of-body experience."

A laugh rumbled in his throat. "Well, I had an in-your-body experience. And it was fucking amazing. Sorry if it was too fast and you missed it."

"It wasn't, and I didn't." I rubbed my palms up and down

his shoulders. "It was perfect. I've never felt an orgasm like that before. I don't know what you did, but if my body has a language, you speak it."

"Good." He sounded smug. Dropping a kiss on my lips, he said, "I'll be right back."

He got off the couch, and I flopped onto my tummy, pulling the cool pillow beneath my cheek. My heart was still beating erratically, and my skin felt puckered with goosebumps, although it was hot as hell in the room. The sheet was damp beneath me.

But I didn't care. My body was completely relaxed, my mind was at ease, and I had the distinct feeling I was exactly where I was supposed to be. Maybe it wasn't my final destination, but it was part of the journey to get there, and somehow I knew I was on the right road.

A moment later, I heard Griffin moving around in the kitchen. "Just feeding the cat," he said. "She's making a bunch of noise in there."

"We probably woke her."

"We probably woke the entire block. My windows are open."

I giggled. "Good thing we're married. Otherwise we'd cause a scandal."

He groaned. "You're as bad as my sister. When are you leaving town again?"

"As soon as you fix my car."

"Oh, right. That's good incentive." The refrigerator door opened and closed. "I'll be right back."

"Sure," I said, my eyelids drifting shut. I was almost asleep when I felt his hand on my back.

"Hey."

I smiled and opened my eyes. "Hey."

He crouched down next to me. "I switched on the window unit in my bedroom. Why don't you sleep in there with me?"

"Isn't that against the rules?"

"Yes. But we've already broken the rules tonight anyway."

"Right." I sat up and looked at him. He'd put on boxer briefs, but the sight of his bare chest threatened to light my fire all over again. In fact, I couldn't stop my hand from reaching out and tracing the lettering on one of the tattoos near his collarbone. "And you think we'll be better behaved in your bedroom?"

"Hard no. But I'm willing to risk it."

Dropping my hand into my lap, I met his eyes in the shadowy dark. "I don't want to make this weird, but are you sure this is okay? In general, I've always been a rule follower, and I want to respect yours, but I also really enjoyed those orgasms, so I—"

"Jesus Christ, Blair." Griffin ran a hand over his hair. "You're not on trial. It's just sex. It's just one night. Now stop talking and come to bed."

When he put it that way, I had to agree. Tomorrow night I'd be somewhere else, so we wouldn't even have to worry about it. Might as well cook while the oven was hot. "Okay."

He took my hand and led me back to his bedroom. As we passed the dining table, I noticed the kitten's crate against the wall beside it.

"You moved her out here?" I asked.

"Yeah. I don't want you to keep waking her up."

"Me?" I laughed as we entered his bedroom.

"Yes, you." He shut the door behind him, ditched the boxer briefs, and pushed me onto his bed.

"You were loud too, you know," I informed him as he moved up my body, his lips pressing kisses on my stomach, my breasts, my throat, until his face hovered above mine in the dark. Against my thigh, I could feel he was already growing hard again.

"Oh yeah?"

"Yes. I think I learned some new curse words tonight."

He laughed—a low, guttural growl—and flipped onto his

back, bringing my body on top of his. "Did I shock your delicate sensibilities?"

"In more ways than one," I said, straddling his hips. "But mostly I'm just glad you made the first move. I was back here in the bathroom trying to think of ways to seduce you in my Snoopy T-shirt and ripped shorts. It was not going well."

"That would have been quite a show."

Leaning forward, I braced my hands above his shoulders and moved back and forth along the length of his cock, my damp hair giving off the apple blossom scent of my shampoo. "I can still try to give you a good show. Minus the Snoopy shirt, of course."

He put his hands on my hips, digging his fingers into my skin, and lifting his mouth to my breast. He inhaled deeply as his tongue stroked my hard, tingling nipple. "You smell so fucking good all the time. It drives me insane. I can't keep my hands off you."

"Good." I moaned as he took the pebbled peak in between his teeth and flicked it with his tongue. "Although it might make our whole boss/employee relationship a little difficult."

His head fell back. "Fuck that. You are not officially my employee yet. That starts tomorrow."

"And this ends?" I rocked back and forth a little faster. I was wet and eager all over again, my desire for him unquenchable.

"This ends," he said, breathing harder. "Do we have a deal?"

"Absolutely. We don't need any complications."

"Good. Now stop moving like that before I lose my shit and come all over my own stomach."

Laughing, I sat back as he reached over to his nightstand drawer for a condom. "Let me," I said, taking it from him.

He lay back on his elbows and watched me open the packet and place the condom over just the tip. Then, hoping to make the opening act of my show more memorable, I leaned forward and used my mouth to slowly push it all the way down, teasing his nipples with my fingertips while I worked. When I picked my head up, Griffin's jaw was practically on his chest.

"Where the fuck did you learn that?"

I smiled like a Cheshire cat. "Boarding school."

"There were boys at your boarding school?"

"Hell, no." I positioned myself above him, and slowly slid down the length of his cock. "But you'd be surprised how dirty a group of seventeen-year-old girls stuck in a dorm with some smuggled condoms and a bunch of bananas can get. And then there were all the fantasies I cooked up when I was alone in bed at night."

He grabbed my ass as his cock twitched inside me. "Tell me."

"Well, I don't know," I teased in a campy Southern belle accent. I covered my breasts with my hands—added bonus, it made them look bigger and perkier—and went on, "I'm actually quite shy. I mostly just spend all my time alone in my room. But I've seen you in town at the service station, and I just love the way you"—I leaned forward here for effect, making my voice more breathy—"pump your gasoline."

"Yeah?" Beneath me, his hips began to flex.

"Yes. It does something to me, watching your hands at work." I piled my hair on the top of my head, circling my hips in a sinuous motion. "I dream about having those hands on me."

Griffin slid his palms up my sides and over my breasts, his breath coming hard and fast. Then he slid one hand down my stomach and used his thumb on my clit.

"Yes, just like that," I breathed. "And I admit I've stared at you like a good girl shouldn't. I've wondered about your body beneath your clothes. I imagined what it would be like to undress in front of you. Where it might lead."

Griffin's breathing had become even more labored, his

cock even thicker inside me. His thumb moved over my clit with quick, insistent strokes, making my entire body radiate with desire.

"Then I snuck into your bedroom tonight," I whispered. "I know it was wrong of me, I know I'll be punished, but when I saw you sleeping there naked, something just came over me. I had to have you." I placed my hands on his chest, playing with his nipples again, plucking at them, running my fingers over the ink on his skin, sliding my palms over his rippling abs. "Your body makes me swoon. All those muscles and tattoos, the way you move. And this"—I stopped, clenching my core muscles around him—"*this*. I took one look at your big, hard cock and knew I had to have it. I had to feel it. I had to make you come inside me, or else I'd go crazy."

"Fuck," he growled.

I knew he was close. I was too.

Time for the finale.

I moved my hands to my breasts, caressing them sensuously. "And I'll confess something else—something so wicked I don't even want to say it out loud—but sometimes I touch myself, and I pretend it's you. Just like you're touching me now. And something happens inside me, and it feels so good I never want it to stop, and I beg you to fuck me—harder, yes, yes, yes, like that"—as Griffin began to rock his hips more violently beneath mine, I fell forward, my hands braced on the headboard—"I beg you not to stop because I want to come all over your cock, and then you—"

But that's as far as I got before Griffin's climax hit and he erupted inside me, groaning long and hard as his cock surged again and again. It set off fireworks in me, and I rode out another earth-shattering orgasm, crying out with every impossibly blissful swell and sighing as the last, rapturous pulses subsided.

When my senses returned, I was still astride him, my chest

flat against his, my face buried in his neck. I inhaled his scent, dizzy with it.

Griffin was silent and still but for the motion of his chest as he breathed. I thought he might have fallen asleep, but then I felt his hands begin to stroke my back.

"You're still awake," I whispered.

"Barely."

"How was the show?"

"Best I've ever seen."

I smiled. "Really?"

"Yeah. Do you do encore performances?"

"Already?" I asked, the shock evident in my voice.

He chuckled. "No. I need an intermission."

"Good. My contract says I get a nap between performances." Dropping a kiss on his collarbone, I peeled myself off him and rolled to the other side of the bed.

He kissed my shoulder. "I'll be right back. Are you thirsty?"

"Yes."

"Me too. I'll get you some water."

"Thanks."

He went into the bathroom, and when he came out and headed for the kitchen, I slipped out of bed and used the bathroom too. When I came out, he was already beneath the covers. "Here," he said, grabbing one of two bottles of water on his nightstand and offering one to me.

"Thanks." Kneeling on the mattress, I took the cold bottle of water from him, uncapped it, and downed the entire thing.

"You *were* thirsty," he said, taking the empty bottle. "Must have been all that talking."

"Admit it." I poked his shoulder. "This was one occasion where you actually wanted me to keep talking."

"Okay, fine. I admit it. That was the best bedtime story I have ever had."

"Good." Although I wanted to snuggle up, I slipped

between the sheets, rolled over and faced away from him, remembering that he wasn't one to cuddle.

Which is why it surprised me when I felt him press against my back, nestling the curve of my spine against his body. "I want another one tomorrow night."

I smiled in the dark. "Is that allowed?"

"Why wouldn't it be?"

"Well, I don't know. Don't you have a rule against it or something?"

"Normally, yes. But nothing about this situation is normal."

"True. What about our deal?"

"What deal?"

"The deal we made saying this thing with us ends tonight since tomorrow you'll *officially* be my boss."

"Hmm. Well, breaking a deal isn't like breaking a promise, right? I mean, if both parties agree to . . . renegotiate the terms, I think it's fair."

"I think so too."

"So we agree."

"We agree."

He wrapped a hand around one breast and kissed my shoulder again. "Renegotiations start at the end of the workday tomorrow." He paused. "Assuming I can wait that long."

I laughed. "I'll try not to tempt you."

"That's the problem, princess," he said. "You tempt me without even trying."

For once, I had no desire to keep a conversation going. I drifted off to sleep with his arms around me, his words even better than a dream.

CHAPTER 9
GRIFFIN

WHEN I WOKE UP, she was gone.

For a moment, I'd forgotten she was ever there, but one deep breath and I could still smell her shampoo or soap or whatever that sweet, mouth-watering scent was clinging to the sheets.

Shamelessly I buried my face in her pillow and allowed myself one more long, slow inhale. Fucking delicious. Then I lay back for a minute, hands behind my head, contemplating everything that had happened.

I'd definitely broken some rules.

And, if memory served, I'd asked Blair for a repeat performance.

How worried did I need to be that any of those broken rules would come back to haunt me? Despite the fact that we'd spent the last thirty-six hours together, how well did I really know her? How well could you know *anyone* after only a day and a half, even if you'd spent some of those hours naked?

But damn, those hours had been good. Better than good. Fucking incredible. She'd surprised me, and very few people did. On the outside, she was all sweetness and light. Politeness and polish. But get her alone in the dark and she was eager and aggressive, loud and feisty. And if I occasionally got annoyed with how much she could talk during the day, I fucking *loved* it in bed.

I'd stayed fairly quiet, even though filthy things had been on the tip of my tongue the entire time. I still wasn't sure how dirty or rough she liked it, so I'd pretty much let her set the tone and followed her lead.

Maybe tonight I'd push the boundaries a little farther.

My dick, already growing hard from the scent of her lingering on the bedding, shot to full mast. Groaning, I flipped the sheets aside and got out of bed.

Work before play—that was a rule I could not afford to break.

"What's this?" I found her in the kitchen hunting through the upper cupboards, wearing her Snoopy T-shirt and purple panties. I could tell they were purple because every time she reached up and opened another door, they peeked out from beneath the hem of the shirt.

"I'm checking for baking supplies."

"Pretty sure I have none."

"Is there a market open early? I'd love to make something to serve in the lobby today."

"There's one on Maple that opens early, I think."

"I also made coffee—hope that's okay. And I fed the cat. I think she likes the sun coming in over by the front windows. She's curled up over there on the floor." Blair set a mixing bowl I didn't even realize I owned on the counter before turning to face me. "Good morning."

"Good morning." I smiled. She chirped like a robin even

at six a.m., but I liked the way she looked, barefoot and messy-haired. "I'm not used to seeing someone else in my kitchen."

She looked a little guilty. "I'm an early bird. And I like to get to work."

"It's fine. I do too."

She picked up her coffee and took a sip. "You're dressed already."

"Yeah. I have to knock off early on Thursdays because it's game night, so I go in early too."

"Game night for your baseball team?" She leaned back against the counter.

"Yeah."

"Can I come watch?"

"Uh, sure. Game's at seven." It was hard not to stare at her bare legs and recall the way she'd straddled me last night. Already I felt another erection coming on. It hadn't been easy to get rid of the first one five minutes ago, so I figured I'd better get out of here fast. "I should go."

"Don't you want coffee?"

"I'll make some downstairs."

"You're out down there, remember?"

"Oh yeah." I frowned. "Maybe you could order some today? My mother always kept us supplied, but I'm not sure where she got it."

"I'll take care of it. In the meantime, I'll pick some up from the market this morning."

"Thanks. Save the receipt and I'll pay you back."

She lifted her shoulders. "I'm not worried."

"Okay." I hesitated, not sure what I was supposed to do here. Did I kiss her goodbye? Toss her a wave as I headed for the stairs? Thank her for last night? Usually I made this kind of post-sex exit under the cover of darkness. This felt really different.

While I stood there debating, Blair set her mug down

and walked over to me, brushed some dust off the shoulders of my navy work shirt, and fussed with one of the buttons. "Have a good day at the office, dear." Then she kissed my cheek and leaned back. "Is that what you were waiting for?"

I scowled at her, grumbling under my breath and I turned and took the stairs down. I could still hear her laughing as I went out the door.

I spent a blissful two and a half hours by myself, save for the two minutes Blair came down with a cup of coffee for me and asked for directions to the Maple Street Market, which she'd verified opened at eight.

"So when I walk out of here, I'd go left on Main, right on Maple, and then down a few blocks?" she asked, staring at the map on her phone.

"Right."

She looked up and squared her shoulders. "Cross your fingers for me. With any luck, I'll be at the desk with fresh coffee and scones by ten a.m. If not, come looking for me. I took a wrong turn."

"Will do." I watched her walk out as I took a sip of the hot black coffee she'd brought me. She wore another short dress today, this one was light blue with white flowers on it. It had some kind of little bow thing that tied at her chest, and while she'd been standing here, part of me had been tempted to take one end between my teeth and undo it. Shaking my head, I set the coffee cup down next to the computer and got back to work.

That girl could distract me like nobody's business—which is why I stayed in the service bay where I belonged even after she poked her head in and let me know she was at the desk with fresh coffee and homemade scones.

McIntyre came in shortly afterward, his expression sulky and his mood sour.

"Emily still mad about the shower thing?" I asked.

"Nope, something totally different. You might be right about this forever thing," he groused. "Is it too late to back out?"

I laughed, saying no more as I continued working on an older Honda whose owner had let her idiot boyfriend swap the original four-cylinder engine for a V6. He'd asked my advice on it while the car was in for a turn signal problem—he was the kind of asshole who wanted to stand there and watch me work, because he knew everything about cars—and I'd told him it *could* be done, technically, but should not be done by anyone who wasn't a certified mechanic because it would require so many modifications.

But did he do it anyway? Of course he did.

And now it was on me to try to clean up the fucking mess he'd made. It was a tedious, expensive job, the kind of thing that normally would put me in a pissy mood. But today, my mood was just fine.

"Are you whistling?" McIntyre asked around noon.

"What? No."

"Yes, you were. I heard it. What happened, you get laid or something?"

"Fuck off." But I was glad he couldn't see my face.

"You did. I know you."

"What? Griffin got laid?" Handme came strolling over, wiping his hands on a blue shop towel. "Was it the new receptionist?"

"Will you guys stop? It's none of your fucking business whether I got laid or not."

"But you did, didn't you?" McIntyre's grin was all-knowing. "Where'd she sleep last night, Dempsey?"

I clenched my jaw and turned back to the Honda.

He burst out laughing. "Yeah, I heard all about how you rescued her from sleeping in her car from Emily. You left out that part of the story yesterday when you told me she was just passing through town."

Fucking Cheyenne. She and Emily were best friends, so no doubt my sister had gone blabbing the moment I'd left the house yesterday.

"So does this mean she's here to stay?"

"No," I snapped. "It means my sister cannot keep her mouth shut to save her life, and it's impossible to keep anything private around here."

"If I were you, I'd keep her around," said Handme. "Did you taste one of those things she brought in this morning? She only let me have *one* because she said they were for customers, but it was really good. And the lobby smells like a bakery."

McIntyre was already heading for the door to the waiting room when I called after him. "Hey! Where do you think you're going?"

"I just want to sniff the lobby, that's all," he said.

I knew what he wanted to sniff out—some gossip—so I followed him, grabbing a towel on my way out. Handme was quick on my heels.

In the lobby, Blair stood beaming behind the desk chatting with old man Dodson, who was eating something. I smelled fresh coffee and something sweet, and she'd propped the front door open, letting in a summer breeze as well as the sunshine.

She waved us in. "Hey, guys. Come try the scones. Mr. Dodson here came in just to taste one. He heard about them already."

"Really?" I asked, moving deeper into the room. My hands weren't clean, so I refrained from taking a scone off the tray—had that been in my apartment?—but I had to admit they looked delicious. Golden and fluffy and dripping with some sort of glaze that caused my mind to wander toward inappropriate territory.

"I sure did." Mr. Dodson finished his scone and brushed off his hands. "I just saw Charlie Frankel at the diner and he said he'd been in here earlier this morning and had the most amazing pastry. He couldn't remember what it was called, but he said he hadn't tasted anything so good in years."

Blair smiled at me and said, "Mr. Frankel came in to make an appointment for a tune-up, and I offered him a scone. Apparently he liked it."

"I'll say he did. He showed up at the diner raving about it, told everyone it was the best thing he's tasted since Betty's apple pie."

"At least *three* other people came in to say hello and taste one after overhearing Mr. Frankel at the diner," Blair said proudly.

"Did they make an appointment?" I asked.

"No," she admitted. "But they all introduced themselves and said nice things about your dad. A couple said they'd be back soon."

"Frankel will probably be back every morning," Mr. Dodson said. "I think he's in love with your wife."

I sighed heavily, my eyes closing. "She's not my wife."

"I also took their names and email addresses down for our new mailing list," Blair continued. "I said I wanted to be sure they got an invitation to our party."

"What party?" Handme wanted to know.

"Is it a wedding reception?" joked McIntyre.

"*No*. We'll talk about it later," I told them, eyeing the tray again. I wasn't even sure what a scone was. "So what's in these things anyway?"

"They're blueberry-lemon-thyme," Blair said. "I call it a BLT." She grinned triumphantly. "Try one. I made plenty."

"I can't. My hands are filthy."

"Here." She picked one up and held it to my lips. I took a bite, conscious of the way everyone in the room was watching us.

But as I tasted her creation, I had to admit I understood why widowed old Charlie Frankel might be back every morning. "Wow. It *is* good. I thought it would be sweet like a donut."

She shook her head and smiled proudly. "My favorite things are both sweet and savory. I love the way the thyme and lemon balance the sugar and fruit. Here, have another bite." She held the scone to my mouth again, and I bit into it once more. As the sugary glaze dissolved on my tongue, I wondered if that's what she would taste like. Why hadn't I tasted her last night? I made a mental note to rectify that as soon as possible.

"Want the rest of this?" Blair held up the scone. "I'll wrap it up for you. You can finish it later."

"Sure." I watched her carefully wrap it in a white napkin, a stack of which sat next to the tray. "Can you set it aside for me? I'll finish it when I break for lunch."

She nodded. "Speaking of lunch, just let me know when you're ready. I can run down to the deli again."

Dodson headed for the door. "Guess I better get home for lunch too. Edna gets cranky if I'm more than five minutes late." He turned back. "But I'm going to tell her to come in and try one of those things. Her car needs an oil change anyway. Think you can fit her in this afternoon?"

"Sure," I said. "But have her come before four o'clock."

"Will do."

Once he was gone, I turned to Blair. "Nice work."

She blushed. "Thanks. It's a start, anyway."

I moved toward the door and pulled it open. "Come on, you guys. Back to work."

"Don't I get to try one of those things?" McIntyre whined.

"Later," I said. "We've got things to do, and we're knocking off early tonight for the game."

But Blair quickly wrapped one up for McIntyre anyway and handed it to him with a finger over her lips. He took it and ducked into the bay, flashing me a triumphant expression.

I was following right behind him when I heard my mother's voice.

"Hello, darlings!" she called as she came hobbling through the open door behind a walker, as if she hadn't been getting around just fine on her own yesterday. "My lands, something smells delightful!"

I turned around and sighed. "What are you doing here, Mom?"

"I came to see what all the fuss was about! It's all over town that Blair is the new Betty."

I shook my head. "Jesus Christ."

My sister strolled in, sipping a cold coffee drink through a straw. "Hey, big brother. How's married life?"

"Will you stop with that?"

"No. I like the way it bugs you."

"What'd I ever do to you?" I asked her.

"Ha! You want the list I started at age seven, beginning with ripping the heads off all my Barbies and burying them around the yard?"

"The other day you said I was the best big brother ever."

She shrugged. "I needed something from you. That's how it works."

I looked at my mother. "This is why I'm not having kids."

Then I ushered the guys back into the garage, letting the door slam shut behind me.

CHAPTER 10
BLAIR

I COULDN'T HELP LAUGHING. "Did he really do that?" I asked Cheyenne. "Bury your Barbie heads in the backyard?"

She nodded. "That and a hundred other mean things. He was the worst. We fought constantly."

"Don't listen to them, Blair," said Darlene, lowering herself into a chair. "Having children is a wonderful, beautiful thing."

I smiled at her. "I'd like them someday."

"Really?" Darlene gave her daughter a look. "Did you hear that Cheyenne? *Blair* wants children."

Cheyenne rolled her eyes. "I've told you a million times, Mom. It's not that I don't want kids. I do, I just don't think there's a deadline. I have plenty of time to find the right person to have them with."

Darlene glanced at the ceiling. "You hear that, Hank? She thinks she has plenty of time." Then she pointed a finger at us. "I'm telling you girls, the biological clock is a real thing, and you won't even hear the slowing of the tick-tock until it's too late. And then there's nothing but sad, lonely silence where the potential for hope and joy once lived." She put a hand on her chest. "Just like in my heart."

I watched Cheyenne take a deep breath, as if trying to keep her composure, and decided to change the subject.

"Would either of you like to try a scone?" I picked up the tray and carried it around the desk.

"Of course." Darlene perked up. She chose one from the tray and took a bite, chewing slowly. Then she put a hand over her heart and explained, "Well, no wonder! These are exquisite! Cheyenne, try one."

Griffin's sister looked at me. "Is it okay?"

I smiled. "Of course."

She tasted one, and her reaction was the same as her mom's. "Oh my God, so good," she mumbled, her mouth full.

"And not dry at all," added Darlene.

"A scone should never be dry, just sort of crumbly," I said. "But also, they're meant to be eaten with a hot beverage. Can I get either of you some coffee? I'd be glad to make a fresh pot."

"I'm good," said Cheyenne, taking another bite. "I should get going anyway. I have an appointment at the salon. Mom wanted to pop in here in case you have any questions about the desk."

"Maybe how to order supplies?" I suggested, glancing at the desk behind me. "Griffin showed me how to schedule appointments yesterday, and the guys have been writing up the estimates and invoices, so . . ." I shrugged. "I've just sort of been chatting with people who call or wander in."

"So I've heard." Darlene nodded enthusiastically. "The whole town is buzzing with excitement."

"It's just some scones," I said sheepishly, setting the tray back on the counter.

"It's fresh gossip, is what it is." Cheyenne popped the last of her scone in her mouth and brushed off her hands. "You're giving all the old biddies in this town something to talk about."

"Cheyenne Dempsey, you hush up. Go to the salon now." Darlene shooed her toward the door. "I need to talk to Blair."

"I'm going. Thanks for the scone, Blair—and let me know if you want to go to the baseball game tonight. I'd be glad to pick you up so you don't have to go early with Griff."

I smiled at her. "Thanks, I'd really like that."

"Get my number from him and shoot me a text later?"

"Perfect."

"So," Darlene said, looking pleased. "You and Griffin seem to be getting along well."

An image of him naked beneath me flashed through my mind. "Um, yes. I think we are."

"Wonderful. Wonderful." She nodded happily. "I'm so tickled, because I'm afraid it's going to be a *little* bit longer until you can move into his room at my house."

"Oh really?"

"Yes, you see, I've been using it as a storage and craft room, and it's just *full* of things I can't get into the basement or attic in my condition." She looked pitifully at her legs. "So I was thinking that maybe you could stay with Griffin a couple more days. Give me a bit more time to get the room ready for guests."

"I understand." I smiled at her. "I'll talk to Griffin, but I think a couple more days should be fine."

"Really?" She looked delighted. "Well, that was even easier than I thought. You're so much more pleasant to deal with than my son. Are you sure you can't stay forever?"

I laughed politely. "I'm sure."

"Because I looked up Cloverleigh Farms, and did you know they had a tornado touch down there a few years back? We've *never* had a tornado touch down here. They're so rare in northern Michigan as it is—that's some bad luck," she said, her tone grave. "And you don't want to move to a place that has a big black cloud hanging over it, do you?"

"I'll be fine," I assured her.

Her face fell. "Too bad. I'd hoped . . ." She sighed heavily. "But I suppose it's a good sign that Griffin's even showing an interest in someone. It's been so long. I worry about him, you know? I don't want him to end up alone."

I glanced over my shoulder at the door to the garage. "I think he likes being alone."

"*I* think it's all an act," she huffed.

"He told me just last night that he likes his freedom."

Darlene looked at the ceiling. "You hear that one, Hank? *Freedom!*" she harrumphed. "I'm not trying to put him in jail, for goodness sake. I just want him to settle down and start a family. He's thirty-two already! He's going to run out of sap!"

I tried not to laugh. "I think he enjoys his independence, that's all."

"He's too independent for his own good," she scoffed, eyeing me critically. "I must say, I'm a little disappointed, Blair. I thought you'd be on my side."

I held up my palms. "I'm not taking sides. I just know that Griffin has very definite opinions on this subject, and he's never going to do anything just because someone else wants him to."

"Oh, he's a stubborn one, that's for sure." She softened her tone. "Don't you think he'd make a good husband, though? And a great dad? He's very loyal. And underneath all that bluster, he's really sweet. He likes taking care of people. He's very protective."

"I agree." I smiled, thinking of the way he'd taken care of me last night—actually since the moment he'd caught me on the sidewalk. "But I kind of like the bluster too, you know? There's something endearing about it."

"I suppose there is. His father was the same way, God rest

his soul, and we were together for almost forty years." She sighed. "So maybe there's still hope."

Griffin and I had a quick working lunch together, during which we discussed a few more ideas for the Labor Day weekend event—he liked my idea for a raffle and gave me several good suggestions for prizes—a budget for some new lobby furniture, and the name of a reporter at the local newspaper who was a good customer and might be willing to give us some press.

"Great," I said, writing down the name and making a note to get an email address or phone number. "Thanks."

"Sure." He crumpled up his sandwich wrapper and stuffed it into the empty brown deli bag. "Hey, you okay?"

"Yeah." I looked up and saw his brow knitted in concern. "Why?"

"I don't know. You seem a little distracted."

"Sorry. A lot on my mind."

He tipped up the last of his iced tea. "My mother say something to upset you?"

"No." I shrugged and looked at my half-eaten sandwich. "Just the thing about the spare room not being ready. You're sure it's okay I crash with you until it is?"

"I'm completely, one hundred percent sure, and you know it. I want my bedtime story. And I have plans for you."

I met his eyes as warmth crept into my face. "You do?"

"Yes. But they have to wait until after the game."

I smiled, perking up again. "I'm looking forward to watching."

"Good. But are you changing the subject because you

don't want to tell me what's bothering you? You've hardly touched your lunch."

Sighing, I set my pen down and sat back, crossing my arms over my chest. "Okay. I got another message from my mother this morning asking me to please call and let her know I'm not dead or kidnapped."

"You haven't called her since you left?"

"No! I'm mad at her. I wanted her support to live my life the way I want to live it, and she wouldn't give it to me."

He rubbed the back of his neck. "Yeah. Mothers can be tough."

"But I did call her back to let her know I was safe."

"Good."

"Of course, once she heard what happened with my car she gave me a big fat *I told you so* lecture. She said it was clearly a sign that I'm not cut out for independence and I should come home immediately before I get myself abducted by sex traffickers on the side of the road."

Griffin rolled his eyes. "Don't listen to her."

"I didn't. I'm not. It's just . . ." I took a deep, shaky breath. "Hard."

"That's life."

"She said I was abandoning my family."

"*That's* ridiculous." Griffin stood up and came around to my side of the table, dropping into the chair next to me. "Listen. It's good that you called her and told her you're safe, but you don't owe her any more than that. Just like I don't owe my mother grandchildren."

"I guess."

"Come on." He chucked me gently beneath the chin. "She obviously raised you to have the backbone and guts to go after your dream, right? She should be proud of you. *You* should be proud of you."

"But I haven't done anything yet."

He took my chin in his hand this time, forcing me to look at him. "You will. Don't quit."

His blue eyes were full of sincerity—he believed in me. It made all the difference. I smiled. "Okay."

After lunch, I went back into the bay and asked Andy for his girlfriend's contact information so I could get in touch regarding a new logo and website design. Then I spent the rest of the afternoon at the desk, dedicating every spare moment I had to the renovation and the grand reopening event. Several people came in inquiring about the scones, and I had to tell them we were all out but to please come back tomorrow—I was planning to make lemon lavender shortbread. At the market this morning, I'd purchased lavender from the local farm, and I couldn't wait to use it.

But in the back of my mind, I kept thinking about the encouragement Griffin had given me, and it warmed my heart every time.

Darlene was right—Griffin would have made an excellent husband and dad. Oh sure, that temper would get the better of him when his sixteen-year-old daughter broke curfew or his seventeen-year-old son tried refusing to stack the tires, but at heart he was kind and patient. He was generous. He didn't like relying on other people, but he knew how to put them first.

Why was he so determined to be alone?

The question grabbed ahold of me and refused to let go.

Around quarter to seven, Cheyenne texted that she'd pulled up in front. Grabbing my bag, I called *au revoir* to Bisou and hurried out to meet her.

"Hi," I said breathlessly after jumping into her car. "Thanks so much for picking me up."

"No problem!" She gave me a grin. "I figured you wouldn't want to spend two hours at the field watching a bunch of old men play catch and thump their chests."

I laughed. "I appreciate it. I love your hair, by the way. It's so cute."

"Thanks. I was in desperate need of a trim. And you gotta love a good blowout."

"I hear you. In my old life, I used to get my hair blown out like twice a week." I shook my head. "Now it seems like such an extravagance."

"Wow. Twice a week?"

"Yeah." I was kind of embarrassed to admit it now. "Wish I could get that money back."

"So you're saving to open a bakery?"

"Eventually. That's my ultimate goal."

"And my mom said you're moving up near Cloverleigh Farms? That is, if she can't convince you that the entire Leelenau Peninsula is plagued by murder hornets, hurricanes, and malaria—and oh, it's going to sink into Lake Michigan any day now. Don't you think you'd be better off right here in Bellamy Creek? Married to her son and giving her grand-children?"

I laughed. "I think that's what she has in mind, yes."

Cheyenne sighed as she turned into the Bellamy Creek High School parking lot. "I love her to death and she's my mom, but she can drive a person plumb crazy. Just ignore her."

"It's okay. She makes me laugh, and she's been really kind to me. Your whole family has. The whole *town* has, actually. I can't tell you how many people came in to introduce them-selves today."

Cheyenne pulled into an empty spot. "Bellamy Creek is a friendly town, but you've also sparked a lot of curiosity.

We're used to the same people in the same places, or tourists coming through. We're not used to beautiful, mysterious women in wedding dresses who charm one of the town's most stubborn bachelors and bake like dear, departed Betty Frankel."

"God, that dress." I laughed ruefully as I unbuckled my seatbelt. "I thought it would bring me good luck in my new life. So far it's been nothing but disaster!"

"Well, I don't know about that," Cheyenne said as we walked toward the field. "I mean, things could have been worse, right? You could have blown that tire on the highway outside town."

"True."

"What were you doing in Bellamy Creek, anyway, if you were trying to get to Cloverleigh Farms?"

"I saw the billboard on the highway about the best apple pie in the Midwest since 1957," I told her, shaking my head. "Of course, now I know that pie doesn't exist anymore, but that's what made me turn off the road and come here."

"So it was fate!"

I laughed as we climbed the bleachers. "You sound like your mom. It was more my sweet tooth—I love me some apple pie. I'm not even sure I believe in fate."

"Why not?" she asked as we found seats about four rows up. The stands were surprisingly crowded—with families, couples, groups of friends. Attending old man baseball games was obviously a popular thing to do on a summer night around here.

"I like to believe we have the power to make our own destiny," I said, tucking my dress under my thighs so it didn't blow up in the breeze. "Otherwise, we're just at the mercy of the stars, right? Everything decided for us? That's no fun."

"I guess. Oh, by the way, I was going to tell you that I know someone at Cloverleigh Farms."

"You do?"

"Yes. Frannie Sawyer—although she got married recently, so her last name is MacAllister now—but anyway, she's my age and I met her when I was student teaching in Traverse City a few years ago. Her family owns Cloverleigh Farms, and she owns a coffee shop downtown. Maybe she's hiring or something? I'd be glad to pass along her contact info."

I grabbed her arm. "Are you serious? I'd love that! Thank you so much!"

"Sure. Just don't tell my mother I helped you leave town. She'll disown me."

Laughing, I drew an X on my chest with a fingertip. "Cross my heart."

"Oh, there's Griff."

I looked out onto the field—and my heart danced a little. Even though he wore a ball cap, I could tell it was him from the way he filled out his Bulldogs team shirt, and it gave me a little thrill to think *I know that body*.

"There's McIntyre from the garage over in the outfield. And that's Beckett Weaver and Enzo Moretti," Cheyenne said, pointing out two other players. "They're two of Griff's closest friends."

I nodded. "I've met Enzo, but not Beckett."

"He's pretty busy this time of year. He runs a cattle ranch just north of town. Oh, and there's Cole." Cheyenne seemed to go a little breathless. "He's Griffin's best friend. And he's a police officer. He grew up next door, and recently he moved back home with his little girl, Mariah."

I looked at Cheyenne, and even though she wore sunglasses, I could practically see the hearts floating from her eyes as she watched Cole Mitchell warm up his pitching arm. "I met him the other night too. So are you and Cole a thing?"

"What? Cole and me a thing? No. *No*." She forced a laugh. "He's never looked at me that way." Then a great big sigh.

"But you wish he would?"

Her nose wrinkled. "Is it that obvious?"

I laughed. "Yes."

"Well, it's also hopeless. I've had a crush on him since 1997 when he rescued all my Beanie Babies from the tree branches where Griffin had thrown them."

"Wow. That's a long time to crush on someone."

"Tell me about it. I'm going on thirty and I still can't meet a guy to take his place in my heart."

"And he's never known how you feel?"

She shook her head, her eyes never leaving Cole. "He had a really serious girlfriend all through high school. Then he married her."

"I heard he lost her when Mariah was born."

"Yes." She closed her eyes and shook her head. "That was so awful. I don't know if he'll ever get over it."

Griffin happened to look over at the bleachers then, and automatically I lifted a hand and waved. He didn't wave back, but he nodded, and I swore I saw him smile. The butterflies in my belly fluttered like mad.

"Did Griffin ever have a serious girlfriend?"

"Not in high school. I mean, he dated around, but he was never serious about anyone back then. His one serious relationship was later. Her name was Kayla."

"How long were they together?"

"Gosh, maybe like five years? He was still in the Marines back then, so he was gone a lot, but I gotta admit, he was pretty devoted to her. I thought they'd get married."

Jealousy stabbed me in the gut. After waiting what I hoped was a suitable interval, I asked, "Whatever happened with them?"

Cheyenne shrugged. "I don't know for sure, but I think she fell in love with someone else while he was deployed the last time. They broke up shortly after he came home."

"Wow. That sucks." And it definitely could explain Griffin's attitude toward relationships. He'd gotten burned.

"Yeah. Griffin was a mess for a while. But he *never* talks

about it, and you can't ever tell him I said anything. He'd kill me."

"I won't," I promised. "Did Griffin ever know about your feelings for Cole?"

"*Hell* no. He would have told Cole for sure, and then he would have made fun of me for the rest of my life." She turned to me and grabbed my arm. "So you can't tell him that either."

"I won't. But Cole is widowed now, right? And he lives right next door to you. Maybe you two could—"

"No." Again, Cheyenne shook her head. "He looks at me and sees that pudgy six-year-old kid with scabby knees and a runny nose, crying over her Beanie Babies. I've always been more like a kid sister to him. That will never change."

"You never know," I told her. "I understand feeling like things are stuck a certain way, but you *can* surprise yourself. You *can* make a change. It's scary, but you can do it."

Just then, Cole looked up and saw us. Gave us a wave.

We waved back, and she sighed. "Maybe. But I won't hold my breath."

Griffin jogged over toward his team's bench and I watched, trying not to drool as I leaned forward to get a better look.

Next to me, Cheyenne laughed. "Speaking of crushes . . ."

"What?"

"Yours is just as obvious."

"Is it?"

"Yes. But so is his, so you're fine."

"You think he has a crush on me?"

She rolled her eyes. "Yes. I go to every one of these old man baseball games, Blair, and I've never seen Griffin look up here *once*. He's done it like twenty times already, flexing his muscles, puffing out his chest, sucking in his gut." She imitated him in an exaggerated fashion.

"He does *not* have a gut!"

"Maybe not, but I could see it when you were at the house yesterday too. He looks at you a certain way. He likes you. Look at all the time he's spending with you."

"Yeah, but he's sort of stuck with me."

She shook her head. "If Griffin doesn't want to do something, he doesn't do it. Trust me. He's got a thing for you."

My tongue felt all tied up after that, but her observation made me undeniably happy.

As the game got started, I started to feel like maybe Cheyenne was right—maybe the dress *had* brought me good luck. After all, it was purely by chance that I'd wound up stranded in *this* town and not another. If I had ended up somewhere else, I probably would have turned around and gone home already. Made a date with the crusty old tycoon. Hung up my oven mitts for good.

Maybe there *was* such a thing as fate.

CHAPTER 11
GRIFFIN

AFTER THE GAME, which we won—thanks to a double from me and a homer from Beckett that allowed both of us to score—a bunch of us went over to the Bulldog for some food and drinks. In addition to Blair, Cheyenne, and me, it was Cole, Moretti, Beckett, McIntyre, and Emily.

We pushed two tables together and sat on the patio, which prompted a boisterous retelling of Blair's now-infamous crash-and-faint episode for anyone who missed it, including the way I'd caught her.

"Oh man, I've never seen Griffin move that fast in my life," Moretti joked. "Why don't you run the bases like that? We might score a few more runs."

"Fuck off," I said, throwing a wadded-up napkin at him. "We won, didn't we?"

"That we did." Moretti held up his beer, and everyone followed suit. "To winning!"

"To defending the championship title!" added Cole.

"To the bride and groom!" shouted my sister, causing half the table to burst out laughing.

I gave Cheyenne the stink-eye as I tipped up my beer.

We put in orders for wings and pizza, ordered another

round of drinks, and rehashed the team's 5-4 win. "Cole, how's your arm?" I asked, leaning back in my chair. "You pitched a fucking great game."

"Thanks." Across the table from me, he rubbed his shoulder. "It's not too bad."

Next to him, my sister put her hand on his bicep. "Want some ice or anything? I can ask for some."

I almost snorted. I knew what my sister wanted to do to Cole, and it wasn't ice his shoulder. She'd been drooling over him since we were kids, and if I wasn't such a fucking nice guy, I'd have been making fun of her for it for years.

"No, thanks," Cole said. "I'm okay."

We sat around, drinking and eating and talking, telling old stories about our youth for Blair's sake, bragging about home runs hit or no-hitters pitched during our glory days, pumping our fists and patting ourselves on the back for still being in such good shape. There was the usual amount of trash-talking about the Mavs and how severely we were going to beat them at the championship game.

Next to me, Blair laughed often and asked a bunch of questions—about baseball, our high school days, the town, our families. Sometimes she put her hand on my leg, and I liked it. At one point, I realized I had my arm around the back of her chair, and she was sort of leaning into me. Cheyenne noticed for sure, and I could just imagine her reporting back to our mother, so I quickly removed it.

"So Blair," Emily said from her place next to my sister. "How long are you in town?"

"Well, I can't go anywhere until Griffin gets the parts for my car, but I'll probably stay through Labor Day. I'm helping Griffin with an anniversary event at the garage."

"I heard about that. Sounds like a great idea. And you're staying . . ." Emily prompted, likely knowing full well where she was staying.

"Right now I'm staying with Griffin, but that's temporary."

"My mother offered to host her," said Cheyenne with a giggle. "Just as soon as she cleans out the spare bedroom, which should only take her about—ohhh, six weeks at the most. She's determined to keep them in the same place as long as possible. I think she's hoping for a grandchild out of this somehow."

"Not going to happen," I said firmly, pulling my wallet from my back pocket. "You ready to go, Blair? I've got an early morning tomorrow."

"Me too," she said, rising to her feet. "I want to make scones again, and some lemon lavender shortbread as well."

"Mmmm, that sounds delicious," Cheyenne said. "I'll have to bring Mom again so I can sneak a taste."

"Don't you dare," I ordered my sister, tossing enough cash on the table to cover Blair and me. "You took forever to come back and get her today, and she drove me nuts."

"Actually, she was really helpful at the desk," said Blair. "Please thank her again for me, Cheyenne. And thank *you* for picking me up tonight."

"Anytime," my sister said with a smile. "I never miss old man baseball. It's the highlight of my week."

I flipped her off and took Blair by the shoulders, steering her down the sidewalk toward my truck. But I took my hands off her as quickly as possible. I didn't want anyone watching us leave to comment.

On the ride home, Blair told me about someone my sister knew who owned a coffee shop near Cloverleigh Farms.

"That's great," I said as I parked the truck. "Maybe she's hiring."

"I hope so. That would be *perfect*. Hey, what's that?" she asked, pointing to a vintage truck parked behind the garage. I kept it beneath a weatherproof cover all year round.

"It's a 1955 Chevy pickup my dad and I rehabbed. I wish I had garage space for it."

We got out of the truck and wandered over to the old pickup.

"Nineteen-fifty-five," she mused, trying to peek under the heavy cover. "That's the year the business opened, right?"

"Right. Why?"

"Because I think you should park it out front during the anniversary event and let it advertise your business. Who doesn't love a fun antique car? And you know what you should do? Paint your new logo on the side!"

"I have a new logo?"

"Don't worry. You're gonna love it." She patted my shoulder. "What color is the truck? I can't see in the dark."

"Red."

"Is it in good shape?"

"Of course it is. I did the work."

She grinned at me, her face lighting up the dark. "Didn't mean to doubt you. Can I have a ride in it?"

"Right now? It's a little late." And I had a different kind of joy ride in mind for tonight.

Her shoulders drooped. "I guess you're right. How about tomorrow after work?"

It was cute how excited she was about it. "Sure."

"Yay!" She clapped her hands, and we started walking around to the front of the building. "It's a date! Or not. Because you would never date an employee. That's not okay."

"But it's okay to sleep with one?" I teased.

"Only the one who tells the good bedtime stories."

"That's right. You promised me another story tonight." I unlocked the door and let her walk up the steps ahead of me. And goddamn, if I lived to be a hundred, I'd always remember the way I liked watching Blair walk up a flight of stairs from below, the way it made me want to grab her from behind, wrap my arms around her, bury my face in her hair.

In fact, the moment we reached the top of the steps, I did exactly that.

She laughed, taken by surprise, covering my arms with hers. "What's this?"

"I don't know. I'm just really fucking glad you're here."

"Me too."

"Sorry I'm sweaty."

"I don't mind."

I inhaled, breathing in the sweet smell of her hair but also my own post-game stench. "One of us smells terrible. Is it you?"

She laughed again. "I don't think so."

"Give me ten minutes to clean up." I let her go and headed for the bedroom.

"Okay. I'll feed Bisou and meet you in the bedroom for story time. I've got a really good one for you tonight."

When I came out of the bathroom, she was waiting for me.

Wearing the ball gown. And the elbow-length gloves. And the tiara.

I was naked.

She stood near the foot of the bed. The lights were off, but she'd managed to find a few candles, which filled the room with low, flickering light. Her eyes traveled over my skin, lingering on my cock, which was already growing hard.

"Once upon a time, there was a princess trapped in a tower," she said in a dreamlike, feminine voice. "Night after night, this unsullied maiden waited for her very own gentleman prince to come find her."

"A gentleman prince, huh?" I moved closer to her.

She nodded. "She was certain her hero would be a prince —a tall, devastatingly handsome man with blue eyes and bulging biceps who rode up on a great white stallion."

"A white stallion. Not a pickup truck?"

"He would climb the tower, fall to his knees, and ask for her hand. Then he would carry her down, and they would ride off into the sunset toward his castle on the hill."

"I see."

"Where they would, of course, live happily ever after."

"Of course." I peeled off one of her long gloves, tossed it aside. My cock was fully erect. "But you know that's not who I am."

"What?" Feigning shock, she put a hand over her heart. "Whatever do you mean, sir?"

"I didn't ride up on a stallion. I don't have any castle on a hill." I peeled off the second glove and pulled it through my fist. "And I'm no gentleman prince."

"Oh dear," she pretended to fret, backing up until she hit the brick wall. "I'm quite afraid I've been found by the villain in my story. Sir, have you come to rescue me or . . . or sully me?"

"Both. Now turn around."

She presented me with her back, and I thought of the evening two nights ago I'd unzipped her dress and run out of the room with a hard-on.

Tonight would go down differently.

Using one of her long satin gloves, I began to bind her wrists, which she obligingly held together for me.

"Struggle," I whispered in her ear.

Trapped between me and the wall, she tried to wrench her arms free, but I was taller, stronger, and much more determined.

"Good girl." I pressed up against her back, caging her in with my palms on the brick. The scent of her perfume filled my head. "Now I'm taking over this story, and the princess is going to do everything I say, or I'm leaving her in the tower forever."

"No," she said forcefully. "You're cruel and vicious. I won't let you have me."

Even though I knew she was faking it, it was still hot as fuck. "You don't have a choice, princess. Now turn around and get on your knees."

She gasped. Then a whisper. "You're good at this."

"Do it," I demanded, then backed up a little, giving her room.

She spun around and dropped to her knees, the dress forming a cloud around her. Her eyes peeked up at me. "What are you going to do to me?"

"Several things," I told her, taking my cock in my hand and beginning to stroke it. "I'm going to fuck your mouth with my cock. I'm going to fuck your pussy with my tongue. And then I'm going to fuck you in that pretty dress you're wearing."

Her eyes nearly popped out of her head.

I decided right then and there I wasn't holding back tonight. I'd say what I wanted, do what I wanted, take what I wanted—and I wouldn't worry about how dirty it was. After all, she'd invited me to play this game.

But maybe I should give her a way out, just in case.

"If you want me to stop, what will you say?" I asked her, my hand continuing to move up and down my shaft.

"Mercy," she whispered.

I noticed the way she couldn't take her eyes off what I was doing. "Do you like watching me?"

"Yes. But it makes me want things I shouldn't."

"Like what?"

She licked her lips. "I want to taste you."

I smirked. "You're making this too easy on the bad guy, princess."

"I can't help it." She met my eyes. "I want you. I can't pretend I don't."

"You want this?" I pressed the tip of my cock against her cheek, brushed it beneath her chin, traced her open lips.

"Yes," she whispered.

"Then open your mouth and take it."

She obeyed the command, and I eased between her lips, just past the crown. Her tongue swept over me in lush circles, sending jolts of electric lust throughout my body. I groaned when she began to suck and pushed in a little deeper. Her mouth was hot and wet and tight—I put my hands on her head and fought the urge to ram my cock to the back of her throat, trying to keep my rhythm slow and controlled.

But that only lasted so long. Her mouth felt too good, and her scent was so sweet, and her noises were so fucking hot— soft little moans and breathless little squeaks and heavy panting when she struggled for air. And she was so damn beautiful on her knees for me.

"Fuck yes," I said, my jaw clenched tight. I watched my cock moving in and out of her mouth and felt heat and power surge through my limbs, and suddenly I was driving in faster, harder, deeper, hitting the back of her throat with every savage thrust. The sounds she made grew louder and more desperate, but I didn't stop.

With my hands in her hair, I fucked her mouth like the cruel and vicious villain I was pretending to be—selfishly, ferociously, mercilessly—until my legs seized up and a snarl ripped from my throat and pleasure was unfurling in me and pouring into her in a hot, pulsing stream.

When I was depleted, I yanked my dick from her mouth and she sat back on her heels, gasping for air. Her face was wet and her mouth was red and raw. Her eyes were closed. For a moment, I thought maybe she was angry. I knew I should have given a warning, but I'd lost control.

"Are you okay?" I asked.

At first she said nothing. Then her lips curved into a slow, sensual smile. Her eyes opened. "Now what?"

Relieved, I helped her to her feet. "Now I'm going to make you come until you don't even remember that fucking gentleman prince on his white stallion."

"You're going to give me something better to ride?"

"Exactly." Backing her against the wall once more, I kissed her hard and deep, sliding my tongue between her lips, stroking hers in a preview of what was ahead. "Now spread your legs, princess. Let me taste you."

Dropping to my knees in front of her, I lifted the bottom of her dress, which was surprisingly heavy. To my delight, she wore nothing beneath it. The sight of her bare thighs parted for me fired up my engine all over again.

Pinning the dress up by her hips, I stroked her with my tongue—long, leisurely sweeps up the center of her pussy that made her writhe and wriggle above me. I lingered at the top, using the tip of my tongue on her hot little button, paying attention to her sighs and moans, learning what she liked best, letting her give me the cue to go faster, to slow down, to flick harder, to lick softer.

She tasted every bit as good as I'd fantasized—and I made it clear that my appetite for her would not be easily sated.

At one point, I reached between her thighs and slung a leg over my shoulder, using the new angle to penetrate deeper with my tongue before sucking her swollen clit into my mouth. Her moans grew louder, and she struggled against the restraint on her wrists. Her legs trembled.

I slipped two fingers inside her, working them the way I knew she liked while devouring her with my mouth.

"Oh God," she panted, rocking her hips over my face, "you're going to make me come. You evil, wicked, terrible, gorgeous—*oh!*"

The leg she stood on buckled and I supported her with my shoulder and hand, her back flat against the wall as her core muscles clenched my fingers and her orgasm beat against my tongue. My name fell from her lips, and the caveman urge to get inside her again overtook me.

Before she could even take a breath, I jumped up, grabbed her by the hips, and swung her toward the bed. Then I spun her around, wrapped an arm around her waist and pushed her forward so her cheek was pressed into the mattress. Her tiara toppled onto the sheets, but her arms were still tied in place, her crossed wrists resting on her back. "Don't. Move."

She stayed still while I grabbed a condom and put it on. Her breath was coming as fast and hard as mine was as I bent down to grab the bottom of her dress.

That's when I spotted the other glove. Snatching it off the floor, I decided to put it to good use.

"Put your feet together," I told her.

She brought one foot in next to the other, and I used the second glove to bind them. Then I gathered the dress and lifted it to her hips. Pausing for a moment, I took a little time to appreciate the sight before me—her heels set primly side by side, her legs straight and pale, her perfect round ass like two scoops of vanilla ice cream waiting to be devoured.

My entire body tensed with anticipation.

She was here. She was mine. She was perfect.

She was completely at my mercy.

And I wanted her more than I'd ever wanted anyone.

Holding my breath, I slid inside her, battling for control. On her lower back, her fingers flexed repeatedly. Her legs quivered. I wrapped my hands around her hips and held her steady while I set a rhythm against her—slow and deep.

Her body was hot and tight and wet around my cock, and it took every ounce of strength I had not to slam into her like a wild animal. My fingers dug into her skin. Watching my cock move in and out of her body made every nerve ending in my body feel like a live wire.

When instinct threatened to take over and tear my self-control to shreds, I reached around and slipped my fingers between her legs. Summoning every last bit of command over my body, I focused on her—holding my cock deep within her while I worked her back into a frenzy with my hand. "Come again for me," I whispered.

"No! I won't let you make me," she panted.

I smiled at her determination. "You're not in control of anything here. Not even your own orgasm."

"You've already had your way with me. Untie me this minute!"

"No." Bracing my other hand on the mattress, I pulled out of her slightly and leaned forward, speaking low in her ear. "You're going to keep your legs together like a good girl should. You're going to admit that you want this."

"I don't," she whimpered, but I could feel her pushing her hips back against me.

"Tell me you want this, princess. Tell me you love my cock inside you. Tell me you're going to come because of the way I'm fucking you."

She groaned in agony, as if torn between her body and her will. "I hate you for this," she hissed as I worked my fingers a little faster, eased my cock in deeper, "but fuck, I love your cock inside me."

"And?"

"And I want this."

I could feel her body tensing around me. "And?"

"Sorry, I forgot the other thing," she whispered, coming out of character. "You have me all—I can't—oh my God—"

"You're going to come because of the way I'm fucking you." I could barely get the words out myself.

"*Yes!*" she shouted, burying her face in the mattress as she tried to buck her hips and take what she wanted. It was the fucking hottest thing I'd ever seen. "*Yes . . . yes . . . yes.*"

I couldn't hold back any longer. With her body still in the throes of climax, I gave in to the instinct to move hard and fast, gripping her hips once more and driving into her with deep, powerful strokes that made her cry out into the bedding. The orgasm tore through my body, making every single muscle clench and shudder with release.

Afterward, I braced myself on two hands beside her, lowering my forehead to her back.

"This is where I beg for mercy," she whispered.

I felt exactly the same.

While Blair slept, I lay on my back, hands behind my head, listening to her breathe, her scent still filling my head. I tried to imagine getting up and leaving right now, which is what I'd normally do at this point in the night, and I couldn't. I tried to imagine letting her get up and leave, and I couldn't. I *wanted* to be right next to her, even if all we did was sleep.

It was really fucking weird.

For me, sex was always about the release, about letting off steam. It was about working off my frustration with life in a physical way, and it had a definite finish line. It *involved* someone else's pleasure, but it was never *about* the other person. The sex and the person were separate—even *I* felt removed from it.

But this thing with Blair was different.

It was impossible to think about what we'd done and separate it from *her*, or how I felt about her. It was about physical release, yes, but it was also about wanting to *be* with her. Share something with her. Give something to her.

And rather than craving distance when it was over, each encounter left me craving *more*.

I hadn't been with the same woman two nights in a row since Kayla and I had split.

Another rule broken.

And I wasn't about to suggest she start spending the night anywhere else. But I also knew that this was all I could offer. A temporary break from my rules while she was here. A little relief from the loneliness. A good time.

But it wasn't like I was using Blair—I genuinely liked her. She was adorable and funny and smart. She was creative and organized, and completely determined to amp up my business. She really cared. She could talk to anybody, and she lured customers into the shop like a siren lured a sailor. She was irresistible—not just to me, to everyone.

And maybe for her, I was part of the rebellious streak she was on. Part of the break from her old life—from guys who wore fancy watches and designer suits, guys who had money in the bank, but didn't have a clue how to please a woman. Maybe this thing with me was what she needed to feel different about herself.

Or maybe for her it was like fucking the help . . . who knew?

Besides, it didn't really matter. In a few weeks, she'd be gone, and things would go back to normal. And as long as she and I were on the same page about what this was, what was the harm in enjoying one another in the meantime?

She rolled over to face me, tossing an arm and a leg over my body. If it had been any other woman, any other night, I'd have felt uncomfortable and desperate to leave. But because it was Blair, I gathered her in closer, glad when she lifted her head onto my chest.

It felt right—for now.

CHAPTER 12
BLAIR

I WOKE up with the sun the next morning. Griffin was still asleep, so I moved as quietly as possible. I managed to slide out of bed, tiptoe to the bathroom and dress without waking him, but before I left the bedroom I couldn't resist studying him for a moment as he slept.

He lay on his back, one arm thrown up above his head, the other on his stomach. The blanket was at his waist, revealing his tattooed chest, which never failed to cause a stir inside me. I let my eyes travel the length of him, feeling a secret thrill as I recalled everything from last night.

Leaning over him, I pressed a light kiss to his jaw. As I straightened up to go, he grabbed my arm. "Trying to escape, princess?"

I giggled. "Never. I just want to get the scones and shortbread going."

"Oh, right. It's a work day."

"Yes. But don't forget our plans tonight."

His brow furrowed. "What plans?"

"You're going to take me for a ride in the old truck, remember?"

"Oh, yeah. I remember now."

I smiled at him. "Good. Okay, you have to let go of my arm now, because I have to go bake."

"Don't you want to come back to bed?"

"Yes, but I can't. I have to get to work, and you do too."

He frowned. "I liked it better when you were trapped in the tower."

Laughing, I patted his shoulder. "You can rescue me again later. This morning, we work."

It was the perfect day.

I spent the early morning in a sunlit kitchen, listening to music, chattering away to Bisou in French, and baking one tray of scones and two pans of lemon lavender shortbread.

Once again, the baked goods were a hit, and a steady stream of people wandered in through the open door to sample a treat, introduce themselves to me, make appointments for maintenance or repairs, and confide that even though they'd tried Swifty Auto last time, it was really just about curiosity and they much preferred to support a local family business. Many of them told stories about Griffin's dad and grandfather, and it gave me an idea.

"Hey, do you have any old photos of your dad and grandfather working on cars? Or of you working alongside them?" I asked Griffin over lunch.

"I'm sure my mom has some. Why?"

"I think we should blow them up, frame them, and put them on the walls in the lobby. They'll be a great visual reminder of your family's history and the garage's place in the community. And they're fun to look at," I said. "People like a glimpse into your personal life."

He raised an eyebrow. "Tell me about it. How many people congratulated you on our marriage today?"

"Just a couple," I said with a laugh. "But don't worry, I set them straight."

"Yeah?"

"Yes. I told them we're living in sin for now, but you've promised to make an honest woman of me sooner or later."

He threw a potato chip at me. "Smartass."

While we were eating, Cheyenne messaged me contact information for Frannie MacAllister, and I called her right away and left a message, explaining who I was and inquiring if there was any possibility she was hiring at her shop. I left my number with her, and hung up, my heart pounding.

"I hope she calls me back today," I said.

Griffin smiled. "I hope so too. Let me know if you need a letter of recommendation."

"From you? What would it say?"

"Hmm. Organized team player with excellent interpersonal skills. Also an unbelievable fuck."

I gasped and threw a chip back at him. "Jerk."

But secretly I was glad for the compliment.

I spent the afternoon scouring Pinterest for lobby makeover ideas, and by four o'clock, I'd ordered new chairs, a rug, two small side tables, and one coffee table. I also called Andy's girlfriend Lola and chatted with her about a redo of the garage's website with a new logo, and also asked her if she might be willing to set up some social media accounts.

"It will be best if they're all branded the same, and they'll need good graphics," I said. "Although finding someone to keep them updated around here might be a chore."

"You know, Andy would be great for that," Lola said. "He's really good with a camera. Photography is a hobby of his. I bet he could come up with content."

"Really?"

"Sure. If you want, I'll talk to him about it."

"That's perfect. Thanks!"

Lola said she'd get back to me within a week, and we hung up. Sitting there studying the walls for a moment, I decided the grungy pale green color had to go, so after securing Griffin's permission to wander away from the desk, I walked over to the hardware store I'd seen on my way to the market. Turned out the store was owned by the Frankel family, and Charlie Frankel was delighted to help me.

"I was at work this morning, otherwise I'd have come in for breakfast again," he said, smoothing the wayward tufts of white hair on his head. "I retired years ago, but now that I'm widowed, I've got a little too much time on my hands. My sons run the place, but I like to come in a few times a week and make sure they're doing things right."

I smiled. "Well, I'm very glad to see you, and I bet you'll be able to help me. I'm going to repaint the lobby at the garage, but I have no idea what I'll need."

He nodded enthusiastically. "Sure, sure. I can get you all set up. What color?"

"I was thinking about a nice clean white."

"No problem," he said. "Are you enjoying life in Bellamy Creek?"

"I really am."

"My family has been here for six generations."

"That's incredible," I said.

"My great-great-grandfather built a log cabin here back in the 1830s and started a sawmill. And my grandfather built one of the first homes on Center Avenue in what's now the Historic District. Have you been over there yet?"

"No, I haven't had a chance, but now you've piqued my interest."

"Number 910. That's our house." The happy expression on his face turned a little wistful. "Betty and I had a lot of good years there. Raised four boys."

"I'll definitely check it out. I love old homes."

"Terrific! Would you like to come for iced tea sometime? After I retired, Betty and I used to have tea and apple pie on the porch every afternoon. I sometimes have it alone now, but it's not the same without someone to talk with. My kids and grandkids visit, but they're all so busy . . ." His voice trailed off, his smile fading.

My heart went out to him. "I'd love to come visit. And I'll bring you an apple pie."

He took my arm. "You're a good girl. Now let's get you some paint."

With Mr. Frankel's help, I chose a shade called White Dove, then I called Griffin to ask what other supplies we'd need to get the job done this weekend. I didn't want to purchase anything he already had.

"We're repainting the lobby this weekend?" he asked, clearly surprised.

"Yes. Do you have painter's tape?" I inquired, looking at the shelves in front of me.

"Yes. And brushes, trays and rollers somewhere. But grab a couple liners and also some caulk."

"Caulk? I don't know what that is, but okay."

Griffin laughed. "Frankel will know. And tell him to put it on my tab."

"Okay."

"How are you going to get everything back here?" Griffin asked. "Should I come get you?"

"He was going to have it all delivered."

"I'll come get you. Sit tight, I'll be there in ten minutes."

"Perfect." I smiled. "Oh, by the way, Mr. Frankel says he'll give us a ten percent discount as a wedding gift."

Griffin exhaled audibly. "I give up. Tell him thanks."

We unloaded the paint and supplies in the lobby and locked the front door. Griffin said he still had some things to do, so while he finished up work, I walked over to the Maple Street Market and bought groceries for the picnic I was planning for tonight.

I had just unpacked the bags when my cell phone rang—it was Frannie MacAllister.

Saying a quick prayer, I answered it. "Hello?"

"Hi, is this Blair?"

"Yes. Is this Frannie?"

"Yes. I'm sorry it took me a while to get back to you. Between my shop and my three stepdaughters, I rarely get a spare minute."

"That's okay. I hope it's all right that Cheyenne gave me your number."

"Of course! She called me this morning and told me about you, and I'm convinced this has to be fate, because I literally just said to my husband the other night, 'I could really use some full-time help at the shop this fall.'" She laughed and lowered her voice. "I'm pregnant with twins, due in March."

I gasped. "Oh my goodness! Congratulations!"

"Thank you. I'm still trying to wrap my brain around it, you know?"

"I bet."

"Anyway, I have someone working for me who's really talented but she's going back to school in a week."

"I'm sort of committed here in Bellamy Creek until Labor Day," I hedged.

"No problem," Frannie said. "I can cover things until you're ready to start. Would there be a day you could come up to Traverse City and interview? We could talk about the position and make sure it's the right fit?"

"I'd love that! I'll need to look at places to live too. I'm sort of . . . starting over from scratch, so to speak."

"I totally understand, and I've lived here all my life, so I can help."

My throat lumped up. "Thank you *so* much, Frannie. I'm about to cry. You have no idea what this means to me."

"You're very welcome. Cheyenne told me your story, and I completely sympathized. I had to get out from under my parents' roof and do my own thing too. It's not easy."

"Well, from what I've heard, you're crazy successful, so I know I could learn a lot working for you. I have to wait for my car to be fixed before I can get to Traverse City, so would next weekend be okay?"

"Sure! How about next Saturday around four o'clock? Week from tomorrow?"

"That sounds good."

"Great. See you then."

I thanked her again and ended the call, put the interview date in my calendar, and allowed myself a little victory dance. Then I turned on some Kacey Musgraves and hummed along as I made dough for a galette, and while it chilled I put together a filling with spinach, caramelized onions, white beans, and Gruyère.

While it was in the oven, Griffin came up the stairs, stopped at the top, and sniffed. "What is that smell? It's fucking amazing."

"It's dinner." I turned down the music and continued rinsing a bunch of grapes.

"You made dinner?"

"Yes."

"I thought you wanted to go for a drive."

"I do." I transferred the grapes to a plastic bag. "That's why I'm packing us a picnic in the basket Mrs. Applebee sent our wedding gift in. Got an old blanket we could use?"

"I think so. Try the hall closet."

"Okay." I dried my hands and turned to face him, bursting with my news. "Guess what?"

"What?"

"I talked to Frannie MacAllister, the woman with the coffee shop near Cloverleigh Farms, and she *is* hiring! I'm going up there to meet her for an interview next weekend!"

"That's awesome."

"Isn't it?" I twirled around. "I'm so happy, Griffin. Finally, something went right! I feel like it's a sign!"

"Good."

Dizzy, I leaned back against the counter and looked at him, unable to stop smiling. "This is the best day ever."

He grinned at me. "And it's not over yet."

An hour later, I squealed with delight as Griffin pulled up in the front of his building in a bright red vintage pickup truck, windows down. "Oh my God! It's adorable!"

After throwing the truck in park, he got out and came around to the sidewalk. "Can a truck be adorable?"

"This one can." But it was Griffin who made me sigh as he opened the passenger door for me. His damp hair was combed but pieces kept flopping over his forehead, his faded blue jeans hugged his butt, the blue of his fitted T-shirt matched his watercolor eyes—my heart nearly jumped out of my chest as he reached for the basket in my arms.

"Here, let me take that." He placed it on the front seat and offered me a hand getting in.

I tried to climb up without flashing my underwear at him, not easy in the short white sundress I wore—although, I admit, I'd chosen the dress on purpose since Griffin seemed to like looking at my legs. In fact, we were only at the first stop sign when I caught him staring.

"You look nice," he said.

"Thanks. I know how you like me in a white dress."

His eyes rose from my legs to my face. "Funny."

I slipped my sunglasses on. "And all yours for the whole night. Lucky you."

He shook his head, grinning as he focused out the windshield again. "Lucky me."

For about twenty minutes, we just drove down country roads with the windows down, listening to the truck's scratchy AM radio as the sun sank lower in the sky. We didn't talk much, but that was okay with me—I was content to watch the scenery roll by, hum along to old-timey tunes, and inhale the fresh air. I felt happier than I had in a long time.

Eventually, he turned off the highway onto a dirt road. Another mile or so down, he turned into a driveway blocked by a rusty gate with a PRIVATE PROPERTY sign on it. Griffin put the truck in park and said, "Be right back."

He opened the gate, pulled the truck just beyond it, then closed it behind us.

"Whose property is this?" I asked once we were moving. The road curved through trees, up and down gentle hills.

"It's Beckett's. He bought the land a couple years back—it borders one end of his farm—and put in a four-acre pond."

"For swimming?"

"Well, you *can* swim in it, but mostly for water storage and irrigation. He stocked it with fish last summer and told us we could come hook our dinner whenever we want to."

I laughed. "Well, no pressure. I packed plenty of food."

Through a clearing up ahead, I saw the pond—a huge, oblong body of water with a wooden dock at the near end. The breeze rippled the surface of the water, and a few geese floated along in the center of it.

Griffin parked the truck and got out, wandering a few steps toward the pond. I hopped out too, following him, looking around from the water to the trees to the sky. The light was golden and soft, the air warm and tranquil. The only sounds were the wind rustling the leaves, the crickets warming up their evening chorus, and the occasional call of a seagull overhead. "Wow. This is really beautiful."

"My dad almost bought this property."

"Really?" I looked over at his strong profile.

"Yeah. He wanted to build a house on it. Retire here."

"Did he change his mind?"

Griffin shook his head. "He was gone before he got the chance."

"I'm sorry." I hesitated, but then moved closer, slipping my arm through his and tipping my head against his shoulder. "I like hearing about your dad. Tell me something else about him."

"Like what?"

"I don't know. What's a lesson he taught you that you still think about?"

He was silent a minute. "Never let a vehicle leave your shop unless you would be comfortable putting your family in it on the highway."

"I love that."

"Treat every little old lady like she's your grandmother."

"Especially the ones who forget their bowling balls in their trunks."

He smiled slightly. "And everybody starts out as the 'stack the tires' guy, even the garage owner's son."

"He wanted to teach you a good work ethic." I squeezed his arm. "And he did. He'd be so proud of you."

"He'd have loved this." Griffin's eyes scanned the pond, the land, the trees beyond. "He'd have built a house over there, a barn over that way, kept a little rowboat tied up at the dock."

I could see it, everything he described. I knew he could too.

"He always said he wanted to spend his golden years fishing, tinkering with old cars, and playing with his grandkids."

"I bet he would have been an awesome grandpa."

"Yeah. He was a great dad."

I took a breath and decided to be brave. "You'd be a great dad too."

He didn't say anything right away. "Well, life never goes as planned, does it?" Then before I could dig in deeper, he went on, "Should we eat?"

"Sure."

But we stood there a moment longer looking at the water, and he surprised me by taking my hand before turning around and walking back to the truck.

CHAPTER 13
BLAIR

"YOU PACKED REAL PLATES FOR A PICNIC?" Griffin stared as I unloaded our basket onto the red plaid blanket we'd spread out in the bed of the old pickup.

"Yes. Picnic like the French. That's my motto."

"Of course it is."

Kneeling, I set out plates and napkins, the galette and grapes. "Besides, you didn't have paper plates. You did, however, have plenty of plastic forks."

"One of the many benefits of frequent takeout. So we're using real plates and plastic forks?"

"I said you *had* them. I didn't say I *packed* them." I pulled two real forks from the basket, the knife I'd included for slicing the galette, the bottle of Moët & Chandon from Mrs. Applebee, and two wine glasses, which I'd wrapped in kitchen towels. "Can you open the champagne?"

He took the bottle from me and carefully popped the cork. "All this is way too fancy to be called a picnic. A picnic is, like, fried chicken and corn on the cob. Potato salad. Beer cans."

"Not if I'm planning it." After taking my sandals off and tossing them to the ground, I set out the glasses and poured us each some champagne. Setting the bottle aside, I lifted my glass and sat back on my heels. "What should we toast? Our wedded bliss?"

"Why not?" He grinned as he touched his glass to mine. "To the wife I never knew I wanted."

I giggled. "And probably still don't."

"You're not so bad." His eyes held mine as we drank, and a funny feeling tugged at my chest—almost like sadness or regret. I realized I was already dreading our goodbye.

But I didn't want to think about that yet.

"Are you hungry?" I asked, setting my glass down. "I'm excited for you to try this. It's one of my favorite things to make."

While I was slicing the galette, he pulled his cell phone from his back pocket and frowned at it. "It's my mother. Do I have to answer it?"

Laughing, I set a plate in front of him. "Probably."

Grumbling, he touched the screen and put the phone to his ear. "Hi, Mom." He looked at me. "Yes. She's right here."

I smiled and added a slice of galette to my plate along with a small bunch of grapes.

"Okay, I'll tell her." He paused and held the phone away from his ear while she rambled on. "It's fine, Mom. Not a problem. I have to go."

A full minute later, he was still trying to hang up, his eyes closed in frustration. "I know. I *heard* you. I *won't*. Goodbye, Mom. Goodbye. I'm hanging up now. Good*bye*." He jabbed a finger at the screen and tossed his phone aside.

Laughing, I popped a grape in my mouth. "What's going on with her?"

"She wants you to know that she's *very* sorry, but she won't have my old room ready for you this week, because she's coming down with something, and she really doesn't have the energy to deal with the mess right now. Nor does she want to expose you to whatever germs she has. She's not sure what it is, but she's positive it's *very* contagious."

I smiled. "Oh, dear."

"She also wanted me to know that she's called around to absolutely everyone in town who might have space to rent, but didn't have any luck."

"Well, it was nice of her to try."

Griffin grabbed his glass and chugged champagne. "I'm positive she didn't make a single phone call."

"Listen, it's fine. Tomorrow I'll call the motel on Highway 31 again. Maybe they've had something open up."

He shook his head. "I'm not putting you at the motel, Blair."

"Why not?"

"For one thing, you still don't have a car. How would you get to work?"

"I don't know," I said quietly, fussing with the hem on my dress, bummed that the reason he didn't want me to move to the motel was because I wouldn't be able to get to work.

"I'd have to come get you every morning and take you back every night. It's not convenient. Plus I don't like the idea of you staying alone at that motel."

"You don't?"

"No. I'm not convinced it would be safe. Neither is my mother—in fact, she is suddenly sure Highway 31 is teeming with serial killers who will murder you in your sleep. She made me promise to keep you at my place."

"Oh."

Safety and convenience and a promise to his mother.

Not sexy.

"Listen, I'm sure I'll be fine at the motel," I said, smoothing my dress over my thighs. "It's only for a few weeks. And maybe I can rent a car or something."

"Blair."

I refused to meet his eyes, embarrassed that I was hurt

over this. "Anyway, I'll figure it out. Sorry this is falling on you."

"Hey." He reached out and grabbed my wrist. "I *want* you to stay with me."

"You do?"

"Yes. I should have said that first. Sorry." He lifted his shoulders. "I'm not good at saying that stuff out loud."

"That's okay."

He smiled, a crooked little half-smirk. "Come here."

I let him tug me toward him, carefully crawling over our picnic so our lips could meet. His kiss was soft and sweet, desire mixed with apology. Pulling back a little, I smiled. "Thank you."

"For what?"

"For being so good to me. I promise you will not be stuck with me forever."

"Let's not worry about it now, okay?"

"Okay." Kissing him once more, I giggled when I heard his stomach roar like an angry lion. "Hungry?"

"Starving."

"Good." I sat back again and picked up my fork. "Dig in."

"What is this called?" he asked, looking at the galette on his plate. "It looks like dessert."

"It's galette. It's a pastry, but it's savory. It's got onions and spinach and Gruyère cheese. Taste it."

He stuck a forkful in his mouth and moaned. "Fuck, that's good."

"Right? It's like dinner and dessert had a baby." I dug into mine too. "I make all kinds of these, some sweet and some savory. They're perfect for lunch. And picnics. They're good hot or cold."

Griffin's was half gone already. "I could eat a whole one by myself."

I laughed. "Have as much as you'd like. I made it for you."

As the sun went down, the gulls quieted and the crickets got noisier. We ate and drank, made plans for painting the lobby tomorrow after the garage closed, and discussed the possibility of Andy taking on the task of social media.

"Would I have to pay him more?" Griffin asked, forking up his last bite.

"Well, yes. But it's going to be worth it. Think of it as an advertising cost."

He grumbled under his breath but eventually conceded. "Fine. You can ask him."

When we were full, I packed up the leftovers while Griffin poured the last of the champagne into our glasses. We moved the basket out of the way and sat hip to hip, our legs stretched out in front of us, my bare feet and Griffin's boots crossed at the ankle. The light was dusky and purple now, the surface of the water totally calm.

I sipped my champagne. "Can I ask you something?"

"I feel like I'm going to regret this, but okay."

"Earlier, when I mentioned that you'd make a great dad, you said something about life not going as planned."

Silence.

"What did you mean by that?"

He shrugged. "Exactly what it sounds like."

"So did you think about having a family at one point?"

He finished his champagne before answering, then reached over to drop the empty glass into the basket. "There was a time in my life I thought I would."

"What happened?"

"I don't really want to talk about it."

"Was it with Kayla? Cheyenne mentioned her last night, and—"

"Jesus Christ, my sister has a big mouth, just like everyone else in this town. I said I don't want to talk about it." His tone was edged with anger, which should have been my cue to shut up, but of course, I didn't.

"Okay, I'm sorry. I was just wondering because—"

"Well, stop wondering, okay? You don't know me at all. You met me three fucking days ago. You have no idea whether I'd make a good father or not, and it doesn't fucking matter, because I don't want kids."

"Got it. Sorry."

"This isn't real, you know," he snapped. "This thing with you and me isn't real. It's just a joke, and it's temporary."

I nodded, feeling like he'd suddenly pulled a knife and gutted me. Hugging my knees, I stared straight ahead. My throat grew unbearably tight, but I refused to cry.

Thirty horrible seconds passed, and then he flopped onto his back. Covered his face with his hands. "Fuck, Blair."

I stayed quiet.

"I'm an asshole."

"Don't worry about it."

"I didn't mean it."

"Yes, you did. But I get it—a girl like me probably does seem like a joke to you."

He sat up and exhaled. "I didn't say *you* were a joke. I said *us*—I meant the marriage thing."

"It's fine."

"No, it isn't." Again, he rubbed his face with both hands. "Look, I don't like talking about the past. With anyone, not just you. And the whole thing about having a family is something I get all the time from my mother, so it sets me off fast. I'm sorry."

"Apology accepted." But I'd been chastised, and it stung.

He leaned back on one elbow, bending one knee. For a little while, we stayed just like that without speaking. The crickets seemed to grow louder as the seconds ticked by, joined by the buzz of mosquitoes. The moon appeared above the trees to our right.

As the silence lengthened, I felt more awkward and stupid. Why couldn't I just keep my mouth shut? He was right—we'd only known each other for three days. I wasn't his wife. I wasn't even his girlfriend. I was living with him because I had nowhere else to go and no way to leave yet. He didn't owe me anything.

I swallowed hard against the lump in my throat as I slapped at a mosquito on my ankle. "Ready to go? The bugs are getting me."

"In a minute." He reached for my arm. "Come here, please."

This time, I didn't let him pull me toward him. But I looked back over my shoulder. "What?"

"Did I ruin your best day ever?"

"No."

"I don't believe you."

I shrugged.

"Are you mad at me?"

I took a breath, fought the lump in my throat again. "I'm more mad at myself."

"Why?"

"Because I say things I shouldn't. And I get carried away."

"I like when you get carried away."

"You know what I mean. I talk a lot, and I let people I like in quickly. I forget other people are different."

"I'm definitely different."

"I know." I took a breath. "And I get that we just met. I know what we're doing isn't *real*. It's just been a while since I've had this much fun with someone. I like you. I want to know you."

"Same."

That made me feel better. "Really?"

"Yes. And you're right. I'm not . . . used to letting people in, or allowing someone to get close to me. I generally push people away who try."

"Why? Sorry." I shook my head. "I did it again. It's like my mouth just shoots out words before my brain gets a chance to stop it. But I swear, I'm only asking because I genuinely care about the answer . . . and about you."

He was silent a moment. "My one serious relationship—with Kayla—ended badly."

"And it hurt?"

"Yeah. It did."

I opened my mouth to ask another question, then thought better of it and closed my lips.

"It's okay. You can ask."

"Are you sure?"

"Well, I'm getting a little impatient to get my hands on you, but I'll give you three more questions to make up for being a jerk."

I smiled. "Thanks. Three's good."

"Okay, shoot."

"Were you in love with her?"

He lay back and put his hands behind his head. "Felt like I was."

"Why did you guys break up?"

"That's a long story."

Falling to my side next to him, I propped my head on one hand. "I *love* long stories."

"Of course you do." He inhaled and exhaled, slow and deep. "Before I enlisted for the second time, we talked about getting married and starting a family when I got out. I asked her to wait for me, and she promised she would. But she didn't."

I bit my lip. "That must have hurt."

Griffin kept his eyes on the darkening sky as he spoke. "When I came home, I bought a ring. My dad loaned me some money, and I put a down payment on a house. I started working long days at the garage to be able to afford it all. Then she finally got the nerve to tell me she'd fallen for someone else while I was away."

"Oh." My heart ached for him.

"There was more to it than that, but you get the idea."

I swallowed hard. His life lessons and rules made more sense now. No wonder he never wanted to rely on anyone but himself. He didn't trust anybody to keep promises. He never wanted anyone to have the power to hurt him again. He'd set his heart on things—a marriage, a home, a family—and wound up alone.

He looked over at me. "Was that three?"

"No, that was only two."

"Are you sure? I feel like I've been talking for an hour."

"I'm sure. But you know what? I'll let you off the hook for the third one."

"Good." He reached for me, and this time I gave in and let him pull me on top of him. His fingers slid into my hair, and he lifted his head so his lips could meet mine. The kiss was sweet and tender and easy, and I felt myself melting for him. It made me so happy that he'd felt safe enough with me to open up a little.

I picked up my head. "Wait, I changed my mind. I want to ask one more question."

He groaned. "What?"

I scrambled to sit up, straddling him with a knee on either side of his hips, my hands on his chest. "What did you think of me the first night we met?"

"Hmm." He ran his hands up my thighs. "I thought you were beautiful. I thought you were a little bit crazy. And I thought you were probably one of those really book-smart people who have zero street smarts whatsoever."

I nodded. "That's fair."

"And I felt protective of you."

My eyebrows rose. "You did?"

"Yeah. I remember watching you get out of your car and walk toward me in that big white dress looking so lost, so confused, and my gut instinct was to—sorry—rescue you."

"No, I think it's sweet."

"Then I remember when you walked out of the garage later that night, carrying your suitcase, I kind of wanted to go running after you and bring you home with me, just to make sure you'd be safe." He paused. "But of course, when I *did* bring you home with me, I started to think about things that were *not* safe."

A laugh bubbled up in me. "I did too."

"Oh yeah?" He put his hands behind his head again. "So now I get to ask you. What did you think of *me* that night?"

"Hmm." I ran my palms over his chest. "I thought you looked like a movie star. I thought you were strong and quiet and manly. I sensed you were a good person."

"You must have, since you spent the night about three feet away from me."

I shrugged. "I felt safe with you."

"You are safe with me," he said quietly.

I lowered my head and slanted my mouth over his, remembering the way I'd looked at him the night we met and wondered what it would be like to be kissed by him, touched by him, desired by him. The kiss grew deeper and more intense, our hands wandering, our bodies straining against clothes. He pushed the skinny straps of my sundress off my shoulders, and I slipped my arms from the dress completely. He groaned as he brought his mouth and hands to my breasts, his cock bulging in his jeans. Weaving my fingers into his hair, I rocked my hips above it until I was panting and bursting with need.

"Should we go?" I whispered.

"No. We won't make it home." He flipped me onto my back and lay beside me, reaching beneath my dress and stroking me over the damp cotton of my panties. "I want you right here. Right now."

I undid his jeans and slid one hand inside, grasping his hot, hard length with one hand. "You can have me."

He wasn't as rough with me as he'd been last night, and

we didn't get naked or play games or whisper dirty things to each other. But it was every bit as intense—more, even—without having a role to play.

It was just me, wanting to get closer to him.

And him, choosing to let me.

CHAPTER 14
GRIFFIN

EARLY SUNDAY MORNING, I met Cole in front of his mother's house for a five-mile run. We jogged the first mile without speaking, letting our bodies warm up, our muscles work out the kinks.

Although I had to admit, my body had been feeling pretty fucking great the last few days. I might have been getting less sleep, but I was having the best sex of my entire life. From the first time on my couch, to the storytelling in my bedroom, to the bed of the pickup truck, to last night after dinner . . . I'd taken her to DiFiore's, an Italian restaurant owned by an uncle of Moretti's. It was a little pricey, which was why I didn't go there too often, but Blair had mentioned how much she liked Italian food, so I splurged for a Saturday night out. She must have appreciated it, because we'd barely made it inside my apartment before she jumped up on me. Her back had to be killing her today, the way I'd slammed it against the thick wooden door.

I wasn't sure if it was Blair herself—although she was *fantastic* in bed and out of it—or if I'd just forgotten how good it could be to get to know someone sexually, let them learn all your favorite things, discover all of theirs, explore their fantasies, share your own, abandon the frantic showmanship of first times and the need to prove yourself, and start peeling back the layers . . . let them know the real you, even if it was dirty and rough and messy and not always nice. It had been a long time since I'd felt so at ease with someone, in bed and out.

I couldn't decide if that was a good thing or not.

Pushing her from my mind, I picked up the pace a little.

"How's Mariah?" I asked. "I saw her last week."

"She told me." He laughed. "She said Cheyenne told her and her friends you and Blair had gotten married, but it turned out to be a lie."

"Fucking Cheyenne," I muttered.

"She said at first she was disappointed, but then she was glad because she wants to be a flower girl at your wedding."

"Well, sorry to disappoint her, but there's not going to be any wedding. I'll take her for an ice cream cone, though."

"A distant second, but she'd like that." We ran in silence a few minutes. "I'm a little worried about her."

I glanced at him. "Why?"

"She's been spending more time alone in her room, and my mom went in there to clean it recently and found this letter to me. It was full of questions."

"Questions about what?"

"About her mother. Things that she's apparently afraid to ask me. She doesn't want me to get mad or be sad."

Pain squeezed my heart. "I'm sorry, Cole. That's rough."

"I don't know whether to confront her about it or not. My mother says yes, but I'm worried about violating her privacy."

"Yeah. That's a tough call."

"I think I'm going to contact a therapist. I feel like this is more than I can deal with on my own."

"That's a good idea."

"I'm also worried about the physical changes coming with adolescence, and having to field *those* kinds of questions."

"Fuck," I said, panicked at the thought of facing that situation.

"And it all just makes me miss Trisha more, you know? We should be facing the teenage years together."

I didn't know what to say to that, so I just gave him a quick clap on the back.

"Anyway, enough of my shit. How are things going at the shop?" he asked.

"Fine. The bank turned me down again, but we were busy enough to pay the bills. This month, anyway. Next month could be different."

"Sorry."

"Yeah, well . . . what can you do? Blair's got some crazy scheme going to get back some of the business we lost to Swifty."

"Yeah?" Cole glanced over at me. "So she's working for you now?"

"I guess you'd call it that."

"I thought she was moving up north somewhere."

"She is. She even has a job lined up already. But I have to get her car fixed first, and since she doesn't have any extra money, she's sort of working off the cost in trade."

"Uh huh. And what all is she trading?"

I glanced at Cole and saw his grin. "Fuck off," I said. But I laughed too. "We're just having fun."

"Fun is good. I vaguely remember that kind of fun."

"So get back out there."

"Nah," he said, picking up his pace.

I pumped my legs harder to keep up. Maybe the late nights *were* getting to me a little. I was usually just as fast as Cole, if not faster.

"So when's she leaving?" he asked.

"In a few weeks. After Labor Day."

"And what happens after that?"

"Nothing."

"Why not? I thought you liked her."

"I do like her. But it's just temporary. Casual."

"You sure about that?"

"What do you mean?"

"I mean, I was there the other night after the game. I saw you guys together. It didn't look like a quick or casual thing. It looked kind of real."

"Well, it's not. She's moving three hours away."

"Couldn't you date her long-distance or something?"

"Why would I do that?"

Cole laughed. "I don't know. Because it's not easy to find someone you have such great chemistry with?"

"Great chemistry isn't the point."

"What's the point?"

I tried to think of the point.

Was it that I was better off alone? Was it that I was too busy trying to keep my business afloat to deal with a relationship, especially long distance? Was it that I didn't want to end up like McIntyre, letting someone else call all the shots in my life? Or was it that no matter how well you thought you knew someone, you could never *really* know them, and finding out you were wrong about them hurt like a motherfucker?

Really, all the reasons converged in one single truth—I didn't want my life to change. It was fine the way it was before Blair got here, and it would be fine again when she left.

"Look, I'm not denying she's hot," I told Cole. "Or that we like each other. She makes me laugh. And yeah, the sex is great. But that's it."

"That's it?" Cole gave me a strange look. "What the hell else is there, Dempsey?"

Then he took off again, leaving me in the dust.

Entering the lobby a couple hours later, I groaned at the sight in front of me. "Blair, that is not how you do it. You're dripping paint everywhere."

"What's wrong?" Blair turned around, roller in hand. "I did it like you said, didn't I? From the bottom up?"

"I said from the top down. And you can't just roll it on aimlessly like that." She'd made what looked like giant white W's all over one wall.

She glanced at her work. "I just wanted to get the most paint on that I could. I didn't know how expensive paint was."

I shook my head. I'd cringed when Blair suggested she could get started on painting the lobby on her own this morning while I was on my run, but I hadn't had the heart to tell her no. "It's fine. Look, why don't you let me do the actual painting?"

"Because I want to help. You did all the prep work yesterday."

"You helped me with the taping off. That's a really important step."

She beamed and wiped her forehead, leaving a smudge of white paint behind. Paint also dotted and streaked the old charcoal-colored T-shirt of mine I'd given her to work in, and from the looks of her butt in those baggy jeans, she'd likely either sat in paint or bumped into a wet wall. "Thanks."

"But I'm going to take over here, okay?" I took the roller from her hand.

"Okay." She looked sad for a moment.

"Hey, I've got an idea," I told her, trying to cheer her up. "Why don't you reach out to my mother and see if she's got any of those old photos you were asking about?"

Excited again, she picked up a wet washcloth lying on top of a step stool and wiped her hands. "Good idea. I'll call her right now."

"Perfect."

She looked around the lobby. "I can't wait for the new furniture to arrive."

"When's it coming again?"

"Friday. Do you think the walls will be dry by then?"

I laughed, shaking my head. "Yeah. They'll be dry by tonight."

Her face lit up. "Yay! I'm so excited for your brand new look. It should all be in place by next weekend. Oh, that reminds me. I have my interview up in Traverse City with Frannie MacAllister on Saturday. Do you think my car will be ready?"

"It should be. I talked to the guy sending the parts yesterday," I said, working the roller in the tray. "They should be here Wednesday."

"Oh. You didn't tell me that." There was zero enthusiasm in her tone. "That's . . . that's good. Wednesday is good." She paused. "So, should I call the motel?"

"The motel?" I started rolling the paint onto the wall.

"Yes. Once my car is ready, I can go stay at the motel. Your mom was very kind to offer a room, but I really don't want to put her out. And I've probably crowded you long enough."

She wasn't crowding me. And I didn't want her to move to the fucking motel. But what reason did I have for asking her to stay? So I could keep banging her every night? That didn't seem right. And besides, I was still kind of bothered by what Cole had said. Maybe if she moved to the motel, that would show people like him that we weren't serious. That I didn't need or want a girlfriend.

Because I didn't. I probably wouldn't even miss her. And if I did, that was a dangerous sign that I was letting her get too close.

"Yeah," I said, without even turning around. "Maybe that's for the best."

She left without saying another word, and it took every ounce of willpower I had not to go after her.

Later that afternoon, after the second coat of paint was on and the mess in the lobby cleaned up, I stored the painting supplies and headed back to my apartment. The aroma that greeted me as I ascended the stairs nearly made my eyes roll back in my head.

"What's that smell?" I asked when I reached the landing and spotted her pulling a tray from the oven. She'd showered and changed into a matching skirt and top. My mouth watered, but it wasn't only because of the scent.

"Dinner rolls. Pesto twists. I told your mom I'd bring them." She set the tray on the stovetop and turned off the oven. "She's expecting us at six."

"We're going to my mom's for dinner?"

"Yes." She pulled off the oven mitts and set them aside.

"I thought she was sick."

"Apparently she's feeling better."

I grimaced. "I thought we could just stop over there this afternoon and look for the pictures. Get in and out fast."

"She said she definitely has some, and she offered to go through her albums this afternoon and find all the best ones for me. Then she invited us for dinner, and I couldn't say no." She started washing a mixing bowl at the sink.

"You're too nice." I couldn't resist pressing up behind her and wrapping my arms around her waist—I liked how her top was a little bit cropped and showed her belly. I kissed the side of her neck. "And you smell delicious too."

"Thank you. Oh, by the way, I did some laundry. I hope that's okay."

"Of course."

"I threw your sheets in as well."

"You didn't have to do that." I pressed my face into her hair and inhaled. Maybe I would miss her.

"I didn't mind. I also called the motel."

"Oh." I released her and stepped back. "What did they say?"

"I have a room booked starting Wednesday night."

"You sure you'll be able to afford it?" I asked, looking for a reason she should stay here . . . one that *wasn't* related to my feelings.

"Yes. They gave me a good deal since I'll be there for over two weeks." She set the bowl on a towel to dry and finally turned to face me with a smile that didn't quite reach her eyes. "So as long as my car is ready by Wednesday, your apartment will be your own again."

Tell her that's not what you want, said a voice in my head. *Tell her you changed your mind, and you don't want her to go.*

But all I did was nod. "Okay. Guess I'll go clean up."

She faced the sink again.

Dinner at my mother's was actually more tolerable than I'd anticipated, mostly because Blair did such a good job of keeping the conversation centered on old family stories, especially about my dad. And she was an expert at veering back on track whenever my mother did her best to stray toward topics like how well we were getting along, how many children Blair might want in the future, and how the Lord worked in mysterious ways to unite two lonely souls in need.

Even my sister rolled her eyes at that. "Mom, jeez. Give them a break. The Lord has better things to do than find Griff a girlfriend."

"Don't sass me, Cheyenne. Your sad and lonely soul is next. The Lord and I are going to have a good long conversation about it."

"On second thought, have at them," Cheyenne said, getting up from her chair at the table. "Sorry, guys. Better you than me."

After dinner, we moved to the den and looked at all the photos my mother had pulled from old family albums. Blair sat in the middle of the couch with my mom on one side of her and me on the other, the stack of pictures in her lap.

"Oh, I love this one," Blair said, picking up a black and white snapshot with a thick white border around it. "Is that your dad and your grandpa in front of the shop?"

"Let me see." I leaned closer, the scent of her hair filling my head, and looked at the photo of a young version of my grandfather holding his toddler son's hand in front of the bay doors. "Yes. That looks like maybe right when it opened? Dad was only a couple years old, right Mom?"

My mother nodded. "He looks exactly like you at that age, Griffin. Look at those ears."

Blair laughed. "So sweet."

We went through the entire pile, and Blair asked questions about every photo, sometimes making notes in her phone. She asked if she could take some with her, and my mother said of course, as long as she got them back eventually.

"I'll take perfect care of them, I promise. I'm just going to have some large prints made." Blair put her hand on my mother's arm. "Thank you for trusting me with your family history. It means a lot."

"You're very welcome, darling. That history is still being written, you know. It would be nice to add another generation of Dempseys to the photo albums." She sighed wistfully.

I stood up. "Time to go. Thanks for dinner, Mom."

"Everything was delicious," said Blair, rising to her feet. "I'd love to get your recipe for those soft white sugar cookies."

"Of course, dear. That was my grandmother's recipe, and I'd be happy to share. Thank you for bringing the rolls. You're *very* talented."

"Thank you."

"Have you thought any more about opening a bakery here in town? At least five people have asked me if you're considering it—and hoping you will, of course."

Blair smiled. "That's sweet."

"The couple who owns the bakery on Main Street is getting on in years. I bet they'd sell cheap!"

"That's enough, Mom," I said firmly. "She's already got a job lined up somewhere else."

My mother's face turned white. "What?"

"Cheyenne put her in touch with someone up in Traverse City who offered to hire her starting right after Labor Day."

"*Cheyenne Dempsey!*" my mother bellowed, whirling on my sister. "How could you?"

While Cheyenne defended herself, I took Blair's arm and started for the front door. "Let's go."

When we got home, Blair wanted to go in the lobby to see if the paint was dry. She turned around slowly, looking at each wall. "I'm picturing where those big photo prints could go," she said.

"Yeah?"

"Yes. I think the one of your dad and grandfather from 1955 should go there. And the one of the three of you over there. Then maybe three smaller ones on this wall—the one of your dad teaching you and your sister how to change a tire here, the one of you and him working on the old truck here, and the one of your entire family at the 50th anniversary ribbon-cutting there. What do you think?"

"I think this place is going to look better than it has in years, thanks to you."

She smiled, her cheeks turning pink. "I just think the reminders that this is a family-owned-and-run business is really important."

"I agree."

She turned to face the wall again. "Someday, the walls of my bakery will have my family photos."

"You teaching your daughters how to bake bread?"

She arched a brow at me over her shoulder. "And my sons."

I smiled. "Of course."

"I want my sons to know how to cook and my daughters to know how to jumpstart a dead car battery," she said, turning to face me. "Which reminds me, do you think you could teach me how to do that before I go?"

My chest grew tight. I didn't want to think about her leaving. "Of course."

"Thanks. I know you're really busy, but I'd like to learn."

"I'm not too busy for you. Should we go up to bed?" I asked, switching off the lights.

"Yes." She headed for the door. "You did a lot of work today. I'm sure you're tired."

"I am, a little," I said, following her out and locking the door behind us. "But that's not the only reason I want to go to bed."

"No?"

"No." I unlocked my apartment door. "It's not even the most important one."

"What's the most important one?" she asked as we went up the stairs.

That I can't stop wanting more of you. That I love having you in my bed at night. That I'll miss you when you're gone. That I'll worry about you alone at that motel constantly. That we only have three more nights together. That in less than a week, you've managed to get under my skin, and I don't know what to do about it—I just know that it feels good to be with you.

But I couldn't admit any of those things to her, so I fell back on sex, which let me show her what I couldn't say.

"This," I said as we reached the top of the steps, spinning her around to take her in my arms and crush my mouth against hers in the dark.

As usual with us, it took no time at all for the fire to ignite. I was even more anxious than usual to get inside her, so anxious I couldn't make it to the bedroom. After yanking off all her clothes, I set her on my dining table and shoved down my jeans just enough to free my bulging cock.

Her legs were wrapped around me and I was about to push inside her when she whispered frantically, "Griffin—wait. It's not safe right now."

"Fuck." I couldn't believe I'd forgotten protection. *That* was a rule we absolutely could not break. Hurrying back to my bedroom, I grabbed a condom from my drawer and tore it open with my teeth on my way back to the table. She waited for me at the edge of the table, leaning back on her hands and breathing hard, her legs spread.

"You have no idea how good you look right now," I told her, rolling on the condom, my cock aching to be inside her again. "This is the picture I want fucking framed on the wall."

She laughed as I slid inside her. "This is for your eyes only."

"Fuck yes, it is." The thought of anyone else getting to see her this way made me insane with rage. Something feral and possessive took over me, and I fucked her more roughly than

I ever had before, almost like I wanted to hurt her. Punish her for showing some future asshole this side of her.

Her cries took on a different tone—I knew I was pushing her limits—and her nails raked up and down my arms like claws. Maybe she'd even drawn blood.

I didn't care.

Unless she asked for mercy, I was going to fuck her the way I needed to, the way my body begged me to. There was something I needed her to understand, and this was the only way to do it.

But she didn't ask for mercy—even though she cried out in pain and gripped my arms like she was drowning and sank her teeth into my shoulder as I poured myself into her.

When it was over, I braced my arms above her shoulders and looked down at her. "Sorry if I was too rough. I don't know what came over me."

"Was it the crop top?"

I laughed. "No, although I do like it."

"What was it?"

"I don't know. Just forgot my manners, I guess."

There was no way I could tell her the truth, which hit me hard as we curled up in my bed and she fell asleep in my arms.

It was panic. Pure and simple.

It was panic that I was about to lose something that mattered to me, and that it would be my own fault. It was panic that a deadline was approaching and a decision had to be made, but I wasn't ready to make it. It was panic that I was on the verge of making a huge mistake, but I didn't know what it was . . . letting her go? Or asking her to stay?

I felt like I was losing my mind.

What I'd told Cole was true—I didn't want my life to change. *I* didn't want to change. I'd put up these walls for a damn good reason, and I wasn't about to tear them down. Not even for her.

But I wasn't ready for this to be over yet either. I needed more time—time for whatever it was I felt for her to run its course. Time for the physical spark to burn out. Time for me to remember I didn't want or need her in my life.

So when the parts for her car arrived early—the very next morning, in fact—I didn't put them in her car.

I hid them.

And I didn't say a thing about it to anyone.

CHAPTER 15
BLAIR

I WAS DREADING WEDNESDAY, but I tried not to show it.

To be honest, I'd hoped Griffin would protest when I brought up calling the motel. Not that I blamed him for wanting his space back. I'd been here a week already. No matter how amazing the sex was, you couldn't just *move in* with someone so fast. I wasn't insane.

But I *liked* him. I didn't want what we had to end.

All day Monday, I kept looking at the clock, dismayed to find that time seemed to be passing more quickly than usual. We were busy at the garage, which was great, but also made the day fly by. Plans for the anniversary event were also keeping me preoccupied. After we closed, I ran over to the print shop Darlene had recommended and ordered the photo enlargements, which the woman at the counter promised to have ready by Friday.

"Perfect," I said. "I also wanted to ask you about printing some flyers for an event we're having on Labor Day weekend."

She helped me with the layout and design, and I hurried back to the garage as the skies darkened, lightning flashed, and thunder rumbled above me. Griffin was standing on the sidewalk in front of the garage as if he'd been waiting for me.

"I was about to get in the truck and come find you," he said sternly, pulling open the lobby door and following me inside. "You weren't answering your phone, and this is going to be a bad storm."

"Sorry. I must have left it on the desk. I was in a hurry to get there because I was concerned about keeping the photos dry."

He frowned. "I was worried about you. Take your phone with you when you go somewhere, okay?"

"Okay," I said, unable to keep from smiling.

"What's funny?" he demanded, his chest puffing up.

"You. Worried about me in the rain. It's cute."

"For the last time, mechanics are not cute."

"Then what do I call a mechanic that makes my clothes fall off and my heart go pitter-pat?" I asked, patting my chest with one hand.

He narrowed his eyes at me. "There better only be one of those."

I kissed his cheek. "There's only you."

Tuesday night, after I showed him how to make penne with summer vegetables and a kale salad—which he grumbled about eating but admitted it tasted better than he thought—he insisted on doing all the dishes. Then we stretched out on the couch and watched a movie together while the summer rain continued to thrum against the windows.

We made it about halfway through the latest Marvel movie before our minds and then our hands started to wander, and we ended up naked and sweaty on the rug between the couch and the coffee table. I don't know what was louder, me or the thunder, but poor Bisou wouldn't come out of her crate for the rest of the night.

"Aww, I feel bad," I said to Griffin when she didn't come out to eat.

"She's okay. I fostered another cat once who was afraid of storms. She'll eat when she gets hungry." But I noticed he set her plate and bowl right outside her crate rather than where he usually kept them.

Eventually we made it into bed, where we snuggled up and listened to the thunder. My head was resting on his chest, my body tucked alongside his. A particularly loud crack of thunder made me jump.

"Do storms bother you?" he asked.

"I was really scared of storms like this when I was little," I explained. "We lived on a golf course, and once when I was small, I heard my parents talking about someone who'd been struck by lightning while playing. I was always convinced it was going to happen to me while I was playing outside."

He held me a little tighter. "What were you like as a kid?"

"Hmmm. Talkative. Definitely talkative."

A laugh rumbled in his chest. "I bet. Did you drive your parents crazy?"

"Yes, but not just them. I'd talk to *anybody*. I'm totally the girl who should have been abducted by the creep in the white van."

"Part of me worries you're still that girl."

I snuggled closer. "I was also lonely."

"Lonely?"

"Yeah, I didn't have any siblings or close neighbor kids to play with. I was always by myself."

"Or with your horse," he teased.

I poked him in the side. "Fine. Or with my horse. But Alistair never wanted to play Barbies with me."

He snorted. "That was your horse's name? Alistair?"

"Yes. Alistair Peacock Beaufort."

"You gave him your middle name, how cute."

I picked up my head. "Did I tell you that was my middle name?"

"No. I saw it on your license the night we met."

"Oh." I grinned. "It's a family name on my mother's side. Did you think it was weird?"

"Kind of. But I thought it suited you."

I stuck my tongue out at him, and he laughed.

"Mostly I thought there was no way Blair Peacock Beaufort would be interested in a guy like me."

"Well," I said, climbing on top of him. "You were wrong."

I woke up Wednesday morning with an ache in my heart. Next to me, Griffin was still asleep, and rather than jump out of bed and get baking like I did most mornings, I lay on my side and watched him for a moment.

He was breathtakingly handsome even as he slept, and the sight of his muscular, tattooed shoulders and chest never failed to rile me up. Before I could stop myself, I reached over and traced the sharp edge of his jaw, then the rounded bulge of his bicep. His eyes opened.

"Hi," I whispered.

"Hey." He stretched, which made his muscles flex and my mouth water. "Is it time to get up already?"

"Pretty much."

"But it's still kinda dark." He reached out and pulled me closer to him.

Smiling, I tucked my head beneath his chin, throwing an arm and a leg over his body. "Can we play hooky today?"

"We could, but I don't think my employees or customers would like it very much."

"Probably not."

"But maybe we could be late," he said, his hands stroking my shoulders, arms, back. "I mean, I *do* own the place."

"That's true," I agreed, my hand sliding down his chiseled stomach to play with his cock, which was rock hard. "Do you always wake up like this?"

"Always? No. Often? Yes."

"And what do you do about it?"

"I ignore it or I take care of it."

"Like this?" I curled my fingers around his shaft and moved my hand up and down his length.

A laugh rumbled in his chest. "Sort of. Only not as gentle. I'm a little more aggressive about it."

Intrigued, I sat up and tossed the covers back. Gave him a devious smile. "Show me."

His eyebrows shot up. "Show you?"

"Yes." I got on my knees and clasped my hands beneath my chin. "Please."

A slow, sexy smile came over his mouth. "You're such a bad girl."

"I know."

Propping himself up on one elbow, he took his cock in his hand, his grip tight as he moved his fist along its length. "Guess you meant it when you said you liked watching me."

I nodded, wide-eyed as he began to move his body, thrusting slowly and rhythmically into his hand. His six-pack abs rippled. I might have whimpered.

"I'm thinking about you," he said, his voice gravelly and deep, his eyes moving over my naked body. "I'm thinking about the way you taste, the way you move, the way it feels to get inside you."

"Oh God," I whispered, dying to touch him but not wanting to interrupt what was happening right in front of me. It was the hottest thing I'd ever seen. Instead, I spread my knees slightly, ran my hands up my inner thighs.

"Fuck yes," Griffin growled through clenched teeth. "Let me watch you. Make yourself come for me."

This was something I had never done before—never even *thought* about doing before—but I wasn't the person I used to be. I felt braver with him. Unafraid to let him see me this way. I licked my fingertips, and his eyes followed my hand as I placed it between my thighs and began to rub my clit. The hum blossomed quickly beneath my touch.

Watching me, Griffin gripped his cock tighter, jerked himself harder, rocked his hips faster. The muscles of his arms bulged and flexed. His breath came in low, hushed exhalations, which grew louder and closer together as his movement got more frantic.

Mesmerized, I couldn't even move my hand as I watched his orgasm unfold in front of me—his eyes closed, his jaw clenched, his entire body going still, and then with a few final, uncontrollable thrusts of his hips and pumps of his fist, he came onto his chest in long, pulsing streams.

It was the hottest thing I'd ever seen—but also the most vulnerable. The most honest. The most intimate. His body was like a work of art. And to watch him take pleasure from it that way, with his own hand, right in front of me, knowing he wanted me to see him like this—it made my heart beat so hard, I thought it might burst out of my chest.

"Fuck." Opening his eyes, he regarded the mess on his torso and looked over at me. "You didn't do it."

Guilty, I shook my head. "I'm sorry. You distracted me."

"That's no excuse, but you can make it up to me in the shower."

"I can?"

He carefully slipped out of bed without getting the sheets messy and held out his hand to me. "Come on, princess. Let's get dirty before we get clean."

Smiling, I took his hand.

Eventually, we made it into work, but I had trouble focusing. Mostly I just sat at the desk, staring into space. Thinking about this morning. Fanning myself with a supplier catalog. Dreading the arrival of those parts for my car.

I felt like those repairs would signal the beginning of the end of something I wasn't ready to let go of. I didn't want to be dependent on Griffin, but I didn't want to say goodbye either. I wished I knew what he was thinking, but I was too nervous to ask. I knew how he felt about relationships, and it didn't seem fair to expect him to change for me.

Cheyenne poked her head into the lobby around noon. "Hey, you."

I stopped fretting for a moment and smiled at her. "Hey."

"Wow, looking good in here. So much brighter," she said, coming inside. "Those photos are going to look great."

"Thanks. I'm excited about them. And about the party. Did Griffin tell you I got him to agree to turn his vintage pickup into a photo booth for the day?"

Cheyenne laughed. "Did you really? Gosh, he and my dad worked forever on that thing."

"He told me about it. I think people would get a kick out of having their picture taken in it—and I convinced him to paint the new logo on the side."

"You're a genius. Will there be food?"

"Yes. I talked to the Bulldog Pub owner yesterday, and she's all for collaborating. We're thinking maybe a little stand selling sliders and fries out front."

"Wow. You're putting a lot of effort into this." She laughed. "Griffin really lucked out when you blew that tire."

"I'm enjoying it. I hope it makes a difference for the business."

"I'm sure it will. So do you have time for a quick lunch? Or does my brother keep you chained to the desk all day?"

I shrugged. "I can probably take lunch now. I'm not getting that much work done today anyway."

"Why not?"

"Just . . . a lot on my mind, I guess." I came out from behind the desk. "Let me go tell Griff. We usually have lunch together, so I'll see if he wants me to bring him something."

Cheyenne tossed a hand in the air. "Invite him along if you'd like."

Griffin was under the hood of a sleek black Corvette. Seeing him at work, all dirty and sexy and hot, did a *thing* to my insides, and I felt my legs go a little wobbly as I got close to him. "Hey, you."

"What's up?" He paused and looked up at me, bracing himself on the car's frame.

"Your sister is here asking if I want to have lunch with her."

"Go for it."

"Do you want to come with us?"

"Nope."

"Can I bring you something back?"

"Nah, that's okay. I'll just run upstairs and eat leftovers from last night." He went back to what he was doing under the hood. "Say hi to Cheyenne for me."

"Okay." I glanced around, scared to ask the question on my mind but wanting the answer. "Did the parts for my car come in?"

"Not yet."

Relief flowed over me. "Okay. Maybe this afternoon or something."

"Maybe." He didn't look up. "But even if they did, I'm not sure I'd have time to do the work today. We're a little busier in here this week than usual, and I want to make sure I have everyone's work done when I said I would."

"Okay," I said tentatively, wondering what that meant.

"You might as well cancel the motel for tonight," he went on. "And probably tomorrow night too. It's game day. Realistically, I don't think I'll get to your car before the weekend." He paused, finally looking over at me. "Is that okay?"

I tried not to shriek with excitement. "Where will I stay?"

"With me." A slow, sexy grin tugged at his mouth. "And before you ask, *yes*—it's what I want."

Feelings for him—huge, monster feelings—rushed through me. I jumped up and threw my arms around his neck, my feet leaving the floor. "It makes me so happy to hear you say that."

Laughing, he awkwardly patted my back. "You're going to be filthy, Blair."

"I don't care." I closed my eyes and breathed him in—the usual sweat and motor oil, plus something uniquely him that made my nether regions tingle. But Cheyenne was waiting for me, so I let him go. "I'll be back soon."

"Okay."

As I turned and walked back to the lobby, I would have sworn my feet didn't touch the ground.

It was a gorgeous day—sunny and mild—so Cheyenne and I decided to take our sandwiches from the deli down to the waterfront park. As we walked, I told her about my phone call with Frannie and my interview on Saturday. "Thank you so much for putting us in touch," I said. "I'm really excited to meet her."

"I'm glad, and you're welcome. Maybe someday my

mother will stop complaining to my father that I've ruined everything with you and Griffin."

I laughed. "Sorry about that."

"So what's the scoop with you two? Do you think you'll keep seeing each other after you move?"

"I don't know. The truth is, I would like to, but I'm not sure he feels the same way."

"Have you asked him?"

I shook my head. "No. I feel weird about it. He's so adamant about his rules and his independence. He made it pretty clear up front he is not a relationship kind of guy. I'm afraid it would freak him out."

Cheyenne was silent for a moment. We reached the park adjacent to the harbor and took a seat on a bench in the shade. "What about you?" she asked as we unwrapped our sandwiches. "Are you looking for a committed relationship?"

"Down the road, sure. But I wanted to get on my feet first, you know? Establish myself. But . . . meeting Griffin has changed things."

"How so?"

"I've just never met anyone like him. He's a *real man*, with real problems, but he faces them. He works so damn hard every single day. He worries constantly about losing the business his father and grandfather built, and he's willing to bust his ass to keep it. What he won't do is lie or cheat or skimp. You have to admire that."

"He's always been honest," agreed Cheyenne. "And he does believe in hard work. Our dad was the same. Not a lazy bone in his body."

"And he's been through a *war*, you know? That's incredible to me. He served his country during a *war*."

"He sure did." Cheyenne's voice was proud. "And I bet he didn't tell you about his Silver Star Medal."

"No. I don't even know what that is," I confessed.

"It's a medal he earned for heroism. He never talks about

it, but it was a big deal in our family. It was the only time I ever saw my dad cry."

My own throat tightened. "He never told me about it. But that's the kind of thing I mean. Most guys I knew in my past life couldn't stop talking about themselves. Their money. Their cars. Their mutual funds. Their connections. And it's all bullshit. None of it matters."

"Yeah, Griff's a cocky bastard, but not in that way." She laughed. "And he definitely doesn't have any mutual funds."

"He doesn't need them. He has so much more to offer." I sighed. "Plus he's hot. Sorry—I know he's your brother—but he's really, really fucking hot."

"Ewwww."

"I know, I know. I'll spare you the details. But he's got that body, and those eyes, and those big hands, and he's so generous. He knows exactly how to—"

"I thought you were sparing me the details," Cheyenne said, holding up a hand.

I laughed. "Sorry. I get carried away thinking about him."

"I can tell."

We ate in silence for a few minutes. Then she said something that surprised me.

"Griffin has a really big heart. He doesn't show it to everyone, and God knows he can be a stubborn, temperamental asshole, but underneath that tough exterior, I agree with you. He's one of the good guys. He just doesn't let people in very easily." She thought for a moment. "I don't know if it was what happened with Kayla or my dad dying or what, but he sort of shut down after all that."

"Really?"

She nodded. "I've watched him grow more and more closed off over the last few years, almost like he's scared to feel things."

I took a bite of my wrap without tasting it.

"But he's definitely different with you."

I swallowed so quickly I almost choked. "What?"

"He's different with you. In the last week, I've seen him laugh more than he has all year. And smile more. And I can see the way he treats you—all hovering and protective. I mean, inviting you to stay at his apartment like that? It's insane!"

"He just asked me to stay a few more days," I confessed. "He said even if the parts for my car arrive today as expected, he won't have time to work on it."

"See? He would *never* do that for anyone else. He'd bust his ass to get that car fixed and have his place to himself again. You're special to him." She laughed. "No wonder my mother is so upset you're leaving."

"I'm not going that far," I said, my heart thumping joyfully at everything she was saying. But was it true?

We finished our lunches, watching kids on the playground equipment and moms pushing strollers and boats moving in and out of the harbor. Several people stopped to say hello to Cheyenne and ask after Darlene, or introduce themselves to me and say they'd heard great things about my baking, and a couple kids shyly approached "Miss Dempsey" and said they hoped she'd be their teacher next year.

"This really is a sweet little town," I said, sticking my napkin and sandwich wrapper in the bag.

Cheyenne nodded. "It is. I mean, you do get sick of the same people all the time when you're young, and I definitely couldn't wait to go off to college and travel and make new friends. I wasn't even sure I'd come back."

"No?"

She shook her head. "But by the time I was ready to find a job and pick a place to live, I missed it. And I couldn't imagine finding anywhere else that would really feel like home. I just feel . . . right in my skin here, you know? It's peaceful. It's friendly. It's safe."

I nudged her foot with mine. "And the law enforcement is especially good-looking."

She sighed. "It really is."

"I still think you should ask him out," I said as we started walking back up Main Street.

"No way. I'm too scared."

"Even if it's just as friends," I said. "Come on, you two have known each other for so long. And I bet he's lonely sometimes. Couldn't you just go have dinner or something?"

"Sure we could."

"So ask him. I bet he'd say yes."

"He probably would. It's not the *asking* I'm afraid of."

I looked over at her. "Then what is it?"

"Falling in love with someone I can't have," she said, "someone that can never belong to me. If we start spending time together, even if it's just as friends, I know I'll be head over heels in no time at all. I know I'll give in if he just wanted sex with no strings attached. I know I'll wind up crying in my pillow just like I did when I was fourteen. Remember that scene in Grease when Olivia Newton-John sings *Hopelessly Devoted to You* while imagining John Travolta's face in that stupid pond?"

"Yeah," I said, trying not to laugh.

"Well, that was pretty much me all through high school. I don't want to go back there." She shook her head as we crossed a side street. "It's bad enough I'm twenty-nine years old, living next door to him again, sleeping in my old bed and having all the same stupid dreams I had about him back then. It's like I'm stuck in this loop and can't get out."

"I'm sorry." I put my arm around her shoulders. "I shouldn't have said anything."

"It's okay. I appreciate the encouragement, but I should really move on. What's the use of wanting something you can't have?"

Her question stuck in my head.

I thought about it that night when Griffin cleared space in his bedroom closet for me and watched me hang up some dresses. I thought about it Thursday evening as I cheered on his team during another big win, wearing his Bulldogs shirt from last year. I thought about it on Friday morning when the new furniture arrived and we set it up in the lobby together, and later that afternoon when we hung the canvas prints of his family on the walls. He looked at the photo of him and his dad for several minutes, saying nothing.

"You look like him," I said. "Which is a compliment, because he's very handsome." It was the truth. Hank Dempsey's good looks were a little darker than Griffin's—although I could see where Cheyenne had gotten her wide brown eyes and full black lashes—but the bone structure was eerily similar. The cut of the jaw, the strong nose, the wide mouth.

Griffin put his arms around me. "He'd have liked you."

"You think so?" My heart warmed at the compliment.

"Yeah."

"Why?"

"Because you're genuine."

Tipping my head back, I smiled up at him. "Keep going."

He laughed. "You're beautiful. You're sweet. You're funny. Even though half the time it's unintentional."

I stuck my tongue out at him.

"You work hard. You smell good *all* the time. And you've got this bottom lip that drives me wild." He took it between his teeth and gave it a tug.

"I don't think your dad would have cared about my bottom lip."

"But I do."

With my arms around his waist and my eyes closed, I pressed my cheek to his warm, broad chest and tried very hard not to feel like I was falling for someone that would never belong to me.

CHAPTER 16
GRIFFIN

EARLY FRIDAY MORNING, a car was towed to the garage with a dead battery. We weren't too busy, so I went into the lobby to get Blair.

"Time for a lesson," I told her. "Go upstairs and put on something grubby."

She touched her chest, looking slightly offended. "I don't own anything *grubby*."

I rolled my eyes. "Do you have a pair of jeans?"

"Yes."

"Okay, put them on and take a T-shirt from my dresser to wear over it. Make sure to put your hair back too, and meet me out in the lot in ten minutes."

She stood up and saluted me. "Yes, sir."

Ten minutes later, she came trotting out to the lot. "Okay, boss, I'm ready."

I took one look at her and started to laugh. She'd traded her usual sundress for a pair of baggy jeans, which were cuffed at the ankle, and one of my T-shirts, which was knotted at her waist. On her feet were a pair of pristine white sneakers, and her ponytail was pulled through the back of a Bellamy Creek Garage baseball cap.

"What's funny?" she asked, looking down at her outfit.

"Nothing," I said. "It's just, you look like Auto Repair Barbie or something."

She put her nose in the air. "Well, Auto Repair Barbie better earn her name by learning a skill. Now are you going to teach me one or not?"

"I will teach you one."

She held up a finger. "With*out* laughing."

I shook my head, grinning even wider. "I will really fucking try."

"Okay," I said. "So to review, once you have the two cars pulled up close enough for the jumper cables to reach, make sure they're both in park, put the parking brake on, and take the keys out of the ignition."

Blair nodded, looking back and forth between my truck and the Ford SUV with the dead battery. They were nose to nose in the lot with their hoods propped open, which I'd shown her how to do. "Got it," she said.

"Okay, now let's look at the battery of my truck. Get up on that stool so you can see."

She climbed up on the stool I'd brought out for her and peered tentatively beneath the truck's hood, almost like she was afraid something might jump out and bite her.

"Know where the battery is?" I asked.

She pointed at the carburetor. "That?"

I tried and failed to hide a grin. "Nope. It's this box over here."

"Oh." She poked my shoulder. "You promised not to laugh at me."

"I'm beginning to regret that promise." I tweaked the cap on her head. "But I'll keep trying."

I explained how to identify the positive and negative terminals of a car battery, then asked her to locate the battery of the SUV—which she did.

"Good job," I said, tugging her ponytail. "Now can you find the positive and negative?"

She pointed to the little red and black tubes on the Ford's battery. "There. Right?"

"Good job. You learn fast."

"Thank you." She smiled proudly. "I didn't think I'd be good at this stuff."

"You'd be good at anything. Now let's look at the jumper cables."

Next, I showed her how to attach the alligator clips of the jumper cables to each terminal—starting with red to dead. "Always start with the dead battery first. That's the safest," I explained. "Leave the black end alone for now, but don't let it touch any metal."

"Got it," she said.

"Next, you're going to attach the red and black leads to the good battery. Start with red." I held out the ends of the cables to her.

"You want *me* to do it?" she asked, shocked.

"Yes. I have confidence in you. Just don't let them touch, and do it exactly the way I showed you."

She took the leads from me, careful not to let them touch, and climbed up the stool again. With her bottom lip caught between her teeth, she attached the red clip to the positive terminal, then the black to the negative. "Like that?"

"Exactly."

She turned to me and held out her palms. "My hands are shaking."

"Why?"

"I don't know. I feel like one wrong move and your car will explode. Along with my face."

I smiled. "I would never let anything happen to that face. You're doing fine."

"Thanks. So now do I attach the last black end to the dead black terminal?"

My heart rate tripled. "No!" I said quickly, shaking my head. "Never do that."

"Why not?"

"It will cause a spark, which could possibly ignite fumes and lead to an explosion."

She blinked at me. "I am so not qualified for this."

"Yes, you are. Come on. We're almost done."

A few minutes later, everything was hooked up. "Now what?" she asked.

"Now I'll start the truck, and we'll let it run for two minutes."

"I'm nervous," she said, wringing her hands together as we waited.

"Why?"

"I don't want to fail at this. If my car dies somewhere and I get stranded again, I want to be able to rescue myself."

I put an arm around her shoulder and kissed the top of her head. "I know. I like that about you."

When it was time to attempt starting the Ford, I asked her to do it.

"Okay," she said, her voice full of doubt. But she got behind the wheel and turned the key in the ignition. It struggled, coughing and sputtering.

Come on, you fucker, I willed the car. *She needs this victory.*

It jumped to life.

"Eeeeeep!" she squealed. Through the windshield, she gave me a blinding grin, and I gave her a thumbs up.

"Leave it running," I called out.

She jumped out of the car and launched herself at me, clinging like a koala. "I did it!"

"You did it." I hugged her back, remembering the excitement of doing this for the first time with my dad.

On her feet again, she looked with amazement from one engine to the other. "I feel like Dr. Frankenstein," she said, pumping a fist in the air. "I brought a dead thing back to life!"

I laughed. "I know the feeling."

"So I should make sure I have jumper cables in my car, right? Do I have to buy them separately? Or are they, like, included when you purchase a new car?"

"Not unless you buy a Rolls Royce," I said wryly.

She sighed. "That is probably out of Auto Repair Barbie's budget. At least for now."

I tweaked her hat again. "I have some extra cables. I'll make sure you have some when you go."

When you go.

I said it, but I didn't want to think about it. And from the look on Blair's face, she didn't either.

But she smiled and thanked me. "I really appreciate the lesson."

"You're welcome. But it's not over yet. I need to show you how to remove the clips."

She paid attention while I demonstrated how to unclip the leads in the reverse order she'd connected them, but the crackle of excitement in the air from a moment earlier was gone.

We'd brought something to life, and it had been easy.

But keeping it alive would be impossible.

Nothing lived forever.

Saturday morning, I went down to work early.

Blair had her interview up in Traverse City today, and I was driving her, which meant I could only work until about noon. She'd offered to drive herself if I'd loan her my truck, but after hearing all the horror stories about her driving record, I said I'd take her. After all, it was my fault her own car wasn't ready yet.

Six days had gone by since I'd hidden those parts. Six fucking days.

On the outside, things were fine. Great, even.

On the inside, I was starting to panic.

My feelings for her weren't going away like I wanted them to. In fact, they were growing stronger. I'd thought for sure I'd get tired of her after a few more days and be desperate to have my apartment to myself again, but I wasn't. At all. I loved having her around, and my mind was starting to wander into dangerous *what if* territory.

What if we kept seeing each other after she moved? What if Cole was right and I was crazy to throw such great chemistry out the window? What if I was wrong about being better off alone?

I tried to wrap my brain around what it might look like. How often we'd see each other. How long it could last.

But every time I thought about it, my adrenaline started to pump like I was in some kind of imminent danger. For years, I'd managed to keep myself immune from this kind of weakness for someone. But she had this way of making me feel strong and helpless at the same time. She made me want to do everything I could to keep her around, and keep her happy. When she laughed at something I said or I saw her cheering in the stands during a game or she came up with yet another idea to help my business, it just made me feel so damn good—like a chemical reaction inside me.

I couldn't deny I had real feelings for her, and that they were growing every day.

I didn't know how to cut them off.

No, that wasn't true. I *did* know how—I just wasn't strong enough to do it.

I was still brooding about it when McIntyre came in around eight. "Hey, did that trailer hitch kit for the Jeep come in yet? I need to get that done this morning. It's for Emily's brother."

"I haven't seen it, but it's possible. We've had several deliveries this week. Check the back."

He wandered toward the back, and I didn't see him for a while. I figured he'd found the hitch and was installing it on the Jeep outside, but about thirty minutes later, he approached me and stood there without saying anything.

"Find the hitch?" I asked from beneath the hood of a Nissan.

"No." He paused. "But I did find the parts for Blair's car. The packing slip said they arrived Monday."

I froze. Didn't look up.

"Did you know they were there all week?"

I continued tightening a bolt. "Yeah."

"Uh, so what gives? Why didn't you do the repair job?"

I straightened up and looked at him. "I haven't had time."

He gave me an odd look. "Do you want me to do it?"

"No," I said quickly. "I'll do it. I want to look everything over myself. Make sure it's safe."

"Okay." He scratched his head. Something wasn't sitting right with him, I could tell.

"I just want to surprise her, that's all. She doesn't know they came in, and I thought it would be fun to surprise her once the work is all done. So don't say anything to her, okay?"

"I won't say a word."

I went back to what I was doing, but I couldn't fucking concentrate to save my life.

McIntyre was silent the rest of the morning too.

I felt like he saw right through me.

The entire ride north, Blair kept up a steady stream of excited chatter, expressing her gut feeling that she and Frannie MacAllister were going to hit it off, fretting about finding a place to live she could afford, and hoping when the day was over she'd be able to call her mother and tell her she'd been wrong.

"I just feel like if this job comes through, that will finally be the thing I need to feel one hundred percent confident," she said. "Like all the pieces will start falling into place."

"What are the other pieces?" I asked.

"Well, I have a one-year plan, a five-year plan, and a ten-year."

"Let's start with the one."

"Okay, in one year I want to seriously reduce my personal debt and be in a position to apply for a small business loan so I can start looking for my own space."

So she was going to spend the next year working her ass off. She wouldn't have time for me anyway.

"How about in five years?" I asked.

"In five years, I'd like my business to be up and running. I'd like to be in my own home, married to a handsome prince, maybe even with a baby or two."

Even better. There was no way in hell I was *that* guy.

I gripped the steering wheel a little harder. "And in ten years?"

"In ten years, I'll be celebrating my fortieth birthday. And honestly, all I want is to look around at my life and be grateful for everything I have. Which is, I hope, a comfortable home, a happy family, good friends, a successful business, and some wisdom to pass on to my kids along with my recipes."

"Sounds good," I said, wishing I knew who this handsome prince was she planned to marry so I could find him and kick his ass.

"What about you?" she asked, shifting to face me on the passenger seat. "Where do you see yourself in a year?"

I shrugged. "At the garage, listening to McIntyre complain about his wife and busting Handme's ass to stack the tires."

She laughed. "How about in five years?"

"Let's see. In five years, I'll be thirty-seven. I hope I still have six-pack abs and a good throwing arm."

"And in ten?"

Ten years. Fuck, I'd be forty-two.

Would I still live in my apartment? Would Moretti be married with nine kids? Would Mariah be out of high school? Would Beckett still be able to hit home runs over the left field fence?

What about my mother? Would she still be around? Would Cheyenne finally get married and give her some grandchildren? Would we all get together for Sunday dinners and talk about Dad and the old days and how much trouble I used to be?

I could picture everyone at the table—my mom, Cheyenne and whatever clown agreed to marry her, a bunch of their rug rats in high chairs or booster seats, or chasing each other around the table like she and I used to do while my mother yelled at us to stop acting like monkeys and sit down like civilized humans. The memory nearly put a smile on my face.

But the thought of the future did not.

Because when I looked at the chair next to mine, it was empty. I was alone.

I frowned. But that was how I wanted it, right? That was how I'd decided it had to be.

Alone was easy. Alone was uncomplicated. Alone was safe.

It didn't have to mean celibate, although the thought of being with someone other than Blair actually repulsed me.

"Griff?" Blair leaned over and poked my leg. "Where'd you go?"

"Ten years into the future."

"And? What did it look like?"

Lonely as fuck, I thought.

"Fine," I said, changing lanes on the highway. "It looked fine."

A few minutes before four, Blair and I arrived at a place called Coffee Darling. The sign on the door said closed, but when we pulled the handle, we discovered it was unlocked.

Inside the shop, I could immediately tell Blair would fit right in. It was bright and modern and girly, with black and white photos on the walls, a long white marble countertop, and glass cases full of colorful cookies that made her gasp.

"Macarons!" she whispered in awe. "Look how beautiful they are."

A woman wearing an apron over her clothes appeared behind the counter with a big smile on her face. "Hi there. I'm Frannie. Are you Blair?"

Blair nodded and held out her hand over the counter. "Yes. So nice to meet you. And this is my friend Griffin Dempsey."

Frannie nodded. "Cheyenne's brother, right? Nice to meet you."

I held out my hand as well. "You too."

"Well, let me show you around and then we can talk. How does that sound?" Frannie asked brightly.

"Perfect," said Blair.

Frannie turned to me. "We're closed for the day, so I don't have a server here, but you're free to have a seat and I'll pour you a cup of coffee. Or you can join us for the tour."

"I think I'll just take a walk around town and meet you back here." I looked at Blair. "Is that okay with you?"

"Of course." She was nervous beneath the smile, but I was positive Frannie wouldn't notice. Grace under pressure was her thing, after all. She'd ace this interview, and the job would be hers.

She'd move up here, accomplish all her goals, and in ten years, she'd have everything she wanted.

I'd be a memory.

Irrationally angry about it, I stomped up and down the streets of downtown Traverse City glaring at happy people, wearing a scowl on my face, confused about what or who I was mad at, and coming to the conclusion that it didn't matter and I needed to just get the fuck over it.

Maybe I would only be a memory to her. But I'd be a good memory. The best-sex-she-ever-had memory.

I'd make damn sure of that.

She got the job—of course she did.

"It's just so perfect," she chirped on the ride home. "I'll be the full-time manager and baker for as long as she needs, and when she's ready to come back after the twins are old enough, I can decide then if I want to stay on or look for a shop of my own."

"Sounds great."

"*And,*" she went on, clapping her hands, "she said she spoke to her parents about renting out her old apartment, which is above the garage at Cloverleigh. Sort of like a carriage house."

"Oh yeah?"

"Yes. It's small, but I don't really need a lot of space, and the rent would only be three-fifty a month. With what she's going to pay me, I can totally afford that, plus I'll be able to pay off all my credit card debt within two years."

"That's amazing." I forced myself to ask the next question. "When will you move in?"

"I told her I can't move until after Labor Day weekend, and she was fine with that."

"If you have to move sooner, it's okay," I said, almost wishing she would. No sense prolonging this. "Don't feel like you have to stay in Bellamy Creek for me. For my shop, I mean."

She reached over and rubbed my shoulder. "Hey. I *want* to stay. After Labor Day is soon enough. I just need my car back by then."

"You'll have it." I cleared my throat. "I'll, uh, put another call into my supplier. Make sure he has the right address."

"I just can't believe it," she said, wiping tears from her eyes. "Everything is coming together."

"Good."

But I felt like everything was falling apart.

CHAPTER 17
GRIFFIN

"WHAT'S THIS?" I asked as Blair set a small frosted cake in front of me. It was late Tuesday night, after nine o'clock, but I'd had practice tonight. Afterward, I'd skipped the usual hangout at the pub to come home, clean up, and eat a late supper with her.

"It's a cake." She lit the single candle standing in the white frosting.

"I can see that, but what's it for?" I looked up at her. "It's not my birthday. Is it yours?"

Smiling, she shook her head. "Nope. My birthday is in June. It's for our anniversary!"

"Our what?"

"Our anniversary. It's been exactly two weeks since we got married." She fluttered her lashes and put both hands over her heart. "The happiest two weeks of my life."

Laughing, I pulled her onto my lap. She was wearing one of my favorite outfits—the blue dress with the little bow in the front, and somehow she looked even more beautiful than usual in it. "You're crazy."

"I know." She kissed me. "And I invaded your space, and

I talk too much, I'm a terrible driver, I'm not good at painting, I spent too much on the new rug for the lobby, I spilled coffee in your nice clean truck—"

"What?"

She winced. "Yeah, I didn't tell you about that. But when I took your truck to get groceries the other day, I spilled my coffee on the front seat. I cleaned it up, though!"

I groaned.

"Also, I might have hit a curb."

I groaned even louder, but it was impossible to be mad at her.

"My *point is*," she went on sweetly, patting my shoulder, "that I know I'm not perfect, but you make me feel good about myself. I'm grateful for you."

"Yeah?"

"Yes. *And*," she said, lowering her voice to a whisper, as if someone might hear her, "you give me the best orgasms I've ever had."

I lifted my chin. "Good."

"Blow out the candle. Make a wish." I blew it out, and she wiggled on my lap. "What did you wish for?"

"A million fucking dollars in my bank account, what else?"

She pouted. "I thought it would be something sexier."

"That is sexy. I'm getting hard just thinking about it." I kissed her, sliding my hands beneath her dress. Actually, I'd been careful not to wish for anything.

"Okay, your turn," she said, a little breathless as my lips traveled along her jaw and down her throat.

"My turn for what?"

She laughed. "For telling me what this marriage has meant to you over the last two weeks."

"Oh." I untied the bow of her sundress with my teeth like I'd wanted to the first day she'd worn it. "Can't I just show you with one of those orgasms? Maybe two?"

"Yes," she said. "But I like to hear words too."

"Mmm. Not good at words. Good at this." I opened up her dress and tugged down the white lace of her bra before swirling my tongue around one perfect nipple.

"Yes, you are *very* good at this." She put her hands in my hair. "But don't you . . . hey, can we talk for a minute?"

"About what?"

"Maybe like . . . what you're feeling? What comes next for us?" She tilted my head up so I was forced to look at her. "I can't think when you're doing that."

"Then you'll have to stop thinking." I stood up with her in my arms and started moving toward the bedroom. The last thing I wanted to do was talk about my feelings right now. I didn't trust myself not to say something stupid.

"Wait, what about your cake?" she cried.

"I'll eat it later. I want you for dessert."

I tossed her onto the bed, pushed up her dress, and pulled down her underwear. "Here's what comes next for us." I spread her legs apart and buried my face between her thighs.

She moaned and clawed at the sheets, rocking her hips beneath my mouth. By now I knew how to make her come easily, but I liked to drag it out, work her into a frenzied state of desperation until she begged me to let her come.

But I didn't tease her tonight. Within minutes, her hands were fisted in my hair, her cries echoing off the walls, her clit throbbing as I sucked it into my mouth.

When she'd released her grip on my hair, I stood up, whipped off my shirt and worked off my jeans. Naked, I pulled her into a seated position and lifted her dress over her head. Then she fell back again, taking me with her.

We kissed and groped and clung and rolled around in twisted sheets, skin to skin, flirting with recklessness. In the back of my head I knew I should stop and get protection, but I couldn't find my voice. *Just for a minute*, I kept telling myself.

I just want to feel her like this for one more minute, and then I'll stop.

But I didn't stop.

I put the tip of my cock inside her, and she moaned. "More," she pleaded.

I gave her one more inch, both of us groaning in agonizing bliss. Her hands were on my back, inching lower. "Don't stop," she breathed, tilting her hips to take more of me.

Clinging to a rapidly fraying rope of self-control, I allowed myself a few playfully shallow strokes. But it was way too good—and then she was grabbing my ass and pulling me in deeper, crying out in frustrated need. Before I knew it I was all the way inside her, driving hard and fast and deep with nothing between us.

And I didn't care. In that moment, I didn't know fear or caution. I didn't care about rules or consequences. I didn't think about the past or the future or anything except this moment, this feeling, this woman, this relentless need for *more, more, more.*

She gripped me tightly and matched my rhythm with her own, our bodies rocking against each other, our skin slick with sweat. We raced toward climax together, spiraling higher and higher until we collided in the sky and burst into flames, then clung to each other as the embers drifted back to earth.

A slow, dizzying, inevitable fall.

After which I hit the ground with a hard, rude *thump.*

"Oh, fuck." I pulled out, as if the risk hadn't already been taken. "Fuck. We shouldn't have done that."

"It's—it's okay."

"No, it's not. You told me the other night it wasn't safe, and I—"

"The timing isn't as dangerous tonight. In my cycle, I mean. I think it's fine."

"You *think*?" I knew shit about timing and cycles, but her

tone was not convincing, and the thought of an accidental pregnancy was scary as hell. "You can't get pregnant, Blair. It would be a fucking disaster."

"Griffin," she said, obviously hurt.

Angry with myself, I got out of bed and went into the bathroom, pulling the door shut behind me a little harder than necessary. I was being a dickhead and I knew it, but she had me all disoriented and confused. I felt like I didn't know which way was up. I had no rules left to break.

What the fuck was the matter with me?

I cleaned up and came out of the bathroom still unsure of what to say. Right away she got out of bed and went into the bathroom, without even looking at me. She shut the door with less force than I had, but with enough to make it obvious she was upset.

I didn't blame her.

Lowering myself onto the edge of the bed, I hung my head. I had majorly fucked up. I'd gotten myself into a place I couldn't get out of without hurting someone who didn't deserve it.

She came out of the bathroom and went over to her suitcase. The bedroom light was off, but the hall light was still on, and I watched her pull on underwear and her Snoopy T-shirt.

"What are you doing?" I asked. She'd been sleeping naked every night—we both had.

"Nothing."

"Come here."

She closed her suitcase and came over to the bed, tentatively sitting on the edge a good three feet from me, her arms crossed over her chest, her knees pressed together. She stared straight ahead.

"I'm sorry," I said. "I was a jerk about what just happened. It wasn't your fault."

She didn't say anything, and I found myself groping for

more words. I felt like I owed her a better explanation, and there *was* one, but it terrified me to think about unlocking that particular vault. Tearing down that particular wall. But I heard myself say it a moment later.

"She was pregnant."

Blair looked at me. "What?"

"My ex, Kayla. She got pregnant right before I left for my final deployment. But I didn't know until I was already gone."

Silence. "Oh."

"I was terrified, but fear was something a guy like me couldn't admit. Couldn't talk about. I'd grown up believing a man should be tough. I'd joined the Marines because they were the most badass. I'd been trained to be a killer ruled by self-discipline, and I was fucking good at it. I didn't feel qualified to be a father yet, to raise a child. Not to mention there was a chance my kid wouldn't ever know his dad. I knew plenty of guys tougher than me who didn't come home."

Blair turned toward me slightly.

"But then, as it sank in over the next few weeks, I started to get really excited about it. The idea of this innocent little being who would need me to protect him or her. I pictured all the stuff I'd done with my dad—playing catch, building a treehouse, restoring an old car. Imagining the life ahead of me got me through my worst days."

"So what happened?" she whispered. "Where's the baby now?"

"She had a miscarriage."

"Oh." She reached over and briefly touched my shoulder. "I'm sorry."

"I was shocked at the way the loss fucking gutted me. But again, I couldn't talk to anyone about it."

"You never told *anybody*?"

"No. There was no one to tell. The guys in my unit didn't

talk about their fucking feelings. We were busy trying to keep each other alive."

"What about your family?"

"They never knew either. Kayla had made me promise not to say anything, because she hadn't told her family yet. They were strict and old-fashioned, the kind of people who would have judged us harshly."

"That must have been hard for her," Blair said softly. "For both of you."

I ran a hand over my hair. "The worst came later. She blamed me for losing the baby. She accused me of not wanting it. She said it was the stress of having to deal with the pregnancy on her own that caused the loss. She said if I hadn't re-enlisted, we'd have been married already, and she'd have been able to carry the baby to term. She said it was my fault."

Blair gasped. "Griffin, you know that's not true."

"I used to think it wasn't. But then I started to believe it. You hear a thing enough times, it starts to feel real."

She touched my shoulder again. "It *wasn't*."

"When I got home, I tried everything I could to make things right, to keep my promises. I just wanted to be able to fucking *fix* things, but I couldn't. The damage was done. She finally told me she'd fallen for someone else while I'd been away, someone who'd been there for her when I wasn't."

"Griffin, she was hurt and angry. She wanted to punish you."

"It worked. I was a fucking wreck of a human being until my dad and my friends sat me down and told me to quit being mad at the world because things didn't go the way I'd planned. And I get it. Life is unpredictable, and shit happens. But I never wanted to be in that place again, so that's why I have all the rules."

"To protect yourself?"

"To protect *everyone*." I stood up, grabbed my boxer briefs from the floor and pulled them on.

"But . . . what if the rules are keeping you from moving on? What if they keep you from being happy?"

"The rules keep me from making mistakes," I said, standing as tall as I could, shoulders back. Walls in place. "At least, they're supposed to."

She wrapped her arms around herself again. "What does that mean?"

"It means what we just did was stupid and reckless."

"Is that all?"

I forced myself to say the words. "And it means we need to stop screwing around with each other. Enough is enough."

"*Screwing around with each other*?" Her mouth hung open. "Is that all this is to you?"

"What else would it be?"

"I don't know, Griffin. I guess I kind of thought we had something special."

"Well, you were wrong."

Her eyes shone with tears that threatened to pierce my resolve. "Where is this coming from? One minute you're apologizing for being a dick and opening up about this traumatic thing from your past, and the next minute, you double down on asshole. I have whiplash."

I shrugged, tripling down. "I never made you any promises."

"I never asked for one!"

"But you would have," I said bitterly. "It was only a matter of time."

"The only thing I was going to ask was to keep seeing you." The tears dripped from her eyes, and she angrily swiped at them.

"No. When you leave, this is over."

"Why? We're good together, Griffin. At least we were up until five minutes ago."

"And then what?" I asked, growing agitated, because I didn't know how to make her understand. "We keep seeing each other, and then what?"

"I don't know! We just see where it goes."

"But there's a limit, Blair. There's a limit to how far we can take this. We don't want the same things." I pointed at her. "You want a fairy tale, and I'm no prince."

"That's not true!"

"Yes, it is. Your ten-year plan doesn't look anything like mine."

"But things could change," she wept. "Couldn't they?"

"No." I started pacing at the foot of the bed. "See, this is why I have the rules. And if I would have fucking stuck to them and kept my hands to myself, this wouldn't be happening."

"But you created those rules for yourself when you were hurting—you needed to heal before you could move on."

"I needed to be real about what I was capable of," I said harshly, turning to face her. "And you do too."

She shrank back almost as if I'd slapped her. "So it really was just about the sex for you?"

I looked down at her crying on the bed, and my hands clenched into fists. My arms ached to hold her. But all that would do was postpone the inevitable. "Yes," I lied, knowing I'd never forgive myself for hurting her this way. "You were right all along. I was lonely, and you were here—I took advantage of it, and I'm sorry."

"Liar!" she cried, jumping to her feet. "You're not sorry! All your apologies are lies. I thought you were different, but you're just like everyone else. I never should have trusted you."

Her words cut me to the bone. She was right—I was a liar, but not in the way she thought.

And I didn't have money or fame or status, but I had honor, and it killed me to let her think otherwise. But before I could defend myself—if it was even possible—she raced out of the bedroom and yanked the door shut behind her.

With a heavy sadness I hadn't felt since losing my dad, I sank down onto the bed, head in my hands.

I was alone again.

But it felt terrible.

CHAPTER 18
BLAIR

FIRST THING I did was throw out that stupid anniversary cake, hurling it into the trash with all the might I could muster.

Asshole! How could you do this to me?

Then I spent the night curled into one corner of the couch, crying my eyes out. Bisou eventually found her way over to me and snuggled up in my lap, but it only made me bawl harder.

God, I was so dumb! So naive! Of course he was just in it for the sex! When had a guy ever truly felt something for me, felt it enough to commit to something that would last?

Never. That was the hard truth. Yet I'd been sucked into believing in the possibility, because deep down, Griffin was right—I was nothing but a little girl who wanted to believe in fairy tales.

"Maybe it's time for some rules of my own, Bisou," I whispered fiercely to the cat. "Number one—no more believing everything a man says, because they lie. All of them."

The cat meowed in agreement.

"Number two—I will work and save, so that I am never

dependent on a man again. I will always be able to support myself."

The cat raised a paw, almost like she wanted a high five, so I gave her one.

Then I thought for a moment. "And number three—I will not get my heart set on anything, because it never ends well."

Bisou was silent, and another sob worked its way up from my chest. Burying my face in a pillow so Griffin wouldn't hear me, I cried until my eyes ran dry, and I fell asleep.

When I woke up the next morning, Griffin was gone. With a lump in my throat and horribly puffy eyes, I walked to the bathroom, which was where I discovered I'd gotten my period.

Relieved that at least I didn't have to worry about an unplanned pregnancy, I cleaned up, got dressed, and packed my suitcase. Then I sat on the bed and called Frannie MacAllister.

"Hello?"

"Hi Frannie. It's Blair Beaufort."

"Hey, Blair! How are things?"

"They're fine." I swallowed hard. "Listen, my plans have changed a little, and it turns out I can move up to Cloverleigh Farms sooner than I thought."

"Oh." A beat went by. "Are you okay?"

"Well, yes and no," I said. "Physically, I'm okay, but something happened, and I need to leave Bellamy Creek." To my horror, I started crying again. "I'm sorry, Frannie. This is so embarrassing. But if I can get myself up to Cloverleigh today, would the apartment possibly be ready for me now?"

"Absolutely," she said. "But how are you going to get here? Is your car fixed?"

I'd told Frannie the story of getting stranded in Bellamy Creek during my interview. At the time, we'd thought it was funny. She'd guessed at my feelings for Griffin based on the way I spoke about him, and we'd laughed that if things worked out, we'd have quite the story for our grandchildren someday. Now it seemed ridiculous I'd even entertained the idea of a future together.

"Not yet," I admitted. "Apparently the guy shipped the parts to the wrong address. But I have some cash saved, and I'm going to try to rent a car."

"Listen. Let me call Mack at work and see how busy he is today. Maybe he can come get you."

"No, please," I begged, sniffing. "You're so sweet to offer, but your family is doing enough for me already."

"Nonsense. I'm calling him. If he's in a meeting, he might not get back to me right away, but don't worry, Blair. We'll get you up here as quickly as possible."

"Thank you so much, Frannie. I really appreciate it."

We hung up, and I looked over at the closet door, where my debutante dress still hung. The sight of it brought a fresh round of tears as I recalled different moments—regaining consciousness in Griffin's arms after fainting, his nervous fingers unzipping it later that night, putting it on and pretending to be the princess in the tower.

I had to admit, a lot of our relationship *had* been about the sex. But *all* of it?

I thought back to other times, moments that didn't have anything to do with sex. Sweet, thoughtful things he'd said or done. Helping me out of the truck. Refusing to let me sleep in my car. Teaching me how to jump a dead battery. Doing the dishes after we cooked dinner together. Encouraging me to chase my dreams. Telling me things about his dad. Confiding in me about the sadness he felt after the miscarriage.

Was all that a lie?

Damn it, Griffin, I thought, wiping away tears. *Which version of you is real? The tough, temperamental asshole who tore my heart out last night and stomped on it? Or the good guy with the big heart hiding behind protective defenses?*

I had to face the fact that I might not ever know.

Around noon, I put on some lipstick, stuck my sunglasses on to cover my red, swollen eyes, and dredged up the courage to go down to the garage and tell Griffin goodbye. I'd heard back from Frannie, and her husband Mack would be in Bellamy Creek around five o'clock to pick me up. Until then, I'd find somewhere to wait that wasn't full of memories of the two of us.

Carrying a folder under one arm, I entered the lobby. At the desk was a platinum blond woman I didn't recognize, chewing gum and filing her nails. "Hi there," she said. "If you're looking for the baked goods, we don't have any this morning, not even if you pay me."

"Uh, I'm Blair," I said. "You must be Lanette?"

Her eyes went wide. "You're Blair?"

"Yes." I set the file folder on the counter. "I just wanted to drop this off. Inside are all the details for the anniversary event. You'll find—"

"Do you know how many people came in here looking for you this morning?" Lanette shook her head, her bob swinging. "Like, a hundred. You are *very* popular."

"That's nice, but—"

"I thought Mr. Frankel was going to cry when I said you'd quit."

"Quit?"

"That's what Griffin told me when he called. He said your car would be ready today so he thought you might be heading out of town sooner than expected. You've got another job somewhere or something?"

"Yes," I said, feeling confused. My car would be ready today?

"He also made me promise I wouldn't call his mother and say anything about you leaving. Paid me an extra twenty for it too." She tilted her head. "Are you okay, honey? You look kinda pale."

"Is Griffin here?" I asked, glancing at the door to the garage.

"I assume so. You want me to go get him?"

"Yes, thank you. If he's not too busy, I need to speak with him."

"Sure thing." She hurried from behind the desk into the service bay.

A moment later, she appeared again. "He says he'll be right out."

"Thank you." I faced the window, looking out at the sidewalk and trying to keep my composure.

A few minutes later, I heard his voice.

"Blair."

I turned to see Griffin standing there in the doorway, tall and solid as a fortress. His blue eyes were bloodshot, his hands curled into fists, but his expression gave nothing away.

"Lanette, could you give us a minute?" he asked.

Clearly hoping to witness some drama, Lanette's face fell. She put her purse over her shoulder. "I guess I'll take lunch now. I'll be in the break room."

When we were alone, Griffin cleared his throat and spoke quietly. "Your car is ready. It's in the lot. Keys are on the front seat."

"That's what Lanette said. I don't understand."

"The parts came in yesterday."

It still didn't make sense. "But when did you do the work?"

"Last night. I couldn't sleep, so I came down here and got it done."

"You worked all through the night?" That explained the bloodshot eyes. On closer inspection I saw the dark circles too. The sallow complexion.

He shrugged. "I figured you'd want the option to leave as soon as possible."

The crazy thing was, I didn't. I wanted to fly at him, beat on his chest, fight back, force him to admit I'd meant something to him. I wanted to try again to convince him that what we had was worth a shot.

But I was too afraid of being rejected again. Realistically, he'd probably worked through the night to get rid of me as quickly as he could.

"What do I owe you for the repairs?" I asked.

"Nothing."

"Griffin, please. Tell me what I owe you."

He shook his head, folding his arms over his chest. "You don't owe me anything, Blair."

My lower lip trembled. When he said my name softly like that, I felt like I couldn't breathe.

"Are you okay?" he asked, his voice cracking.

I pushed my sunglasses up on my head. "I'm not pregnant."

He looked relieved. "Are you sure? Already?"

"I'm sure."

"Well . . . that's good."

"Yes. But to answer your question, no. I'm not okay."

"I'm sorry," he said, moving close enough that I could smell the motor oil on him. "I wish things could be different."

"Me too." I laughed, but it wasn't funny. "I wish so many things. Mostly, I wish the man I thought you were really existed."

"He does," Griffin said, his eyes full of torment. "He just can't give you what you want."

"I feel like I must have imagined everything," I said, tears filling my eyes. "Imagined that you cared about me."

"You didn't imagine it."

I shook my head. "Why should I believe anything you say?"

"Because it's the truth." He took me by the shoulders. "I'm sorry about what I said last night. It wasn't just sex, okay? It was a lot more than that, but you have to go now."

"Why?" I said, tears splashing down my cheeks. "If you feel something for me, why are you sending me away?"

"Goddammit, Blair." He crushed his mouth to mine, and in his kiss I felt desperation and agony, a heartbreak that rivaled my own. He broke it off abruptly. "You have to go," he repeated, breathing hard. "I made a mistake keeping you here so long."

"What do you mean, keeping me here?"

"Nothing." He stepped back from me. "Don't make this harder than it has to be."

"I don't understand you, Griffin. If it's so hard to say goodbye, why do it at all? Why can't we give this a chance?"

"Because we just can't!" he yelled. "We're not the same, okay? We're too different. From different worlds. It never would have worked. I'm doing you a favor."

"That's bullshit. I left my superficial world behind looking for someplace better. Someplace real. Someplace that would welcome me with open arms and make me feel like I belonged. Someplace that made me feel loved."

He clenched his jaw. "I hope you find it." Then he shouldered past me and pulled the door open.

What choice did I have?

He was holding the door open for me to leave.

He was holding the door open for me to leave, because he'd had his heart broken in the past. Because he'd spent years building up this emotional armor. Because he wanted to hide behind his rules and his solitude and call it freedom.

I knew he had feelings for me. I knew not all of what we'd shared had been a lie. I knew, if he begged me right now to stay here in this town and take a chance on him, I'd say yes.

But he didn't.

He was holding the door open for me to leave, and there was nothing left for me to do but walk through it.

CHAPTER 19
GRIFFIN

SHE WALKED OUT.

Like I had known she would since the night I met her. Like she was supposed to. Like I wanted her to. So why the sight of her leaving made my chest feel like it was caving in, I had no idea.

I'm not sure how long I'd been standing there wanting to put my fist through all the walls we'd just painted together when Lanette snuck back into the room.

"Wow," she said, her eyes wide. "That was intense. Sorry, I couldn't help overhearing."

Which meant the news of our farewell fight would be all over town by dinnertime.

"Are you okay?" she asked.

"I'm fine."

I stormed back into the garage and stared under the hood of some vehicle without even registering what it was or what I was supposed to be doing. Five minutes after I'd been frozen there like a statue, Handme said, "Hey. Isn't that Blair going by? She's carrying a suitcase. Is she leaving now?"

"Yes," I said, refusing to look out the open bay doors. She'd been wearing that short yellow dress with the flowers that she'd had on the very first day she worked the desk. I loved her in that dress. I loved her in anything. I couldn't believe I would never see her again. Touch her again. Kiss her again.

"Well, should we go say goodbye?"

"Handme, don't you fucking dare."

I tried to work, but my head was a mess. I was exhausted, miserable, angry, resentful, and suffocating with guilt. I had hurt her. I had wrecked something good. I was supposed to feel better now that she was gone, more in control, but I didn't. I felt like I was completely losing my shit.

I took it out on the people around me, of course. I lost my temper with Handme for not folding the towels the way I wanted them. I screamed at McIntyre for an invoicing mistake I'd made a hundred times. I hung up on my mother after she called me demanding to know why she'd heard from at least two people that Blair had suddenly quit working for me and left town. And I was grumpy with Lanette when she came into the garage with a file folder in her hands.

"Hey, have you seen all this?" she asked. "It's really impressive. Blair did a *ton* of work."

"Yes, I've seen it," I snapped. "But I'm too busy to take it over. Give it to my mom or Cheyenne."

"Everything is pretty much organized. Someone just needs to be on site coordinating. I can handle that."

"Fine."

"Although I can't bake like she does. So we'll have to either scratch the sweets table or see if Louise from the diner can do it."

I frowned. No one liked Louise's baking. "Scratch the sweets table."

"Too bad Betty Frankel never had any daughters. I wonder if—"

"Just scratch the damn sweets table, Lanette! Betty and Blair are both gone, and neither of them are coming back!"

Surprised by my outburst, my cousin backed off. "Okay, okay. I'm just trying to help."

I turned back to the engine I was working on, muttering about the constant interruptions, wishing Blair Beaufort had never crashed into my life, and refusing to let my mind wander to her on the road . . . was she okay? Was she halfway there yet? Was she still crying? Had she believed me when I told her that she hadn't imagined I cared?

Because I did. And for the rest of my days, I'd probably remember the two weeks I spent with her as the most fun, the most happy, the most alive I'd ever felt.

After leaving the shop later than usual—I wasn't looking forward to going home alone—I locked the door behind me and trudged slowly up the stairs to my apartment, thinking about all the times I'd followed her up the steps.

Inside, I stopped and looked around. It was big and empty and silent. Even Bisou was nowhere to be seen. I inhaled, but there was no lingering scent of something baking in the oven, no hint of Blair's perfume or shampoo.

I walked back to my bedroom and saw that her suitcase was gone, the bed was made, and her dress no longer hung on the back of my closet door. A pang of regret stabbed me in the side.

I'd made a mistake.

I'd been wrong to send her away. Wrong and mean and stupid, and now I was going to spend all my nights alone in this bed where she'd made me feel so good.

I wanted her back.

Panicked, I grabbed my phone from my back pocket and was about to call her when a text came in from Cole, asking if I wanted to take a run with him. It reminded me of the last run we'd taken, when he'd prodded me about dating Blair long-distance, and I'd insisted that wasn't going to happen, because I didn't want my life to change.

I looked at my bed. At the closet door. At the phone.

If I made this call, it would change everything. I'd have to admit I'd been wrong—to everyone, not just Blair. To my mother, my sister, my friends, my co-workers, this town.

I'd have to acknowledge I'd been weak. That I wasn't as strong as I'd bragged about being. That there was someone who had such a powerful hold over me after only two weeks that I was willing to take back all the things I'd said and upend my life to be with her.

I couldn't bring myself to do it.

This was temporary, and it would pass. I'd gotten through hard times before, right? I'd lost people who'd mattered to me, people I loved. I'd hit rock bottom. I'd clawed my way out. I'd made my peace with the kind of life I'd have.

Ignoring the text for now, I took a shower and crashed into bed. It was impossible not to feel surrounded by the memory of her—I could still smell her shampoo on the pillow. Bisou wandered in and nosed around the room like she was looking for something—or someone—and then jumped up on the bed, tucking herself in along my side, sort of the way Blair used to. She meowed a few times, and I stroked her soft black and white fur.

"Sorry, Bisou. She's gone, and you're stuck with me."

The cat continued to make sad little noises, but I shut my eyes and fell asleep.

CHAPTER 20
BLAIR

AFTER LEAVING Griffin in the lobby, I'd gone directly upstairs and texted Frannie that I wouldn't need a ride after all because my car was ready. She'd texted back right away.

Oh, that's good news! her message read. **Drive carefully and call me when you get to town.**

Next I'd said goodbye to Bisou, hugging her close to me as I choked back tears. *"Tu vas me manquer, ma chatounette."*

Then, with my heart in pieces, I grabbed my suitcase, folded my white dress over one arm, left Griffin's spare key on the table, and walked out.

Sunglasses back in place, I didn't even look in the windows of the lobby when I passed by, and I kept my head straight and my chin up as I passed the open service bays. Was he watching?

In the lot, I found my car, and opened the trunk. Inside it were jumper cables, which made my throat catch and my nose tingle. Pushing them aside, I loaded my suitcase in the trunk and carefully laid my dress on top of it. For a moment, I stood there looking at the gown, remembering how I'd thought it would bring me good luck. Hope. Opportunity. But now every time I looked at it, I'd think of Griffin, and he was now the opposite of all those things.

On impulse, I grabbed the dress from the trunk and marched over to the dumpster.

But I couldn't bring myself to actually open the lid and toss it in.

Instead, I draped it over the top before hurrying back to my car and sliding behind the wheel. Through tears, I grabbed the keys off the passenger seat and started the engine.

I pulled out of the lot and turned right onto Main Street, although I had no idea where I was going. I drove aimlessly for several blocks, realizing I was going to have to pull over and use the GPS on my phone to get to Cloverleigh Farms.

But when I came to the stop sign at Center Avenue, I remembered that I'd never visited Mr. Frankel for tea. I had no idea whether he'd be home or not, and I didn't have that pie I'd promised him, but I figured I'd at least try to honor my word to stop in. He'd seemed so happy when I said I would.

I turned onto the pretty, tree-lined street, admiring the colorfully painted Victorians on either side. I remembered Mr. Frankel had said his address was 910, and found it on the second block. Turning around in the driveway, I pulled up at the curb in front of his house, a beautiful Queen Anne right out of a storybook, complete with wraparound porch, bay windows, stained glass, and even a turret fit for a princess. Its roof shingles were dark red, and it was painted a deep shade of moss green with amber trim.

I took a moment to blow my nose and mop up my eyes, but in the end there wasn't much I could do to make it less obvious I'd been crying. Hopefully, Mr. Frankel's eyes weren't as sharp as Lanette's.

At the front door, I knocked three times. Less than a minute later, Mr. Frankel pulled it open. His face lit up. "Blair!" he exclaimed. "I thought you'd left town!"

"I'm on my way out," I told him, "but I remembered I'd promised you a visit."

"Have you come for tea?"

"I have," I said, holding up my empty hands. "But I'm afraid I'm *sans* apple pie."

"Oh, that's all right. My housekeeper, Mrs. Moon, made some lemon cookies this morning. They're not as good as anything you bake," he added in a stage whisper, "but they're better than nothing."

I smiled. "That sounds lovely. Should I wait out here or help you with the tea?"

"I'll get the tea and cookies. You have a seat out here on the porch." He started to go back in the house and then smiled at me again. "I'm so glad you came by. I was about to go down to the store just to have someone to talk to."

"I'm glad too, Mr. Frankel. I could use a friend today as well."

He nodded like he understood. "Some days are just like that. I'll be right back."

Two hours later, I was still sitting out on the porch with him, finishing a third glass of iced tea, laughing at his terrible old man jokes and listening with rapt attention to all his stories about growing up in Bellamy Creek. I especially loved hearing about how he'd fallen in love with brown-eyed Betty Brinkerhoff the day he first saw her in the second grade, but he hadn't worked up the nerve to talk to her until high school.

"Her family owned the diner, and I'd go there every day after school for a chocolate soda just to see her behind the counter," he reminisced. "I didn't even like chocolate soda."

I laughed. "True love."

"I finally invited her to go to a movie with me, and her answer was, 'Well, it's about time, Charlie Frankel.' I think I asked her to marry me on our first date," he said, chuckling fondly. "And she said she would."

"That's sweet," I said. "Sometimes you meet someone, and you just know."

He nodded. "Exactly right. And if you know, what's the use of wasting a whole lot of time hemming and hawing about it? Everyone said we were too young to get married—we were only eighteen—but I'm telling you, we just knew. And we had seventy years together. Isn't that incredible?"

My throat tightened. "Yes. It is."

He sighed. "I miss her every single day. But I feel lucky I had her as long as I did."

"I've heard wonderful things about her baking," I said. "That apple pie must have been something else."

"It was. It was."

"Do you know that's what brought me to Bellamy Creek? I saw the sign on the highway advertising the best apple pie in the Midwest since 1957, so I got off the road and came looking for it."

"Isn't that something?" Mr. Frankel looked pleased.

"Of course, I was sad to learn the pie doesn't exist anymore."

He shook his head. "No one can replicate it, although plenty have tried. But Betty had a secret recipe she never shared with anyone. It won a national contest. That's how she got such a big reputation."

"Wow. I'm impressed."

"I always told her she should open up her own bakery, but she never wanted to. She said she was content baking pies and things in small batches for the diner just like her mother had, and raising her family. She volunteered a lot too. She loved this town. And people loved her."

"I can tell."

"She was special," he said, getting misty-eyed. "And I want people to remember her. If just anyone could bake that pie, they'd forget her."

I reached out and put my hand on his arm. "I don't think this town will forget her. I never even met her, but I can picture her behind the counter just like you described, with her big brown eyes and curly dark hair, wearing a white apron and waiting every day for you to come in for a chocolate soda you hated."

The smile was back on his face. "She knew I hated it too. Later she confessed she and her sister Louise would laugh about how funny my face looked as I choked the last of it down."

I laughed, patting his arm before rising to my feet. "Thank you for sharing your memories with me. I needed to smile today."

"Anytime." He stood too. "I'm sad you're leaving, Blair. I've really enjoyed your company, and we've talked all about me the entire time." He shook his head. "Betty would be in fits!"

"That's all right. I don't really have a story to tell yet anyway. I'm sort of . . . a thirty-year-old work in progress." I smiled and felt my throat catch. "But I hope I find a happily ever after as wonderful as yours."

He smiled. "You will."

"You think so?"

"I know it. Now you might have to be a little patient," he said as he walked me down the porch steps toward my car. "As my wife would attest if she could, sometimes it takes boys more time than it takes girls to work up the kind of courage you need for a love story. I mean, even two people who are meant to be together are going to have their trying times and misunderstandings. You're going to say things and hear things that sting. But you don't give up."

I turned to face him. "I won't."

"Thank you for coming to see me today. I don't get many visitors."

Something occurred to me. "Mr. Frankel, do you know Doris Applebee?"

"Sure, I know Doris. She grew up over on Elizabeth Street. I knew her husband Roy too. He passed a few years back."

"Well, Mrs. Applebee was in the garage the other day, and she happened to mention how much she loves chatting about local history. In fact, she mentioned some interest in putting together a walking tour of the historic district."

"Did she? That's a good idea."

"I think so too, and with your knowledge of the homes on this street and your family's heritage, I think you'd be a real asset to her. Maybe you could invite her for tea sometime."

"Oh, I don't know." Mr. Frankel looked distressed. "People might talk."

"So let them!"

"And she might not want a partner on the project."

"Well, you can find out, can't you?"

"And I wouldn't want anyone to think I was trying to replace Betty."

"I don't think a single soul would imagine that."

"I'll . . . I'll consider it." Lost in thought a moment, he gathered himself and focused on me. "Now don't be a stranger, okay? You come back and see me. Turn off the highway when you see the sign for the pie."

Laughing, I rose up and kissed his cheek. "I will. But they should probably take that sign down, don't you think?"

His cheeks turned red. "Can I tell you a secret?"

"Sure."

"That's my sign. I keep it up because I want people to remember her," he said sheepishly. "But I'm sorry that it led you off course."

"You know what?" I smiled at him, even though my heart

was heavy. "I think the best journeys have a lot of twists and turns, don't you? They're not just a straight line. And you have to be open to following your heart and seeing where the road takes you. My heart brought me here, and I'm not sorry."

But as I drove out of town and got on the highway, I cried like a baby.

CHAPTER 21
GRIFFIN

THE NIGHT AFTER BLAIR LEFT, we lost our baseball game to the Mavericks.

It wasn't the championship game or anything, but it was the final game of the regular season, and losing to them sucked.

The entire game was a shit show. Moretti reinjured his groin sliding into third, Cole threw more balls than strikes thanks to his sore shoulder, and I got into it with the first base ump after he made a bad call in the bottom of the ninth. The Mavs' runner was clearly out—I know I was on the bag with the ball in my glove when he ran past me, but the call was "safe."

Since I was already in a shit mood, my temper flared and I argued it, getting in the guy's face, poking my finger against his chest, asking him if he was fucking blind or just stupid.

Of course, he threw me out of the game, and I called him some other names I regret, because then he started threatening to ban me from the league.

From behind the plate, Beckett pushed his catcher's mask up and came jogging over to first base. "Hey, hey," he said, pushing me back from the ump. "That's enough. What are you doing?"

"This guy's a fucking asshole," I said. "He can't throw me out of the league."

"Wanna bet?" said the ump, going toe to toe with me again.

Beckett pushed me back again and stepped between us, facing me. "My guess is that he can, Griff, so just calm down, okay? This isn't like you. Smithy's gonna come in and cover first. You go sit down."

"No. Fuck this guy."

"I said *go sit down*." Beckett glared at me, and since I didn't want to get in a fight with him too, I tugged my cap lower on my forehead and shouldered past both of them. After striding over to the dugout, I threw my glove to the ground, and plunked myself onto the bench next to Cole, who was sitting with a plastic bag of ice on his shoulder. He said nothing as the game started up again, which pissed me off.

"What?" I said angrily.

He glanced at me. "I didn't say anything."

"The guy was out," I stated as if Cole had argued with me.

"Okay."

"That ump is a fucking moron."

Silence.

"What, you don't agree with me?"

"I don't know if that guy's a moron or not. But I know my daughter is in the stands watching this game."

"Sorry," I muttered, feeling guilty for the first time.

We watched as the Mavs scored two more runs, and we struggled to get to two outs.

"We look like shit tonight," Cole said, shaking his head. "We're just not playing good ball."

"The calls have been against us all night," I insisted.

"Maybe. But we're making a lot of mistakes too. We're just not on."

"Yeah." Watching Moretti blow an easy throw to first, I shook my head. "Maybe you're right. I know I'm off tonight."

Cole readjusted the pack on his shoulder. "I heard Blair left town yesterday."

"From who?"

"A few people." He was silent a minute. "You gonna see her again?"

"I already told you. *No.*"

"That her choice or yours?"

"It was a mutual decision," I lied. "And I'm done talking about it."

"Okay."

The game ended five minutes later when the Mavs' biggest hitter homered with two guys on.

"At least our record still gets us into the championship game," said Cole as we packed up.

"We better get our shit together by next weekend." I glanced at his shoulder. "Rest that arm."

"I will."

The guys all wanted to go drown their sorrows at the pub, but I decided to call it a night. I wasn't in the mood for people, even my friends. Instead, I offered to take Mariah out for ice cream and told Cole I'd drop her off at home afterward. "Is that cool?"

"Yes!" Mariah jumped up and down and clapped her hands. "Say yes, Dad!"

Cole shrugged. "I guess it's okay."

"Good." Then I tugged one of Mariah's braids. "I'd have taken you no matter what he said."

She grinned. "Can we go to the place by the water with the waffle cones?"

"We can go anywhere you want."

"Why don't you come by the pub after you drop her off?" Cole asked.

"Nah," I said. "I don't feel like it tonight."

Twenty minutes later, I was walking along the pier next to Mariah, who was doing her best to devour a massive amount of Mackinac Island Fudge ice cream in a waffle cone. The sun was going down, but it was still hot out, and rivulets of chocolate were running down her face, the cone, and her hands.

"We should have gotten more napkins," I said. "You're a mess."

"I don't care." She licked the inside of her wrist. "I saw you get mad during the game."

"Yeah. Sorry about that."

"You said cuss words."

"I did. Sometimes I do that when I get mad. But it wasn't very nice."

"When Daddy says those words, Grandma says she's going to wash his mouth out with soap."

I laughed. "She's been threatening to do that since your dad was your age."

"Did you know my dad when he was my age?"

"I did."

"What was he like?"

"Hmm, let's see. He was a fast runner—but not faster than me—and a great swimmer, and he loved Power Rangers and magic tricks—although he wasn't very good at them."

Mariah giggled. "He still isn't."

"But he was the nicest guy in the class, and everyone wanted to be his friend."

"What did you guys like to do during the summer?"

I thought back to those hot, sticky, sunny summers of our youth. "We played a lot of baseball. We rode our bikes. There used to be a treehouse in my backyard, and we spent a lot of time in there."

"Doing what?"

"I don't even remember. Talking about baseball and trying

to keep out the girls." I paused. "Until we wanted them to notice us."

She was quiet for a minute, trying to keep up with the melting ice cream. "Did you know my mom?"

"I sure did."

"What was she like?"

I remembered what Cole had said about Mariah being curious about her mother and afraid to ask him. My heart ached as I thought for a moment, trying to remember all the best things about Trisha. "She was really cool. She was a softball player, and we used to joke she could hit better than your dad. She was crazy smart and teachers loved her. She was our class president. And she was a really good nurse too. One time, I cut myself on something at work and she came over and stitched me up."

"She did?" Mariah looked impressed.

"Yes. And it didn't even hurt."

"Grandma says I look like her."

I glanced down at her and smiled. "I agree. And that's a very good thing because your mom was cute but your dad looks like a grumpy old troll."

She giggled. "Sometimes he acts like one too."

We walked a little longer in silence. Mariah finished the cone and licked her fingers, palms, and wrists. Even so, she was a mess when I dropped her off at Cole's house—chocolate ice cream like a beard on her face and all over the front of her pink shirt.

"Sorry," I said to Mrs. Mitchell at the door. "She's a little chocolaty."

Cole's mom laughed and patted Mariah's head. "That's okay. She's going straight into the tub. Did you have fun, sweetie?"

"Yes!"

"Say thank you."

Mariah turned and wrapped her arms around my waist,

her cheek pressed against my ribs. "Thank you, Uncle Griffin."

I hugged her back. "You're welcome."

"I love you," she said, surprising me. She'd never told me that before.

"I love you too, kiddo." I couldn't even remember the last time I'd told someone that. Or heard someone say it to me. I'd forgotten how deeply the words could burrow into your bones.

On my way home, I thought about how lucky Cole was to have a daughter.

Back in my apartment, I popped the cap off a cold beer and studied the contents of my fridge. Blair had gone grocery shopping while she was here, so there was a lot more to choose from than usual, but I didn't feel like making anything. I was about to order a pizza when I heard someone knock on my door.

Puzzled, I went down the stairs, beer in hand. The door had no glass pane, so I had to open it to see who was there.

It was my sister.

She held up a brown paper bag. "I have food. Can I come in?"

"I guess. Since you have food."

She followed me up the stairs and started unpacking takeout from the pub on the kitchen island. "When you didn't show up, I figured you were back here nursing your sore ego, so I thought I'd play good sister and bring you dinner."

I gave her the finger. "Want a beer?"

"Yes, please." She took the plastic cover off a container

holding a burger and fries and lifted the top of the bun before sliding it toward me. "This one's yours. Mine has no onion."

I popped the cap off a bottle of Two Hearted Ale and handed it to her. "Thanks."

Cheyenne sat on one of the island stools across from where I stood, and we dug into the meal. "So," she said after a couple minutes. "Rough game."

"Yeah."

"You'll get 'em next weekend."

"I hope so." I took a long swallow of my beer.

"That doesn't sound like your usual cocky self talking."

I shrugged. Took another sip.

"Poor Cole," she said with a sigh. "Do you think his arm will be okay?"

"If he rests it." Then I couldn't resist a little jab. "Why don't you offer him a massage?"

She rolled her eyes. "Very funny."

"Come on. You've been wanting to get your hands on him for twenty years."

"What?" she shrieked. "I have not."

"Please." I took a huge bite of my burger and chewed while I watched her face go from pink to purple. "I'm not an idiot."

She grabbed her beer and tipped it up. "Does he know?"

"I have no idea. He's never said anything to me about it."

"You can't tell him," she said. "Ever."

"Why would I tell him?"

"I don't know." She set her beer down, picked up a fry and put it down again. "Now my stomach hurts."

"For fuck's sake, it's not that big of a deal."

"Yes it is, Griffin!"

"So if you feel that strongly about it, why not ask him out or something?"

"Because I can't! I just can't." She shook her head. "And anyway, he always says he doesn't want to date."

"True," I admitted. "Guess it sucks to be you."

Frowning, she picked up the fry again and threw it at me. "You're such an asshole."

"I'm kidding." I picked up the fry from the floor and tossed it into the trash. "And maybe he does want to date, but he's worried about Mariah."

"What makes you say that?"

"I don't know. I'm just thinking that it can't be easy to think about dating when you're trying to raise a kid on your own. He worries about her all the time. In fact, I meant to ask you if you knew any child therapists. He's looking for one."

"He is?" Cheyenne's face grew concerned. "Is Mariah okay?"

"I think so, but she's dealing with some stuff, and he thought it would be helpful for her to talk about it with someone that's not him."

She nodded. "Totally. And yes, I do. Should I reach out to him?"

I thought for a moment. "You know what, I'll tell him to reach out to you."

"Perfect."

We finished eating and opened two more beers. "So can I ask about her now?" Cheyenne ventured.

"No."

"Griffin, come on. What happened?"

I took a long drink. "I made a mistake."

"How so?"

"Letting her stay here."

"Well, what choice did you have? Blair was broker than her car, Mom was being top-shelf manipulative, and every place around here was booked. She had nowhere to go, Griff. Were you supposed to put her on the street?"

I said nothing and took another sip.

"I mean, I guess you could have loaned her some money

so she could've stayed at the motel and rented a car. But you liked having her around, didn't you?"

"For a while."

"I could tell. So what changed? Why the big blow-up?"

I rolled my eyes. "I take it Lanette called you."

"I saw her at the game tonight."

Shrugging, I tipped my beer up again. "It was bound to happen."

"Was it? I had lunch with Blair last week, and all she did was gush about you the *entire* time. I literally almost vomited in my lap, it was so disgusting. She has real feelings for you, Griff."

"What did she say?" I asked, then immediately regretted it. "Never mind. I don't want to know."

"She called you a real man. She said how much she admired you for your work ethic, and your honesty, and your commitment to Dad's legacy."

"I said I didn't want to know," I snapped.

"She mentioned your bravery, the fact that you served your country. She hadn't heard about your Silver Star, but don't worry, I filled her in about that."

I breathed hard, my nostrils flaring.

"And then there was all this stuff about your blue eyes, or maybe it was your big hands or your muscles—I don't know, I was pretty grossed out, so I made her stop talking."

"Can I make *you* stop talking?"

"My point is," she went on, "the woman wants to be with you, Griff. Like, really, really wants to be with you."

"Well, I'm sorry, but it's not possible."

She stared at me, took a sip of her beer, and sighed. "I wasn't going to do this, but okay."

"Do what?"

"I know about the parts."

"What parts?" I asked, although I had a sinking feeling I knew exactly.

"The parts for her car that came in more than a week before you actually installed them."

Furious, I finished off my beer and cracked open another. "Fucking McIntyre. He told Emily?"

"Uh huh."

I shook my head. "I swear to God, there is *no* privacy in this town."

"I'm not judging you, brother." She held up her hands. "I get it. You didn't want her to leave. What I *don't* get is why you didn't want her to stay."

There was no way to make her understand without telling her the entire painful history, and I just couldn't bring myself to do it. I loved my sister, but I couldn't share everything with her.

Not like I could with Blair.

The realization that I trusted Blair more than I'd ever trusted anyone made me squirm. "I realized I'm better off alone, okay? Let's leave it at that."

She sighed. "Whatever you say." Then she looked around. "Where's Bisou? You'll be glad to know I think I found a home for her."

"Already?"

"Yeah. Just waiting on final confirmation." Then she looked at me. "If that's okay. You can keep her if you'd like. I just thought—"

"I'll keep her."

Cheyenne's eyebrows rose. "Really?"

"Yeah. I want to keep her."

What the hell was I doing? That damn cat was just another reminder of Blair, and I didn't need it.

I already had one hanging in my closet.

CHAPTER 22
BLAIR

I COULD NOT HAVE ASKED for a better start to my new life.

My carriage house apartment was adorable, fully furnished, and perfectly sized for one person. Frannie's parents, John and Daphne Sawyer, could not have been nicer or more welcoming. The evening I arrived, they insisted I join them for dinner along with Frannie's family. On Sunday, I was invited to supper again, and I got to meet all five Sawyer sisters, their significant others, and Frannie's niece and nephews.

They were a huge, loving, noisy bunch, and they made me feel right at home.

But something was missing. I felt like I'd left a piece of me behind.

It wasn't that I was unhappy—I wasn't. I just missed him. I wanted to hear how he was doing. Was business picking up at the garage? Were people excited about the anniversary event? Did anyone ask about me? Had they won their old man baseball game?

More importantly, did he ever think of me? Did he lie

awake remembering things we'd said and done? Did he regret pushing me away?

Or was he happier being alone?

The unanswerable questions tortured me endlessly.

Thankfully, I had work to distract me, and I threw myself into making a fresh start with everything I had.

The coffee shop opened at seven, and I'd arrive by six, turn on the oven, throw on my apron, put my hair up with a bandana, and get to work. Frannie's kitchen actually had windows, which was amazing because many kitchens can feel like dungeons.

The morning routine, performed like a ballet while the sun came up, was comforting to me. First, I'd pull the yeast doughs from the cooler. While they were proofing, I'd start the scones. Frannie and I had discussed the menu and decided on two batches of sweet and one savory each day.

While the scones were in the oven, I'd fill the case up front with items made the day before—cakes, shortbread, galette, strata. At this point, I'd often enjoy a quick cup of coffee, inhaling the scent of baking scones and my favorite dark roast with a little cream. Frannie would arrive by seven to greet customers, and I loved hearing them ask who the new baker was and compliment my pastries.

The break didn't last long, though, because there were cookies to bake, dough to make, questions to answer about specific ingredients because of allergies, and the occasional introduction to a happy customer who wanted to meet me. I was always hustling to keep the cases filled and rarely got a lunch break, but that was okay. Being busy meant less time for my mind to wander toward Bellamy Creek.

By three o'clock, I'd be dead on my feet, and Frannie would try to shoo me home. "Go," she'd say. "You open, I close. Remember?"

But I didn't mind staying to help her close up, and we

often ended up having one last cup of coffee and chatting at the long marble counter.

I really did love the job, and I was so grateful to Frannie for giving me the opportunity.

But that tug on my heart refused to leave me be.

If only it wasn't trying to pull me back where I wasn't wanted.

One afternoon a week after I'd arrived, Frannie poked her head into the kitchen just after closing and smiled. "Hey. You have a visitor."

"I do?" Immediately I thought of Griffin—he knew where the coffee shop was, after all—but I didn't want to get my hopes up. Still, I brushed some flour from my apron and tightened the bandana knot on the top of my head.

But when I walked out, it was Cheyenne I saw.

"Hey stranger," she said with a grin.

"Cheyenne!" Excited to see her, I flew around the counter and hugged her. "What a great surprise! It's so good to see you."

"You too. How are you?"

"I'm good. Busy."

"Frannie said things are going well here."

"She's amazingly talented," said Frannie, who was wiping down the glass cases.

My cheeks warmed, and I tucked my hands into my apron pockets. "I really love it here. The shop is great, the people are so nice, and Frannie's family has been wonderful."

"She's like an honorary Sawyer sister already," joked Frannie. "My dad can't get enough of her southern comfort strata. I think he's been in here every day this week for lunch!"

Cheyenne smiled. "That's wonderful."

"How's *your* family?" I asked.

"Well, my mother still isn't speaking to me, and Griffin isn't speaking much to anybody."

"Why isn't your mother speaking to you?" asked Frannie.

"Because I aided and abetted the escape of her future daughter-in-law, AKA the mother of her future grandchildren."

"Griffin isn't speaking to anybody?" I wasn't sure how I felt about the news. I went back and forth between wanting him to be as heartbroken as I was and hoping he was doing okay.

"Nope. And when he does, he's grouchy as a bear." Cheyenne dropped onto a counter stool. "The damn fool is lost without you, but he's too stubborn to admit it."

"Men," said Frannie with vehemence, rubbing at a stubborn smudge on the glass. "What's Griffin's problem exactly?"

"His last relationship ended badly," I said, hoping I wasn't betraying a confidence. "And he sort of made up his mind at that juncture of his life that being alone suited him better."

"But everybody has baggage," Frannie said. "Right?"

"Griff also gets a lot of pressure from our mom to 'find a nice girl and settle down,'" added Cheyenne, hooking her fingers into air quotes. "And there is nothing that makes my brother angrier than being told what to do. He's got an independent streak a mile long, always has. Frankly, I'm surprised he lasted as long as he did in the military."

"I think he liked the military for what it taught him about self-discipline," I said.

"He needed it." Cheyenne laughed. "All that adrenaline was too much for one small town when he was young. But it's amazing to me the way you understand him, Blair. It's so obvious how good you are together."

I shrugged helplessly. "Not much I can do if he doesn't feel the way I feel."

"But he *does*." Cheyenne banged her palm on the marble. "That's what kills me—he *does*. I can see it. My mother sees it. The whole *town* sees it!"

"You know, if it makes you feel any better, Blair, Mack gave me a really hard time too," offered Frannie.

"Really?" It shocked me, because he was so crazy in love with her now.

"Oh, God yes. You can ask his girls sometime. He was awful. He ended things because he was convinced that he would never get married again or have more children, and he knew I wanted those things. He looked at it like he was doing me a favor—breaking it off quickly so that I'd move on and find the right person for me."

"That's what Griffin said too! That he was doing me a favor." I shook my head as my eyes filled. "But it's not true."

"Of course it's not," Frannie said, taking my hand. "What he's doing is what Mack did—retreating so he doesn't have to deal with his baggage. Face his fears."

"Exactly," Cheyenne said.

"And the worst thing is, there's nothing you can do about it." Frannie squeezed my hand. "He just has to be miserable enough without you to come to the conclusion that what you have is worth the risk."

"I don't think that's ever going to happen," I said sadly. "And the sooner I face reality, the better."

"Listen, my bullheaded brother isn't really why I came to see you. I have something for you." Cheyenne pulled a large yellow envelope from her bag and slid it across the counter toward me.

"What is it?" I picked up the envelope and looked at it. On the outside, my name was written in wiggly black ink.

"It's from Charlie Frankel," she said with a giggle. "Maybe it's a love letter."

"Who's Charlie Frankel?" asked Frannie.

"He's a cute old widowed man in our town with a gigantic crush on Blair," said Cheyenne. "He was devastated when she left Bellamy Creek."

"He liked my baking," I explained, sliding my finger along the envelope's seal.

Cheyenne laughed. "I'm pretty sure he liked the entire package. He's rich too, you know. Maybe he can be your sugar daddy."

I rolled my eyes. "No, no. He's more like the grandpa I never had."

"Anyway, he went over to the garage and gave this to my mother—she's back behind the desk now—and Mom asked me if I could get it to you. I was going to mail it, but I decided to come for a visit instead."

"She called me yesterday to tell me she was driving up," explained Frannie with a guilty smile, "but I wasn't allowed to say anything."

"It's a great surprise," I said, smiling as I pulled two pieces of paper from the envelope. "Thank you."

"So what is it?" Frannie asked curiously.

The top page was a handwritten note from Mr. Frankel on plain white paper. "Looks like a letter and . . ." I looked at the second page, which was considerably older than the first. It was lined paper that might have been white once upon a time, but was yellowed now, its texture as soft as cotton, its corners frayed. I gasped. "It's a recipe!"

The handwriting was faded, but I could make it out. Betty's Apple Pie, it said at the top.

I scanned the list of ingredients and the instructions as a lump formed in my throat. I could see how over time, she'd adjusted things, changed her mind about certain amounts or techniques or spices. "Lard in the crust, doesn't surprise me. But cardamom does!" I exclaimed in surprise. "She used cardamom in her filling!"

"Is that . . ." Cheyenne's tone was reverent, her eyes wide. "Is that *Betty Frankel's* apple pie recipe?"

"Yes," I said.

"Oh, my God! It exists!" Cheyenne squealed. "All these years there were people who claimed to have seen it, but no one was ever able to find it. It was like the Loch Ness Monster of Bellamy Creek!"

"Who's Betty Frankel?" asked Frannie.

While Cheyenne explained the story, I turned to Mr. Frankel's letter and read it with tears in my eyes.

Dear Blair,

I hope this letter finds you well. Since you left Bellamy Creek, I have been doing a lot of thinking about different things you said. I want to thank you again for visiting me and listening to me ramble on about the past. It meant so much to me.

But I have been thinking about the future too, and I have realized that you were right about life's journey being full of twists and turns. Some of the most joyful things in my life were the most unexpected, born of following my heart. I hope you continue to follow yours.

You mentioned ending up in Bellamy Creek because of Betty's apple pie. Although that pie hasn't existed here in several years, I am sending you this recipe in the hope that it may again someday. (And then, you see, that little twist will become a loop . . . and perhaps a knot will be tied.)

Or perhaps I am just a silly old man with romantic notions. I will leave that to you.

Anyway, I kept the recipe to myself in the years since I lost Betty for several reasons—denial that she was never coming back, a selfish desire to keep something of her to myself, fear that if someone else were to bake her pie the magic surrounding her memory would vanish. But I know better now. And I trust you with her legacy.

She would have loved your generous spirit . . . even if she might have been a little envious at how much I enjoy your baking!

Sincerely yours,

Charlie Frankel

P.S. I have taken your advice and contacted Doris Applebee about the idea of a historic walking tour. We are meeting Friday afternoon for tea to discuss it. I suppose I am still a work in progress at age eighty-eight!

"What did he say?" asked Cheyenne.

"He said he kept the recipe to himself for personal reasons, but now wants me to have it because he trusts me with her legacy," I said, wiping away tears.

"Oh, that's so sweet." Frannie put a hand over her heart.

"It really is," Cheyenne added, her eyes shining. "Are you going to bake it?"

"I want to. But it doesn't feel right to just bake it and sell it here, you know?"

"Hmm." Cheyenne thought for a moment. "Hey, I've got an idea. Why not bake some for the cakewalk my mom organized for the anniversary event at the garage this weekend?"

"She organized a cakewalk for the event?"

"Yes, and ticket sales will benefit the animal shelter."

I smiled. "That's a great idea."

"So you'll do it? I think there would be a lot of excitement once word got around that Betty's apple pies are up for grabs!"

I nodded. "Definitely. What are you serving in the lobby with coffee?"

Cheyenne looked guilty. "Store-bought cookies."

"Good Lord. No." I shook my head. "Let's think—today is Thursday, the event is Saturday. I can make them tomorrow, along with a sheet cake for the lobby, and then drive them down in the morning."

"That would be perfect," Cheyenne gushed.

"I would be happy to help," offered Frannie. "You can use the kitchen here, and we can even bring the girls in on it. You'll have five sets of hands."

"You're the best, Frannie." I smiled at her. "I'd love that."

"So I'll see you Saturday morning?" Cheyenne asked.

"Yes. But Cheyenne . . ." I stopped and took a breath. "I don't want to run into Griffin. Can I just drop everything at your mom's house?"

"Of course," she said. "But are you sure you don't want to just stop in and say hi? Maybe it would kick his ass into gear."

"Feel free to take the entire day off," Frannie said generously. "The girls and I can cover the shop."

I shook my head. "No. He made his wishes very clear when he told me to go. Seeing him won't help."

Cheyenne sighed. "I understand."

Frannie and Cheyenne invited me to have dinner with them, but I declined—I had a lot of baking to do. I did, however, ask Cheyenne if she'd mind stopping by Cloverleigh Farms before she drove home. I wanted to show her my new apartment, but I also wanted to send something back to Bellamy Creek with her.

She said she would, so after they left, I went home and baked up a batch of blueberry lemon thyme scones for Mr. Frankel. Then I ran out to the drug store and grabbed a card. I wanted to write back, thanking him for his kindness.

Dear Mr. Frankel,

What a wonderful surprise I got today! Thank you so much for sending me a letter, and for the precious gift of Betty's apple pie recipe. I have been reading over it nonstop, and I've so enjoyed imagining her rolling out the crust, adding a little more of this or that to the filling, brushing the top with cream and sprinkling the sugar on top. I cannot wait to try it out this weekend.

I understand completely your reasons for keeping the recipe close to your heart, and I do not believe anyone would blame you. I certainly don't. But I also love that you're looking toward the future now rather than clinging to the past. You deserve a lot more happy days!

Get that historic walk all planned out—I hereby request you take me on it someday. Bellamy Creek is such a lovely place, and I think of it often. I hope you enjoy these scones and think of me fondly.

You take care of yourself, my friend.

Sincerely,

Blair Beaufort

P.S. I like thinking of us both as works in progress. If we were already masterpieces, there would be nothing to do!

I sealed the card inside the envelope and slipped it beneath the string of the cardboard bakery box full of scones.

When Cheyenne arrived, she marveled over my carriage house home, took a walk with me across the grounds, peeked inside the inn and winery, and gave me a tight goodbye hug in the driveway. "I'm so glad to see you doing so well," she said.

"Thanks. I really do love it here."

"But . . ." she said as she released me, because she knew.

"But I miss him." I wrapped my arms around myself. "I keep waiting for the morning I wake up and he's not the first thing I think about. Or the night when he's not the last thing. I know it's only been a week or so since I left him, but it just feels like this ache is never going to go away."

She sighed. "Don't give up, okay?"

My throat closed. "I don't want to feel this way forever."

"You won't." She bit her lip. "I shouldn't tell you this, because he'd string me up by my toes if he found out, but then again, he's the one being a big jerk. And I have gone over the conversation again and again, and I swear he didn't *specifically* tell me not to tell you."

Dizzy, I shook my head. "I speak three languages and I'm still not sure what you just said."

She took a breath and closed her eyes a second. "Griffin had the parts for your car for over a week before he put them in."

My mouth fell open. "What?"

"He didn't install them because he didn't want you to go."

"I don't believe it!"

"Believe it. McIntyre found them, confronted him, and he admitted it. Oh, he made up some bullshit story about wanting to surprise you, but we both know what's what. McIntyre told Emily, Emily told me, and I asked him if it was true."

"And he said it was?"

She nodded. "He did. He was pissed as hell that his secret was out, but he didn't deny it. He was falling for you, Blair," she said. "And when he realized it, he panicked and retreated, just like Frannie said. Because he thinks that will be easier than taking a chance on love again."

Of course, I knew there was more to it than that, but Griffin had told me things in confidence I'd never whisper to another soul. "Maybe."

"I only hope he gets over himself before it's too late. I mean, look at this place." She held out her arms and glanced around. "It's beautiful here. You have a great job. You've got a built-in family. And pretty soon, some guy is going to come walking into that coffee shop, eat a bite of that strata, and fall to his knees. It'll be too late for Griffin."

I sighed. "Part of me hopes you're right."

"And the other part?"

"That would be my heart." Smiling sadly, I lifted my shoulders. "And it's set on someone I can't have."

CHAPTER 23
GRIFFIN

SINCE THE LEAGUE championship would be played on Saturday of Labor Day weekend, we didn't have a game on Thursday. Instead, the team got together for an extra practice, during which we felt pretty good. We were confident our last game had been an aberration and looked forward to decimating the Mavs in this weekend's matchup.

Well, most of us were looking forward to it. I couldn't seem to work up much excitement about anything these days. Not even baseball.

On Friday after work, I went over to Cole's house for a run. When I got there, Mariah was jump-roping in the driveway.

"Hey, kiddo," I said. "What's new?"

She shrugged. "Nothing much. Lots of my friends are out of town for the holiday weekend, so I'm kind of bored."

"Well, there's going to be lots to do tomorrow. We're having a big party at the garage."

Her face lit up. "I know. Miss Cheyenne asked me if I wanted to help her run the cakewalk. I'm going to play the music."

"Perfect. We'll need lots of help, because we're going to be really busy. I hope." I crossed my fingers and held them up.

Cole came out a minute later, and we set off at our warm-up pace.

"How was your week?" he asked.

"Fine," I answered.

A total lie. I'd been miserable since Blair left. It had been ten days, and every one of them seemed more lifeless and flat. Just twenty-four hours to get through before another one started over again. There were no bright spots whatsoever.

I missed her behind the desk at work—my mother was back in the chair, passive-aggressively ignoring me with her sighs and silences—I missed her smile and her voice and her scent in my apartment at night. I missed her singing that song about the rainbow in the shower, loud and off-key. I missed holding her close at bedtime, and every time I opened my closet door, I saw that fucking dress hanging there. Haunting me.

But I couldn't let it go. The sight of it draped over the dumpster had gutted me, and I'd snuck it up to my apartment when no one was looking. I'd even had it dry-cleaned, and when the woman behind the counter had raised an eyebrow at me, I'd given her my grouchiest glare and said, "Don't. Ask."

"Should be a fun day tomorrow," Cole said.

"Yeah."

"And a good game."

"I guess."

"You guess?" Cole looked over at me like I was nuts. "We've been waiting all summer for this game. And your family has put a lot into the party, haven't they?"

"Yeah. Blair did most of the legwork." God, why had I used that word? Now I was thinking about her legs.

"Think she'll make an appearance?"

"Nah."

"Why not?"

"Because I told her she had to go, and she knew that I meant it."

"I thought you said it was a mutual decision."

"When did I say that?"

"Last week at the game we lost to the Mavs."

"Oh." I gritted my teeth. "I lied. It wasn't mutual. She wanted to stay, and I told her she had to leave."

"Why?"

"Because I had to!" Suddenly words were tumbling from my mouth like an avalanche. "I was starting to feel things for her that were not okay. I kept getting distracted by these stupid ideas about us."

"Like what?"

"Like—just—having her in my life. Her staying here. Us being together."

"What's so stupid about that?"

"Because it's not what I want!"

Cole gave me the side-eye. "You sure about that?"

"Yes," I said, aggravated. "I made up my mind years ago that I was never going to be in the position of needing some-one. I was never going to fall in love again. Because it *sucks* when it all goes wrong."

"I'm not sure that's a thing your mind can decide," Cole said in his assured, easy way. "You just fall for someone. You don't really choose it."

"You know what I mean. Even if you feel something, you don't have to act on it. You have free will. You can choose to be strong enough to resist or ignore the feelings."

"Or you can choose to be strong enough to take the risk. But I agree that it sucks when it goes wrong."

I glanced at him, softened my tone. "Sorry. I wasn't trying to compare our situations. What you went through was a lot worse."

"I didn't think you were comparing. I was just agreeing

that losing someone you love hurts like hell. But there isn't one day with Trisha I'd take back, even knowing how it ended."

Ashamed, I fell silent, and spent the remainder of the run trying to think of reasons why Cole was wrong and I was right. He didn't say anything more until we were nearly back at his house again.

"We've been friends a long time," he said. "What, like twenty-five years?"

"Something like that. Yeah."

"You were the best man at my wedding. You're my daughter's godfather. If anything were to happen to me, I trust you to raise her."

I glanced at him. No matter what was coming, I had a feeling I wasn't going to like it. "Yeah."

"So I would expect that if I was fucking something up in a big way, and being a real asshole about it, you'd tell me. Right?"

"Right."

"So I'm going to tell you this." He stopped running, so I did too. He put a hand out and grabbed my shoulder, holding me at arm's length. "You're fucking something up in a big way, and you're being a real asshole about it."

I shoved his arm off my shoulder. "Fuck off, Cole. You don't know anything about this."

He parked his hands on his hips. "You think I don't know you? You think I haven't picked up a few things in the twenty-five years I've been your best friend? You think I can't see when you really care about something?"

I clenched my jaw. Dug in harder.

"I was there, Griffin. I was there when you came home and Kayla abandoned you. I know what you went through when your dad died. I know you think having control over your life means never needing someone you could potentially lose. But none of those things are reasons to shut out someone you love."

"I'm not in love with her," I snapped, although I wasn't entirely sure about that.

"But you could be."

I didn't admit it. Couldn't. Instead I doubled down on asshole, which I always did when I felt cornered.

"And what about you? I don't see you putting yourself out there."

"Our situations are totally different, and you know it. But you can be damn sure that if someone came along who got to me the way Blair gets to you, I wouldn't push her away."

I felt my armor cracking. "I can't undo what I've done."

"Are you sure?"

"I wouldn't even know what to say to her. She probably hates me. I don't even think she'd listen." It was an excuse, and my best friend knew it.

"She'll listen. If you say the right thing."

"What's the right thing?"

"That you were wrong. That you're sorry. That you said things to her you didn't mean because you were scared."

Jesus. Could I say that to her? "It's not . . . easy for me to admit those things."

"It's not easy for anyone, Griff. Every time you step up to the plate, there's a chance you'll strike out. But there's also a chance you'll knock it out of the park. Don't blow this by not even taking a swing."

I exhaled, my shoulders sagging.

"Take the risk, man." Cole's voice quieted. His blue eyes were intense. "Do you know how lucky you are? How much you'll regret doing nothing when you could have had everything? Just . . . take the risk."

He left me standing there and went in to eat dinner with his family, and I went home alone to eat by myself.

Later that night, I lay awake, thinking about what Cole had said. Was he right? Was I fucking this up? Would I regret not even *trying* to make things work with Blair?

Maybe I would. Being alone was not the salve on the wound I'd hoped it would be. I missed her too much. I'd had a taste of what life could be like with her in it, and now that she was gone, it was like endless rainy days stretching out in front of me without any chance for sun. Things that I used to enjoy—even baseball—had lost their shine.

I thought about the kind of closeness I'd had with her. It was unlike anything I'd ever experienced before. She made it so easy to share things about me that I'd never shared with anyone. She made it so easy for me to be myself. She made me want to be a better version of that self. More patient. Less angry. More hopeful. Less bitter.

She made me want to loosen the reins and open myself up to new possibilities—a different kind of future.

I didn't want this lonely life for myself. I wanted to eat meals she cooked and do the dishes for her when she was done. I wanted to hold her during thunderstorms and tell her everything would be all right. I wanted to hear her chirping like a robin in the morning and telling dirty stories at night. I wanted to admit I'd been wrong, tear down my walls, and build something new with her right beside me.

But was I ready for the kind of change she would bring?

I stared at my ceiling in the dark, as if the answer was written there, and by morning I'd be able to see it.

"Wait—Blair was *here*? *Today*?" Panicked, I looked around the garage's newly renovated waiting room like I might have missed her in the crowd. All morning I'd been smiling absently at the people milling around, shaking hands with old and new customers, fielding compliments on the new look. But I was totally preoccupied with thoughts of Blair. *She should be here*, I kept thinking. *This doesn't feel right without her.*

The event was a huge success, as far as I could tell. From the moment we'd opened the doors, we'd had a steady stream of people in and out. The Bulldog Pub had a little sidewalk stand out front serving sliders and fries, and my '55 Chevy was parked at the curb, where kids could climb in the back or get behind the wheel and have their pictures taken. The new logo Lola had designed was painted on the side of the truck in fresh white paint, and every time I looked at it, I wished Blair could have seen how great it turned out, since it had been her idea.

Everything had been her idea.

She should be here. This doesn't feel right without her.

"When was she here?" I demanded.

"Not here at the garage," my mother said. "She came to the house this morning to drop off the pies and the cake. Just look at these beauties." She gestured toward six apple pies that did indeed look delectable. "It's like Betty Frankel rose from the grave. To think Charlie had the recipe the whole time!"

"I don't understand," I said, caring less about the pies themselves than the woman who'd made them. "Blair baked these?"

"Of course she did. And the cake too."

I looked at the cake—a large, rectangular cake covered in sky-blue frosting and decorated with a vintage red Chevy truck with our new logo on the side. I thought my mother had ordered it from a bakery or something. "*Blair* made the cake?"

"Yes. Your sister can tell you the whole story. She drove up to visit Blair on Thursday."

"But you saw her this morning?" I asked, following my mother into the break room, where she grabbed more cups for the coffee in the lobby.

"Of course I saw her."

Agitated, I trailed my mother back out to the front, where she stacked the cups on a table. Music from a live band up the street filtered in through the open door. "Why didn't you say anything to me?"

She gave me a look. "*Now* you want to talk about Blair? After almost two weeks of telling me to mind my own business?"

"Yes. Now I want to talk about her."

She faced me and crossed her arms over her chest. "What do you want to know?"

I shifted my weight from foot to foot, agitated. I felt like a swarm of bees was under my skin. "How did she look?"

"Beautiful."

"Was she . . . did she seem okay?"

"She seemed fine. We didn't chat long because she was in a rush to get back up north to her job."

"She likes it up there?"

"She said she loves it."

My chest ached. Maybe she didn't even miss me. Maybe she loved her new life so much, she never gave me a second thought. Maybe she'd even met someone new already.

The thought made me feel sick. How had I let her go?

"Did she ask about me?"

My mother huffed. "No, she didn't. And I don't blame her. After what Lanette told me about the way you sent her packing, I wouldn't ask about you either!"

I frowned. "Lanette owes me twenty bucks."

"You know, all this concern for Blair would have been nice before she left," my mother snapped. "Oh, I see how broody and miserable you are without her, and it's your own fault. I don't feel sorry for you!" She turned to greet an old family friend, and I went outside, searching out my sister. Spotting her by the truck, I stormed over and grabbed her by the elbow.

"What the hell?" she said as I dragged her up the sidewalk a little, away from the crowd.

"Mom says you saw Blair on Thursday."

She yanked her arm back from me. "Yeah, so?"

"So did she say anything about me?"

My sister shrugged. "She might have. I don't remember exactly."

I was at the end of my rope. "Cut the crap, Cheyenne. Did she say something or not?"

"Why do you want to know? I thought you decided you were better off without her."

"Look, I may have been wrong about that, okay?" I ran a hand through my hair. "I'm . . . I'm thinking about things."

My sister's eyebrows rose. "Don't hurt yourself."

"Could you just give me a break, please? I'm a fucking wreck, Cheyenne. I can't stop thinking about her. I can't sleep. Nothing tastes good or feels right. I can't focus at work. I'm not even excited about the game tonight."

"Whoa. This *is* serious."

"That's what I'm saying." I rubbed my face with both hands. "So can you please just help me out? Did she say anything?"

My sister relented and spoke softly. "Of course she did, Griffin. She's in love with you."

My heart immediately shot into my throat. I fisted my hands in my hair. "She said that?"

"No, but she didn't have to. I could just tell."

I dropped my arms. "I don't know what to do."

"If you want her, go get her back. But I'll tell you this, Griff." My sister's voice took on a warning note. "Do not mess with her. She has a really great thing going up there. A place to live, people that care about her, a job she loves. She's definitely hung up on you, and if you apologized and asked for another chance, I bet she'd give it—but you better be sure it's what you want."

I didn't even have to think about it. "It's what I want."

"*Finally.*" She opened her arms and gave me a hug that felt surprisingly good. "I love you, you big jerk. Why do you have to make things so difficult?"

"I don't know," I said. "I guess I just like to fight."

She laughed and patted my back. "Well, now you have something worth fighting for. Go get her."

Later that afternoon, I was still trying to think of what I could say to Blair that would convince her I deserved a second chance when Charlie Frankel approached me. "This is wonderful, wonderful," he said, shaking my hand.

"Thank you."

"Your dad and granddad sure would be proud."

"I appreciate that."

"Did you see those apple pies over there? Blair baked them. With Betty's recipe." He looked sheepish. "I had it all this time, you see. I had my reasons for keeping it to myself, but Blair reminds me so much of Betty—such a good heart and a bright spirit—I knew she was the right person to trust with it."

I swallowed hard. "Blair will take good care of it."

"She stopped by to see me today."

Jealousy kicked me in the gut. "Oh?"

"Yes. She brought me a pie of my own, and we sat on the

porch and had a piece with some tea, even though it was just nine in the morning." He chuckled at the thought.

I swallowed hard. "Sounds nice."

"We had a nice chat," Frankel went on, scratching his head, "and she talked a lot about this event and all she'd learned working for you. I hope you won't think this too forward, but she also mentioned that the bank has been reluctant to give you a loan."

"Reluctant is one way to put it," I said stiffly.

"Well, I was thinking. I'm a very good customer at that bank. My family has been for generations. And I bet if I co-signed on that loan, they'd be more willing to approve it."

My jaw dropped. "Are you serious?"

"Sure. I see the good work you're doing here, and I know how hard it can be to keep a small, family-owned business running. I believe we have to invest in the people we know, the people who make this town what it is. Your family has been in business here a long time too, and I'd like to keep it that way. Let me help you."

I felt like the wind had been knocked out of me. "I don't know what to say."

"Say you'll come over sometime soon and we can talk about what you need. Then I'll make an appointment with the bank, and we'll go in together."

I held out my hand. "It's a deal, Mr. Frankel. And thank you."

"You're welcome, Griffin. Now can I offer a piece of advice?"

"Sure."

"Girls like Betty and Blair don't come along too often. They're special. One in a million." He put a hand on my shoulder. "I probably shouldn't tell you this, but I offered Blair the loan first. I thought she could use it to start her own bakery in town, but she said no. She said if anyone deserved the help, it was you."

Again, I found myself at a loss for words, which made Frankel laugh.

He gave my shoulder a squeeze. "Don't let her get away, son."

I swallowed hard. "I won't. I promise you, I won't."

That evening, Cole and I sat side by side in the dugout, waiting for the game to start. "Hey, I'm sorry about yesterday," I said.

He gave me a funny look. "You don't owe me an apology."

"Yes, I do. You were trying to be honest with me, and I didn't want to hear it, so I was a dick. It's not you I'm mad at."

He laughed. "I know. I've been your best friend for twenty-five years, remember? I see through all your bullshit by now."

I laughed too, feeling better. "Anyway, thanks for the advice."

"You gonna take it?"

"Yeah. But don't let it go to your head." I grinned at him. "Now let's win this thing so I can go fix what I broke."

The game was a nail-biter—no score until the top of the seventh, when Cole's arm started to give him trouble and the Mavs scored a two-run homer. Thankfully, I managed to get on base in the bottom of the eighth, Moretti hit a double right after that, and then Beckett ripped a monster line drive up the third baseline that the Mavs' third baseman couldn't get a glove on and the left fielder fumbled. I scored, Moretti scored, and Beckett made it to third. But the batter after that struck out, and we took the field for the final inning with a tie game.

Thanks to Cole's resilience and a kick-ass double play, we managed to keep them from scoring during the top of the ninth. All we needed was one run to win this game and keep our championship title—which we got when I swung at a fastball at the top of the strike zone and sent it flying over the fence in left field.

I ran the bases with a smile on my face and crossed home plate to celebrate the win with my teammates, who were rushing out of the dugout, hands in the air, yelling at the top of their lungs.

That's when I looked up in the stands and saw her. She was in the visitors' section of the bleachers, wearing the white dress she'd worn the night of our picnic, a floppy sun hat on her head, and sunglasses covering her eyes.

At first glance, I thought maybe I'd been mistaken. My mother and Cheyenne had both insisted Blair had left the house as quickly as she'd arrived this morning, claiming she had to get back to her job.

But it was her. I knew it because she took off her sunglasses right then, and the moment we locked eyes, my heart exploded. She immediately shoved them back on and started making her way to the end of the row, as if she were trying to make a quick escape. I wanted to stop her, but I felt myself being hoisted onto my teammates' shoulders and paraded back to the dugout. By the time they set me down, she was gone.

I didn't wait around. I grabbed my keys and took off running. If I didn't catch her on foot, I'd catch up to her on the highway. There was no fucking way I was letting her go again.

"Dempsey! What the hell! Where you going? Come back!"

Ignoring the jeers from my team, I sprinted toward the parking lot and was halfway to my truck when I heard the boom of a tire blow out.

With a glance at the sky, I picked up my pace.

CHAPTER 24
BLAIR

NO.

This couldn't be happening.

What the hell did the universe have against me?

Had I been a total jerk in a previous life? Was this some karmic bullshit I couldn't escape? Maybe there *was* such a thing as fate, and my stars were way, *way* out of alignment.

Just like my steering wheel.

I flopped forward and banged my head against it.

I'd only wanted to see the game. It had been so important to him, to everyone. I'd thought if I sat in the visitors' section, wore a hat and sunglasses and stayed quiet, I'd go unnoticed.

But he'd seen me, I knew he had. We'd locked eyes, and I hadn't been able to breathe.

Then I'd panicked—it was so embarrassing! So obvious that I was still clinging to hope, even after he'd told me in no uncertain terms we were through. I'd rushed out of the stands and raced toward the parking lot, praying I could get out of there before anyone else spotted me. Jumping into my car, I tossed my hat aside and took off so fast, my tires spit gravel.

But I was flustered and I'd gotten turned around in the lot, unsure which way the exit was. Was it over there by the tennis court? Over this way by the soccer field? My eyes blurry with tears, I found myself speeding up and down row after row like I was in a maze I couldn't get out of. There were a bunch of orange and white barrels everywhere, and the pavement was all rocky and pockmarked. Finally, I saw a way out, and I hit the gas.

And then—*boom*! I felt a familiar explosion beneath my car and slammed on the brakes.

My car skidded sideways, wobbled and shuddered, jumped the curb and struck a huge boulder on the school lawn that had two words painted on it: WELCOME BACK!

God. This was so unfair.

I choked back a sob as I got out of the car.

"Blair!"

Startled, I looked to my left and saw Griffin running at me across the parking lot as if his life depended on it. Reaching my side, he fell forward, hands on his knees, breathing hard. "Blair, are you okay?"

"I'm fine. Are *you* okay?"

"Yes." He straightened up, still huffing and puffing. "Just don't faint yet. I need a second to catch my breath."

My face burned, and I shook my head. "I'm not going to faint."

"Good. Are you sure you're all right?" He took me by the upper arms, and gooseflesh rippled across my skin.

"Yes. I'm just really embarrassed." Fans from the game were heading toward their cars now, and many of them were staring at us.

"Why?"

"Because I didn't want you to see me here. And I just blew another tire. Also I might have damaged this rock that's probably been here for a hundred years." I gestured toward it.

"I'm sure you were legally parked when it hit you."

I almost smiled. A tear slipped down my cheek. "I'm a disaster."

"Stop it. You're beautiful." He brushed it with his thumb. "Do you know how happy I am to see you here?"

My heart stopped beating. "You are?"

He took my face in his hands. "If it weren't for that game, I'd already be on your doorstep right now, begging your forgiveness."

"You would?"

"Yes. I'm so sorry, Blair. I was wrong to send you away like that. I lied about how I felt because I was scared. I swear to God, the *minute* you were gone, I realized my mistake, but I was too stubborn to admit it."

"You really hurt me," I said quietly.

"I know. And I'm sorry. I hated myself for it. You just . . . took me by surprise. I had no idea someone like you even existed, and I was totally unprepared for the way you made me feel. But I don't want to fight it anymore."

The crowd behind him was closing in around us, and I could hear some people murmuring with curiosity, and others shushing the murmurers so they could hear better.

"Um, we're surrounded," I whispered.

"Doesn't matter," he said with a wry, crooked grin. "It's not like it's possible to have any secrets in this town."

"True."

"Nothing was good without you, Blair. I need you in my life. And I don't care who knows it."

"Griffin," I said, tears splashing down my cheeks.

He wiped them away with his thumbs. "Say you'll give me another chance."

"I want to, but I'm scared. I trusted you."

"Don't be scared." He pressed his lips to my forehead. "I *am* the man you thought I was, Blair. Let me prove it to you."

I felt like the crowd was holding its breath right along with me.

"Say yes! He means it!" someone shouted.

"Mariah, be quiet!" a man's voice scolded.

"But Dad, you can tell he does. And she's wearing a white dress. Maybe this means they'll get married for *real*."

I started to laugh, even though I couldn't stop crying. "I really do love this town."

"Does that mean you'll come back?"

"It means you can have your second chance. Beyond that, we'll talk."

Then his lips were on mine, the crowd around us cheered, and I felt myself being lifted right off the ground.

That's when I knew—if a place could love you back, or grow arms and hug you, that's what this place would do.

After we towed my car to the garage, I called Frannie to let her know what happened.

"Oh my God, really?" she shrieked. "You blew *another* tire? That's some seriously bad luck."

"Or good luck, depending on how you look at it." I exchanged a smile with Griffin as he opened the door of his truck for me.

Frannie laughed. "Right! So you guys got back together right there at the scene? With a crowd around you?"

"Yes," I said, climbing into the passenger seat. "We've given them something to talk about tomorrow for sure."

"I can't wait to hear all the details," she squealed. "Listen, don't worry about coming back tonight. Just stay there and enjoy."

"Are you sure? Griffin said he'd be glad to drive me."

"I'm positive. And since we're closed on Mondays, you don't have to rush back tomorrow either. Take the whole weekend."

"You're the best, Frannie. I'll see you Tuesday."

"All good?" Griffin asked, sliding behind the wheel.

"All good. You don't have to bring me back right away."

He grabbed my hand and kissed it. "I might never want to bring you back."

I smiled. "We'll talk."

Griffin and I met up with the rest of the team at the pub to celebrate. The moment Cheyenne saw me, she hugged me hard and dragged me into the bathroom to get the scoop.

"Did he grovel?" she squeaked. "I can't believe I missed the big scene!"

I laughed. "Kind of. He was pretty apologetic and took all the blame. He asked me for a second chance."

"Good. He told me earlier today he was going to get you back, and I was so worried he'd mess it up."

I shook my head. "He didn't. We still have some things to figure out, but I have a really good feeling we can make it work."

Cheyenne grinned. "Me too."

"You know what this means, though," I said as we walked back to the table.

"What?"

I steered her toward the empty seat next to Cole. "It's your turn next."

"Bisou!" The moment I saw her, I dropped to my knees on the floor and scooped her up, misty-eyed. "I missed you so much!"

"She missed you too," said Griffin. "I'm going to grab a shower, okay?"

"Sure. I'll feed her." I snuggled the cat for a minute before setting her down, but even after I stood, she wound herself around my foot and rubbed her head against my ankle. Laughing, I reached down to pet her again. "I'm not going anywhere yet," I promised.

I fed her, turned out all the lights, and undressed in Griffin's bedroom. When he came out of the bathroom, I was already under the covers.

"God, you have no idea how happy I am to see you back in my bed," he said, crawling in beside me. "I had no idea how lonely this place could be."

We lay on our sides, facing each other. "I was lonely too," I told him, running a fingertip over the ink on his chest.

He pressed a kiss to my forehead. "Can you forgive me for being such a stubborn jerk?"

"Maybe." I smiled mischievously. "But I get to ask you some questions first."

He groaned. "I forgot about you and the questions."

"Those are my terms."

"Then I guess I have to meet them. Ask away."

"Were you really going to drive up north to get me back today?"

He nodded. "I promised both my sister *and* Charlie Frankel I would. They will vouch for me. And speaking of Charlie Frankel, he offered to co-sign a loan for me at the bank."

"He did?" My heart trilled happily. "Did you say yes?"

"Of course I did. If you're stuck in a tower and someone offers to lend you a ladder, you'd be stupid not to use it."

I laughed. "Right."

"I know it was you that encouraged him to make the offer, Blair. And I can't tell you how much that means to me. To my family."

"Well, you deserve it. You work so hard. How was the event?"

"It was amazing. And it sucked."

I gasped. "It sucked? Why?"

"Because you weren't there. And you'd done so much to make it the success that it was. I kept looking around all day, hoping to see your face in the crowd."

"I made myself stay away," I told him quietly. "I was scared I'd break down if I saw you."

"What made you come to the game?"

"Are you kidding? I couldn't miss the old man baseball league championship!" I slapped at his shoulder. "I lied and told your mom and sister I was going right back to Traverse City so they wouldn't look for me. But the truth was, Frannie had given me the whole day off in case . . . just in case." I sighed. "So I hid out at Charlie Frankel's house all day. He was the only one who knew I was there."

"He adores you."

"He's sweet."

"I adore you." He ran a hand over my hip, and his cock stirred between us. "And I can't wait to show you how much. Are we done with questions yet?"

"Nope. I get two more. Is it true that you hid the parts for my car for over a week because you didn't want me to leave?"

He sighed. "It's true."

"You big lug, why didn't you just *say* you wanted me to stay?" I shouted, although it made me happy to hear him admit what he'd done.

"Because saying that out loud would mean owning up to feelings I did not want to have," he said.

"So what was the plan, you were just going to keep me stranded here until your feelings for me went away?"

"I really didn't think it through, Blair. All I knew was that I couldn't let you go."

"But you did," I reminded him, poking his chest.

"I did. Because I freaked out. I thought I might have gotten you pregnant, and that triggered a real shit show in my head."

"I know. That was a scary moment, I agree."

"Then I freaked out because I'd never told anyone about the miscarriage, and there I was spilling my guts to you."

"I was glad you did," I said softly, looking up at him. "It helped me understand you better. I don't think you're any less of a man for being sad over the loss, Griffin. I don't think anyone would think that."

He was silent a moment, then he rolled onto his back. "You're probably right. But it never felt like something I could talk about. Until you."

I threw an arm and leg over him and pressed my cheek to his warm, bare chest. "I know you'll never be a talker like me. But no more hiding the big stuff, okay? That's the only promise I'll ask you to make."

"No hiding things? And I get my second chance?"

"No hiding things. And you get your second chance."

"Then there's something I need to show you." He sat up, bringing me with him.

"What is it?"

He switched on the bedside lamp, got out of bed, and went over to his closet door. "I swear, this is the *last* thing I was hiding."

I gave him a strange look. "Okaaaay." Then he opened the closet door, and I gasped. "My dress!"

"I rescued it from the dumpster."

Scrambling out of bed, I went over and looked at it, all wrapped in dry cleaner plastic, looking as fresh as the day I'd bought it. "I don't believe it!"

"I remembered how you were wearing it the night we met. And how you said to me that you couldn't let it go because it made you feel beautiful and hopeful. Like your life was just beginning."

My throat closed up, and my eyes filled. "That's right."

He drew me into his arms. "I want you to feel that way again."

"I do." I laughed, even as tears leaked from my eyes. "I honestly do."

"Good." He lifted me off my feet and carried me back to the bed, turning off the lamp before stretching out above me. "Because I've gone and gotten my heart set on you, Blair Peacock Beaufort. And I come from a long line of men who are awfully stubborn once they get their hearts set on something."

I wrapped my arms and legs around him. "I'm so glad you were there that night, to catch me when I fell."

"I'll always be there to catch you," he whispered as his body began to move above mine in the dark. "In my arms is where you belong."

CHAPTER 25
GRIFFIN
ONE YEAR LATER

"BLAIR! YOU READY?"

"One minute!" I hurried out of the bedroom and saw him standing at the top of the stairs, keys in his hands. "Sorry," I said breathlessly. "This thing takes a minute to get on. Can you zip me up?"

"I'm better at unzipping this dress, but sure."

I laughed, turning my back to him. When I was all zipped up in my strapless white gown, I faced him again. "I'm lucky this thing still fits. How do I look?"

"Like a debutante ready for the ball—or at least a photo shoot."

"Is my tiara on straight?"

He pretended a close assessment. "It's perfect."

"Is my lipstick smudged?"

"Nope."

"Good." I looked him up and down, and my entire body tingled. "You look cute too."

He glowered at me. "You know how I feel about cute."

I laughed. "I can't help it. The baseball uniform gets me. I know you weren't actually wearing it the night we met, but I think for the photo shoot, it's perfect."

The Bellamy Creek Gazette was running a series on how local couples had met and fallen in love, and Cheyenne had submitted our names and the details. The editor had gone crazy for the story of how I'd gotten myself stranded here after my car broke down and then fallen for the mechanic who fixed it. She especially loved the detail about my wardrobe, and how Griffin had caught me when I fainted. She wanted us to re-enact the scene.

The only difference, besides putting Griffin in his Bulldogs jersey, was that she wanted the photos taken in a different location—rather than in front of the credit union, where it had actually happened, the editor wanted the photographer to snap us in front of the shop I'd just opened up: The Bellamy Creek Boulangerie.

I'd cut the ribbon over the Fourth of July weekend, and business had boomed from the start. Betty's apple pie was a huge draw, of course, but with Mr. Frankel's blessing, I'd tweaked things here and there to make it my own. After tasting it, he told me Betty would have been proud. I also served all kinds of cakes and pastries, strata and quiche, rolls and doughnuts, muffins and scones, along with coffee, tea, fresh lemonade, and mimosas on weekends.

Frannie and her family had come down for the ceremony, pushing their new babies in a double stroller—twin girls they'd named Audrey and Emmeline. It meant everything to me to have her there, since she'd been so supportive of me throughout the previous year.

As promised, I'd stayed on at Coffee Darling throughout her entire pregnancy, taking over full-time while she was out on maternity leave. It hadn't been easy, because at the same time, I'd been in the process of buying the old Main Street Bakery in Bellamy Creek, lining up the financing, designing and overseeing its renovations, and planning for a summer opening.

It was exhausting—but Griffin had been my rock. We

dated long-distance all through the fall and winter, trying never to go longer than a week without seeing each other, although it hadn't been easy. The drives were rough, especially in bad weather, and Griffin always insisted on being the one to trek through the snow. He'd had to hire another mechanic to cover Saturdays so he could spend them with me.

But he never once complained. He knew how important it was to me to establish myself independently, to work for myself, support myself, feel steady on my own two feet. He understood me, and I fell more in love with him for it every day.

By springtime, we knew we couldn't be apart any longer. After talking it over with him and asking Frannie's advice, I made the decision to approach the older couple who owned the Main Street Bakery and offer to buy them out. They were thrilled with the idea, since they'd been wanting to retire to Florida for years and just needed the push to do it.

I'd moved in with Griffin in May, and I'd never been happier. Glancing over at him as we drove to the shop, I felt a rush of affection and gratitude. I reached out and took his hand.

"What?" he asked.

"Nothing. I'm just in love with you."

He lifted my hand to his lips and kissed it. "I love you too."

"You must, since you agreed to this photo shoot. I know you hate being the center of attention."

"Well, you said it would be good for business. After what you did for mine, how could I refuse?"

I smiled. Griffin had invested the loan Mr. Frankel had helped him get in tools, training, advertising, and more help at the garage, and it had paid off. Andy had the social media accounts up and running, and Darlene picked up baked goods from me every morning to serve in the lobby. Swifty

Auto was still the bane of his existence, but it wasn't the threat it had been before.

Life was good.

For now, we were still living above the garage, although we sometimes talked about the day when we'd be able to afford a house. Griffin wanted some land, I wanted a little more kitchen space, and both of us wanted a family, but we weren't in any rush (much to Darlene's dismay).

We'd learned some things from each other over the last year. I'd learned not to ask so many questions and let things unfold a little more naturally, and Griffin had learned to ease up on his need for control and to trust his feelings.

"Looks like the photographer is there already," I said as we pulled up in front of my bakery. As always, I had to pinch myself when I saw its black-and-white striped awning, the elegant script on the valance, the polished wood of the front door, the two little café tables in matching windows on either side of the entrance.

Inside, the kitchen was full of light, and every morning I woke up excited to put on the coffee, get the ovens going, and greet smiling customers who left their homes to come taste what I created. It meant everything to me.

It was hard to believe it was really mine—any of it, the shop, the man beside me every night, the love we shared, the life ahead, this place I called home, this hope in my heart.

It was better than a fairy tale.

"So you think we got the perfect shot?" I asked as Griffin pulled away from the shop.

"Considering that she took at least a hundred pictures, I hope so. We can't be that un-photogenic. Well, *you* can't."

I took his hand. "That was fun, wasn't it? I hope we get on the front page."

"Everyone will think we're married again."

"Oh my God, remember that?" I laughed, recalling the way the rumor had spread. "As if that could have actually happened."

"People like a good story."

"Yes, they do. Hey, where are we going?" I asked when he drove past the garage without stopping.

"I thought maybe we'd take a drive."

"Dressed like this?" I looked down at my gown.

He shrugged and gave me a little sideways grin. "I have a surprise for you."

I gasped. "I love surprises!"

"I know."

"Can I try to guess what it is?"

He laughed and shook his head. "If you want to."

Craning my neck to look out the windows on all sides, I tried to figure out what direction we were headed in. "Are we going to your mom's house for dinner?"

Griffin grunted. "Do you know me at all?"

I giggled as he got on the highway out of town. "Hmmm. The pond?"

We sometimes took a picnic over to the pond for a date night, just like we had the first week I was here. Those evenings lying in the back of his '55 Chevy under the stars were better than any I had ever spent dancing with millionaires in hotel ballrooms.

"Nope," he said.

"Hmmm." I tapped a finger on my chin, confused when he exited the highway, looped around, and got on again going the opposite direction. "Did you miss your turn or something?"

"Did you know," he said, "that tonight marks exactly one year since you blew that tire on Main Street?"

I gasped. "Does it really? One year to the day?"

"I checked the original invoice."

"You still have the original invoice?" My voice was high-pitched with excitement.

"Of course I do."

"I don't even think I ever saw it because you wouldn't let me pay for the repairs."

"I didn't want your money," he said, pulling onto the highway shoulder. "I wanted something more."

My heart was pounding hard as he shut off the engine. "Griffin, what is this?"

"Stay there." He jumped out of the driver's side and came around to me, pulling the door open and lifting me down, just like he had that first night. But this time, he kept his hands on my waist. "I didn't know it then—in fact, I would have argued with anyone who tried to tell me—but I wanted you to change my life. We joke a lot about me rescuing you that night, but now I see it was the other way around."

I smiled up at him. "But I was the one with nowhere to go."

"You did have somewhere to go. But you followed your heart instead."

"Sort of." Giggling, I lifted my shoulders. "I followed a sign, remember?"

"I remember. And I hope you'll follow it again."

For a second, I was even more confused. Then I looked beyond his shoulder, and I saw it—the billboard.

My jaw dropped, and I sucked in my breath.

It had once advertised the best apple pie in the Midwest since 1957, with a cartoon drawing of the pie and the diner's logo. Now it had only four words on it:

WILL YOU MARRY ME?

Griffin got down on one knee and took a small ring box from his pocket, and I covered my mouth with both hands. My eyes blurred with tears.

"That sign changed everything for me," he said, his voice cracking. "I don't know what my life would've been like if you hadn't seen it."

"Or if I paid more attention to potholes," I squeaked, my throat tight.

"I will happily spend the rest of my days fixing all your blown tires if you'll let me. And now, for once, it's *my* turn to ask a question." He opened the box, and a diamond winked at me in the light of the setting sun. "Blair Peacock Beaufort, will you marry me?"

"Yes!" I shouted, jumping up and down, my tiara coming loose on my head. "Yes! Yes! Yes!"

Grinning, he plucked the simple, classic solitaire from its satin cushion and slipped it on my finger. Then he rose to his feet and embraced me, lifting me right off my feet. I threw my arms around his neck and held on tight as happy tears dripped down my cheeks.

When he finally set me down, I looked at the sign again and shook my head. "I just can't believe it! Was Mr. Frankel in on this?"

"Of course he was."

"Who else knew?"

"Cheyenne, my mother, Althea Bond at the jewelry store, McIntyre, Cole and Mariah, Moretti and Beckett—"

"Oh my God, you told *everybody*!"

"I had a little trouble keeping it secret," he admitted. "I was really excited."

"I can't believe they all kept it from me!"

Griffin shrugged. "Turns out, they can be trusted when it really counts."

My heart spilled over with joy, and I rose up on my toes to kiss him. "This is the best day ever."

He laughed. "You say that all the time."

"Because you keep giving me all the best days!"

"This is only the beginning, Blair." He kissed me, soft and sweet. "I promise you, the best is yet to come."

THE END

Thank you so much for reading Blair and Griffin's story! I hope you had as much fun taking their journey as I had writing it. If you didn't get enough of them, sign up for my newsletter, and the first thing you'll get is a Drive Me Wild bonus scene!

Click here to sign up!

If you'd like to try your hand at some of Blair's creations, recipes are up next—just keep swiping!

Next up in the Bellamy Creek series is Cole and Cheyenne's story, MAKE ME YOURS—it's coming your way on November 23rd! Keep reading for a sneak peek!

BONUS EPILOGUE

GRIFFIN

"So what did you think?" I took Blair's hand as we walked down the cracked cement path from the house's front door to the sidewalk.

She didn't even glance at the FOR SALE sign on the lawn. "It's okay," she said with a heavy sigh, kicking a pebble with the toe of her sneaker.

Okay was actually pretty generous. I'd thought the place was ugly, decrepit, and smelled like moldy carpet. It wasn't even the best one we'd seen today, let alone in the three months we'd been looking. But my surprise would make a bigger impact if I played with her a little. "Okay but not perfect?"

She shook her head. "Not even close. The kitchen looked like 1975 and 1995 had an ugly baby—sorry, I know all babies are supposed to be beautiful, but I can't with the knotty pine soffits and the stained formica counters."

"We can always remodel a kitchen."

"Not right away. We don't have that kind of money. And I

need a kitchen I can at least live with for a while. It doesn't have to be perfect, but I don't want to hate it."

"The three bedrooms were nice and big."

"But there's only one and a half baths. I really think we need two full."

"It had a decent-sized yard, though."

"I guess. But that deck is practically falling off the back of the house. It's all rotted."

"I can fix that." We reached the truck and I unlocked it before pulling open the passenger door for her.

"I know." She looked up at me, her expression guilty. "Am I being a princess?"

I laughed, dropping a kiss on her lips. "No."

"I'm sorry, I swear I am trying not to be too picky, and I know we've looked at like every house in our price range in Bellamy Creek, but . . ." She twisted her hands together. "I just haven't felt right in any of them. I feel like when I walk in to the right one, I'll know it."

"It will give you a hug?" I teased her.

Her cheeks grew pink, and she laughed. "Yes."

"Listen," I said, slipping my arms around her waist. "I want you to be happy in our new house. You deserve to have all the things you want."

Brightening, she threw her arms around my neck. "Me too. I know I said the apartment was feeling a little cramped, but I can be patient. Let's not rush."

"It wouldn't feel so cramped if we hadn't gotten so many wedding presents."

"I can't help it if our friends and families are generous!"

"Seriously, how many kitchen utensils and mixing bowls does one woman need? And when are we ever going to use those fancy plates your mother sent?"

"That was my grandmother's china, and I happen to think it goes perfectly with your great-grandmother's silver, so I'm planning lots of formal dinner parties."

I groaned. "I'm sorry I asked."

We got into the truck, and I started the engine. "Want to go for a little Sunday drive?"

"Sure." She rolled down the window and let the early autumn breeze ruffle her hair.

A few minutes of silence later, I glanced over at her, surprised she wasn't chattering away as usual, and saw that she'd fallen asleep.

It concerned me a little—she'd been napping a lot more than usual lately. We'd been married about ten months, and I knew she got up really early every morning to open her bakery, but in the last few weeks she'd been more exhausted than usual. It seemed worrisome to me that she was falling asleep in the middle of the day more and more. Three times in the last week I'd come home from work to find her passed out on the couch—once she hadn't even taken her shoes off. I'd asked her about it that day, but she'd brushed off my concern and simply said she hadn't been sleeping well, maybe because of the heat. It *had* been an unusually warm fall so far, so I hadn't pressed her. But I made up my mind to ask her about it again.

She was everything to me, and I wanted to take care of her.

She woke up when I turned off the highway onto the familiar dirt road, sitting up straighter and rubbing her eyes. "Sheesh, how long was I out?"

"About ten minutes." I glanced at her again and took her hand. "You feeling okay?"

"Yeah. I feel great." She looked around, recognizing where we were heading. "Hey, are we going to the pond? I didn't pack a picnic."

"That's okay." About a mile down the dirt road, I turned into a driveway. Putting the truck in park, I jumped out and unlocked the gate with the sign on it that read PRIVATE PROPERTY.

Soon, if all went well, it would be our property—at least part of it.

Back in the truck, I pulled past the gate and drove slowly through the woods until we reached the clearing. Over to the left was the pond with the little wooden dock at one end, and somewhere beyond the trees ahead was the lake. We were at the height of the season for fall colors, surrounded on all sides by shades so vibrant you could almost taste them—honey and pumpkin and cinnamon and sweet potato and cider. Blair and I often came here for date nights, preferring the quiet intimacy of a picnic to a restaurant or bar.

But this afternoon was about something else.

I got out of the truck, and she followed suit. "Come here," I said, taking her hand and leading her toward the dock.

"Are we going fishing?" she asked.

"Not without a pole."

"Oh, right. Skinny dipping?" she joked, squeezing my hand.

I laughed. "We could. Might be a little chilly."

We reached the dock and walked out on it. Then I turned her toward the clearing where the truck was parked and put my arms around her. "Look over there," I said softly, my lips next to her ear.

She put her arms over mine. "What am I looking for?"

"Something that isn't there yet. You have to imagine it."

"Imagine what?"

"A house."

In my arms, she shivered. "Whose house?"

I wrapped her up tighter. "Ours."

She sucked in her breath. "What?"

"Ours."

"But how?"

"Beckett offered to sell me some acreage—not a lot, but enough for us to have some space of our own."

Another gasp, and she turned to face me. "Griffin, can we afford it?"

"Yes. He's being extremely generous with the sale price."

Her eyes teared up. "He is?"

"Beckett's a good guy."

"And we can build a home here?"

I shrugged. "I mean, we could pitch a tent and call it a day, but I thought you might like to build your dream house complete with the perfect kitchen."

She sniffled, swatting at my chest. "It's too good to be true!"

I turned her around again, keeping her wrapped in my embrace. "But can you see it?"

"Yes," she whispered. "I can."

"Tell me."

"It's white, and it has a big wraparound porch."

"Yeah?"

"Yes. And on the porch are rocking chairs and a hammock and all kinds of hanging flower baskets."

"Where's my three-car garage?"

"Hmm. That's not coming to me."

Laughing, I scooped her off her feet and pretended I was going to toss her in the pond. "Maybe it'll come to you after a swim, Mrs. Dempsey!"

"Griffin, don't you dare!" Squealing, she flailed and kicked in my arms. "I see the garage! I see the garage! Oh my God, it's huge! It's massive! It's bigger and nicer than the house!"

Grinning, I set her on her feet again. "Now you're talking."

She nestled her back against my chest again, and I looped my arms around her waist. Placing her hands over mine, she played with my wedding band. "I see something else," she said.

"What?"

"Bedrooms."

"Mmm." I kissed her temple. "Our bedroom?"

"Yes. But not just ours. I see the baby's room too."

I went completely still. "Baby?"

"Yes." She took my hands and flattened my palms over her belly. "I'm pregnant, Griffin."

My entire body warmed, flooded with five different feelings at once—love and joy and shock and fear and above all, a ferocious, all-consuming sense of protectiveness. "Are you sure?"

"Yes. I've taken like five tests. I didn't want to tell you unless I was positive." She turned to face me, putting her hands on my chest. Her smile was tentative. "Are you happy?"

"Are you serious? Of course I'm happy!" I crushed her body against mine, lifting her off her feet. "We're going to have a baby—you and me!"

She grinned. "Yes, we are."

"I didn't think it would happen so soon." We'd only decided to stop using protection a month ago. Then it hit me —the reason she'd been so tired. I set her down and looked at her. "*That's* why you keep falling asleep."

"I think so."

"Are you feeling okay? Jesus, I shouldn't have threatened to throw you in the water like that—I'm such an asshole!"

"It's okay," she said, laughing. "I'm not breakable, all of a sudden. And my body is going to have to withstand a lot more than an unexpected swim."

"Are you nervous?" I asked, overwhelmed with love and gratitude and awe at the journey she was willing to take for me, for us. "Don't be. You're stronger than you think, and I am going to be here with you every step of the way."

"I know you will." Rising up on her toes, she kissed me. "I feel very lucky."

I kissed her back, hoping she could feel how much I cherished her, wishing I could think of words to say that would make her understand how fiercely I would protect her and our children, how hard I would work for them, how deeply I would love them. On impulse, I dropped to my knees on the dock, lifted up her shirt, and put my hands on her stomach again. "Hey, you."

Above me, she giggled. "I don't think he has ears yet."

"He might. Our kid is gonna be ahead of the pack on everything."

"Of course." Her hands played in my hair.

"Hey in there. It's your dad." But then I found myself too choked up to speak, and all I could do was close my eyes, rest my forehead against my wife's belly, and thank my own father for sending me this angel—and the one inside her.

"I love you," Blair whispered.

I swallowed hard, and pressed my lips to her skin.

My heart was too full for words.

BLUEBERRY LEMON THYME SCONES

Ingredients
    3 3/4 c. all-purpose flour
    2 tsp. salt
    2 Tbsp. baking powder
    1/2 c. sugar
    1 tsp. lemon zest
    1 pint blueberries
    2 1/2 c. cold heavy cream

Glaze:
    1 tsp. fresh thyme leaves
    1 c. powdered sugar
    4 Tbsp. lemon juice
    1 tsp. lemon zest

1) Preheat oven to 375 degrees.

2) Mix together the flour, salt, baking powder, lemon zest and sugar.

3) Add the blueberries and incorporate into dry ingredients so they are evenly distributed. Add the heavy cream and mix just until it comes together in the bowl.

4) Turn dough over on table and fold a few times.

Note from Blair: "I like to knead until the blueberries start to break up, resulting in a nice jammy scone."

5) Shape into a ball and pat down to form a 10" circle. Cut into 8 slices and place on parchment sheet. Make sure the scones have at least 1/2" separation between them. Bake at 375 degrees for about 20 minutes.

Glaze: Mix all ingredients together and spread on scones once they have cooled.

LEMON LAVENDER SHORTBREAD

Ingredients
    2 c. all-purpose flour
    1/2 tsp. salt
    1/2 lb. unsalted butter
    1/2 c. sugar
    1 tsp. vanilla
    2 tsp. lemon zest
    1 1/2 Tbsp. lemon juice
    1 Tbsp dried lavender

1) Preheat oven to 300 degrees.

2) Spray 8 or 9" round cake pan. Line bottom with parchment.

3) Beat butter and sugar until light and fluffy. Add vanilla, lemon zest, lemon juice, and lavender. Mix until well combined.

4) Combine dry ingredients. Add flour mixture and mix just until combined. Spread mixture into prepared pan.

5) Bake at 300 degrees for about 25 mins or until edges are golden.

Glaze:
    1 c. powdered sugar
    2 Tbsp. unsalted butter at room temp
    1/8 c. lemon juice

Beat ingredients until smooth.

Once cooled, spread glaze over top and sprinkle with more dried lavender.

SPINACH, CARAMELIZED ONION & GRUYÈRE GALETTE

Dough:
  1 1/4 c. all-purpose flour
  1/4 tsp. salt
  8 Tbsp. cold unsalted butter
  1/4 c. sour cream
  1 Tbsp. lemon juice
  1/4 c. ice water

Put the flour and salt in a food processor and pulse in chunks of butter until it's pea-sized. Combine cold water, sour cream and lemon juice in separate bowl. Add to flour mixture and pulse just until it comes together. Cover in plastic wrap and chill for an hour.

Note from Blair: "I usually triple the recipe and have portions of dough ready to go in the freezer. I take the dough out of the freezer and put it in the cooler so it's ready for me to roll out in the morning."

Filling:

    1 lb. of spinach
    3 cloves garlic, sliced
    1 c. caramelized onions (how-to below)
    olive oil
    1 14.5 ounce can white beans, drained
    2 cups of shredded Gruyère
    salt, pepper

Egg wash: 1 egg with 1 Tbsp. water

Caramelized Onions
    2 yellow onions
    3 Tbsp. butter
    1 tsp. salt

Thinly slice the onions. Melt butter in saucepan over medium/high heat. Once the butter is melted, add the onions. Cook the onions, stirring constantly until they start to soften. Add 1 tsp. salt. Turn heat down to medium low and cook the onions until they are dark amber and jammy. This will take about 30 minutes. Make sure to stir the onions every few minutes to prevent burning.

1) Preheat oven to 375 degrees.

2) Sauté garlic until golden, and then add the caramelized onions. Mix that until it's warmed up, and then slowly add the spinach. Season with salt and pepper. Once that is cooked down, let cool.

3) Assembly: Roll dough out into a 12" round. Spread shredded Gruyère evenly over the dough, leaving a 2" border of dough all around. Next, evenly sprinkle drained white beans over the cheese. Top this with an even layer of your spinach/onion mixture.

4) Fold the border of dough over the filling. Brush border with egg wash and bake at 375 degrees for about 30-40 minutes, or until crust is golden brown.

PESTO TWISTS

Note from Blair: "I make two versions of these savory rolls: red pepper rolls and pesto twists. The dough is the same for both. Filling and shaping methods are different."

Dough:
    1 c. lukewarm milk
    2 1/4 tsp. active dry yeast
    4 1/2 c. all-purpose flour
    1/4 c. sugar
    1 3/4 tsp. salt
    2 large eggs
    1/3 c. unsalted butter, diced

1) In a small bowl, combine milk, yeast and 1 tsp. sugar. Let sit for 10 minutes in a warm spot.

2) In bowl of a stand mixer with dough hook, combine flour, milk mixture, sugar, salt, eggs and butter on medium until it comes together. Then knead on high for about 10 minutes until smooth and soft. Transfer dough to oiled bowl and cover

with plastic wrap and let rise for about 1-1 1/2 hours until double in size.

3) Punch down the dough.

PESTO TWISTS

I make a pesto using spinach, pistachios, olive oil, parmesan, garlic. Roll dough into rectangle. Spread the pesto on the dough. Sprinkle with parmesan and mozzarella. Fold dough. Cut into strips, and make twists.

RED PEPPER ROLLS

I make a paste with roasted red peppers (in a jar), almonds, Parmesan, garlic, oil, and sriracha. I roll out the dough into a rectangle and spread this savory paste on the dough. I then scatter strips of red pepper over the paste and sprinkle with mozzarella. Roll it up, cut into 12 pieces. Proof, and bake. Brush with garlic butter as soon as they come out of the oven.

Author note: "Blair, what the hell do you mean by 'Proof'?"

Blair: "Proofing just means to let rise. Usually you let dough rise until double in size, for about an hour."

SOUTHERN COMFORT STRATA

Ingredients
18 eggs
5 1/2 c. Half and half
2 tsp. cumin
1 tsp. thyme
1 Tbsp. salt
2 tsp. pepper
1/2 tsp. cayenne
2 tsp. garlic powder
1 tsp. turmeric
2 bunches of Swiss chard, roughly chopped
1 c. cooked chopped bacon
2 cups cooked chopped ham
1 large onion
5 cloves garlic
1 c. chicken stock
24 oz day-old bread cubes
12 oz Gruyère, shredded
4 oz Parmesan, grated
24 oz canned white beans

1) Slice onion and garlic. Cook until golden brown. Add chopped Swiss chard. Season with salt and pepper. Cook for about 5-8 minutes or until Swiss chard starts to cook down.

2) Add chicken stock and cook until chard stems are soft. Drain any excess liquid and set aside.

3) Mix together eggs, heavy cream, and all the herbs and spices with an immersion blender or a whisk. Set aside.

4) Spray 12x18" roasting pan. Add layer of half of the bread cubes to bottom of the pan. Top with half of the Swiss chard mixture. Sprinkle half of the bacon, ham and beans over the Swiss chard. Then spread half of the cheese over that. Repeat once with remaining ingredients.

5) Carefully pour the egg mixture evenly over the top of the ingredients. Let soak for at least 2 hours or overnight.

6) Bake at 350 degrees for about an hour or until golden brown on top.

BLAIR'S APPLE PIE WITH MASCARPONE CREAM

Crust

- 2 1/2 c. all-purpose flour
- 3 Tbsp. sugar
- 1/4 tsp. salt
- 2 sticks (8 oz) butter
- 6 Tbsp. water

Filling

- 3 lbs Granny Smith apples
- 1/4 c. brown sugar
- 1/2 c. granulated sugar
- 2 Tbsp. all purpose flour
- 3/4 tsp. cardamom
- 1/2 tsp. cinnamon
- 1/4 tsp. salt
- 2 Tbsp. unsalted butter cut into small pieces

Heavy cream and sugar as needed for brushing the top

Crust:

1) In a large bowl, stir together the flour, sugar and salt. Using a pastry cutter or fork, cut the butter into the flour mixture until the mixture resembles a coarse cornmeal. Add the water and mix with a fork just until the dough comes together.

2) Cut dough into two equal pieces and form into flat disks. Refrigerate for one hour.

Filling:

1) Peel, core and slice apples into 1/2" wedges. Toss with remaining ingredients and set aside.

2) Roll pie dough into two 12" rounds that are 1/8 inch thick. Transfer one of the dough rounds to a 9-inch pie pan or cast iron skillet, fitting the dough into the bottom and sides of the dish. Trim the dough, leaving a slight overhang. This can be done with scissors. Spread the apple mixture into the crust and scatter the bits of butter over the mixture.

3) Place the second dough round over the apple filling. Trim the dough so it is even with the bottom crust. Fold the overhang under and crimp by pinching or using a fork. Cut a few slits in the top crust.

4) Brush top with heavy cream and sprinkle with sugar.

5) Place pie on a lined baking sheet. Bake at 400 degrees for 15 minutes, then turn temperature down to 350 and bake for another 45-60 minutes or until top crust is golden brown.

Mascarpone cream:

4 oz Mascarpone
    1/4 c. powdered sugar

2 c. heavy whipping cream
1 tsp. vanilla
1 tsp. cinnamon

In a medium bowl, beat mascarpone And powdered sugar until soft and fluffy. Add 1 tsp vanilla and 1/2 tsp cinnamon. Slowly add 2 cups of heavy whipping cream and beat on low speed until combined. Turn speed up to high and beat until stiff peaks form.

RASPBERRY PISTACHIO TORTE

Ingredients:
- 3/4 C. Sugar
- 4 oz. unsalted butter, room temp
- 2 eggs
- 1 tsp vanilla
- 1/2 C. all-purpose flour
- 1/2 C. almond flour
- 1 tsp. baking powder
- 1/8 tsp salt
- 12 oz of raspberries
- Juice from half a lemon
- Sugar and cinnamon for sprinkling
- Handful of coarsely chopped unsalted, roasted pistachios for garnish
- Powdered sugar for sprinkling

1 Preheat oven to 350 degrees.

2 Grease 9" pan with baking spray. Line bottom of pan with parchment.

3 Beat Butter and sugar until light. Add eggs and vanilla. Mix until combined. Add dry ingredients.

4 Spread into prepared pan. Top with fresh fruit. Make sure to cover the top.

5 Sprinkle with lemon juice, sugar and cinnamon. Then sprinkle with chopped pistachios.

6 Bake for about an hour at 350 degrees. Once cooled, sprinkle with powdered sugar.

Unforgettable

The Bellamy Creek Series
Drive Me Wild
Make Me Yours
Call Me Crazy
Tie Me Down

Cloverleigh Farms Next Generation Series
Ignite
Taste
Tease
Tempt

Co-Written Books
Hold You Close (Co-written with Corinne Michaels)
Imperfect Match (Co-written with Corinne Michaels)
Strong Enough (M/M romance co-written with David Romanov)

The Speak Easy Duet

The Tango Lesson (A Standalone Novella)

Want a reading order? Click here!

NEVER MISS A THING!

For exclusive behind the scenes information, sales and freebies, cover reveals, recommendations, and sneak peeks to what's coming, subscribe to my mailing list using the QR code below!

ACKNOWLEDGMENTS

DRIVE ME WILD was very much inspired by Schitt's Creek, a show I discovered during quarantine that brought laughter and joy to days that were often sad, challenging, and uncertain. I knew in my gut that I wanted the next book I wrote to bring that kind of hope, love, and levity to my readers—so I hope Blair and Griffin's story made you smile, and I am grateful to the brilliant Dan Levy for creating such a wonderful series about family, friendship, belonging, and acceptance.

I need to thank incredibly talented baker and special effects makeup artist Dina Cimarusti for all the delicious recipes in this book, both sweet and savory! She was the inspiration behind all of Blair's creations, and I hope you enjoy making them yourself.

As always, my love and gratitude to the following people for their talent, support, wisdom, friendship, and encouragement...

Melissa Gaston, Brandi Zelenka, Jenn Watson, Corinne Michaels, Nancy Smay at Evident Ink, Julia Griffis at The Romance Bibliophile, proofreaders Michele Ficht and Shannon Mummey, the Shop Talkers, the Sisterhood, the Harlots and the Harlot ARC Team, bloggers and event organizers, my Queens, my betas, my proofers, my readers all over the world...

And once again, to my family. We've spent a LOT of time together over the last few months, but you're my favorite people in the world, and there is no place I'd rather be than home with you, eating takeout and watching Schitt's Creek. ("Congratulations on your ongoing love for each other. You did it!")

ABOUT THE AUTHOR

Melanie Harlow grew up attending her dad's "lawyer league" old man baseball games. She writes sweet and sexy contemporary romance from her home outside of Detroit, where she lives with her husband and two daughters. When she's not writing, she's probably got a cocktail in hand. And sometimes when she is.

Find her at www.melanieharlow.com.